Lupe's Dream

and Other Stories

Lupe's Dream

and Other Stories

Margaret Randall

San Antonio, Texas
2022

First Edition
ISBN: 978-1-60940-621-9

E-books:
ISBN: 978-1-60940-622-6

Wings Press
P.O. Box 591176
San Antonio, Texas 78259

Wings Press books are distributed to the trade by
Independent Publishers Group
www.ipgbook.com

Acknowledgments:
"The Photograph" first appeared in *Sinister Wisdom*, Fall 2021. "Wind" first appeared in *Unfit Magazine*, Summer 2021. "The Table" first appeared in *Unreal Magazine*, Summer 2021. Both of the latter stories were nominated for Pushcart prizes by the magazines' mutual editor. "The Invitation" appeared in *Mystery Tribune*. An earlier version of "The Ring" appeared in *The Morning After: Poetry and Prose in a Post Truth World* (Wings Press, 2017).

This book is for Martin Randall

Contents

My flowers [art] will not come to an end,
my songs will not come to an end,
I, the singer, raise them up;
they are scattered, they are bestowed...
Even though flowers on earth
may wither and yellow,
they will be carried there,
to the interior of the house
of the bird with the golden feathers.

—Nezhualcoyotl

Storytelling reveals meaning without committing the error of defining it.

—Hannah Arendt

Lupe's Dream

Bernie walks slowly through the antiseptic white prison halls. His world is brightly lit but monotonous, unbroken by the slightest show of affection or interesting happening. He has been here for more than a decade now. His son Mark hanged himself in his apartment, pushed to defeat when his glittering world was suddenly ripped to pieces by the father he idolized. When that father calmly admitted he'd taken hundreds of trusting clients for 170 billion dollars over a period of twenty years. His other son, Andrew, succumbed to lung cancer a few years later. His wife Ruth—they'd been sweethearts since high school—will no longer take his phone calls. He is inexplicably, devastatingly, alone.

The scheme had been simple. He sold favored clients on what he assured them would be extraordinarily lucrative stocks. Then he pocketed the money and sent them yearly statements showing fake earnings, which he paid from the funds new clients deposited. His status in the financial world kept him from being investigated by the agencies charged with doing so. Bernie expected to be able to go on like that forever. Then the 2008 financial crisis intervened. Suddenly, he no longer had the money to cover his fiction. He had no alternative but to confess to the largest pyramid scheme in history.

"Guilty... guilty... guilty... guilty," they'd all heard him respond, as each charge was called out in a courtroom filled with many of the super-rich who'd lost millions, some of them billions, because of what he'd done. Some were still stunned. Surely they would be able to get some of their losses back. Bernie stood, turned and told them: "I will face you. I'm sorry." His countenance was an emotionless mask.

Although defined by guard towers, razor wire, regimental cells and rigorous rules, medium security has its advantages. Many of Bernie's victims think he got off easy, even with a sentence of 150 years. Most of the day he's not confined to his cell. He gets a daily shower and exercise, has access to a library, could work if the jobs offered weren't so beneath him. He can make phone calls and is able to communicate with the outside world. Though a far cry from the opulence in which he once lived, his surroundings are clean and protected. He is an anomaly, a man who did the unthinkable when ordinary success just wasn't enough. Some of the guards ask him questions about finances from time to time. He is still an authority.

The loudspeaker blares: "Inmates: fifteen minutes to lockdown." Or: "Visitor hours ending." Bernie still doesn't quite believe these regulations apply to him. After all, he shares this place with common criminals, burglars and forgers, the lowest of the low.

Lately time plays tricks on Bernie. It alternatingly feels foreshortened or elongated, depending on his ability to hide inside himself. Just last week, as he made his slow way back to his cell from the bank of public phones, he thought he saw his Degas hanging among the informational signs and keypads that dot the cellblock walls. He stopped and stood before it for a moment, recalling with a burst of satisfaction how he'd outbid everyone else. The ballerina reminded him of Ruthie when they met, the same pure complexion and aura of innocence. The painting held pride of place over the fireplace mantle in the living room of their Fifth Avenue mansion. Guests often complimented him on it and he remembered how that made him feel. In an instant the Degas is gone, the walls institutional once more.

Everyone has abandoned him. Family, friends, business associates, those few who knew about the Ponzi scheme and the many who didn't. It had been absolutely brilliant of course. If it hadn't been for the crisis, he'd never have been caught. No question. He'd long since admitted to himself, although not to others, that he didn't care about the people he hurt, not really. Less sleep lost, fewer people to whom he had to feel accountable, fewer questions to answer. He's a different kind of person, one in a million.

Even the press has lost interest. Maybe there'll be an interview or a special of some sort on the twentieth anniversary, or the thirtieth. If he's still alive. The press. Such pedestrian minds. In a feature story the writer equated him with one of those Muslim terrorists who flew a plane into the Twin Towers. And the journalist who made the outrageous comparison let it stand without comment. He still shakes with rage when he remembers. "Can you believe it? I didn't intend to hurt anyone. And they bear some responsibility, after all. They could have asked more questions." Some of his victims have been quoted as saying he deserved the death sentence.

A reporter who'd interviewed him shortly after going to prison asked if he regretted what he'd done. "I said I was sorry," he told her, lips moving below vacant eyes. "I said that at the trial. And I pleaded guilty to all charges. I have to live with this every day of my life. What more do you want from me?"

❀

Halima was an infant when what was left of her family fled Somalia's civil war, joining the endless migration making its way across the plains into Kenya. A human ribbon, struggling, falling, picking themselves up and going on. Vast desert interrupted by occasional oases, endless sand. Like the sand that covers this camp, stretching to distant mountains off limits to the refugees. This is her memory. She is eight now.

Hagadera is where they live, one of the three camps that make up Dadaab. Thousands of tents, tens of thousands of families. Her mother and uncle speak less and less of their homeland, neighborhood, family members she doesn't know except in their stories, that are fewer as the years pass. She cannot remember the desperate human stream, the exhaustion and uncertainty, walking for days until they reached safety. Of course, she wasn't walking; she was carried: shifted from uncle to mother and back again. When they left Mogadishu, they had a small cart, but a wheel fell off after a few days and they had to abandon it. The ancient port city and its elegant gardens, sparkling by the Indian Ocean, was only memory now.

When they finally arrived, they claimed their regulation canvass tent from the UNHCR. United Nations High Commissioner for Refugees. Halima has never seen this Commissioner, doesn't know what he looks like, only that his initials rule her life.

She knows about the Return Program, sometimes hears people arguing its pros and cons. Some families have left. They don't hear about them again. Hers has opted to stay in the camp, imagining a future homeland here or in Europe, maybe even America. Rumors have become their daily bread, hope what keeps them going.

For her mother, fear still clouds any thought of going back. She rarely speaks about life before. She rarely speaks at all. Halima has never known what it was like to have a toilet for her family alone, running water closer than a quarter mile away, the luxury of privacy or peace or silence. She has never been to a place called school, where her mother says even girls can learn to read and write.

Lately there is talk about Kenya issuing some sort of special residency card, so her people can leave the camp, look for work, contemplate a different life. This sort of chatter always intensifies at moments of political change, then dissipates as the government in power is forced to confront its own people's needs. Halima's uncle says that's what politics is, a game in which their hopes are raised and then dashed again. "Better to make the best of what Allah has given us. May his name be blessed."

Her mother seems numbed after all these years. She wakes, bargains for firewood and food, cooks over the fire she tends with diligence, watches her daughter, keeps their tent as clean as possible and sleeps when the sun goes down. Each day is identical to the one before, her life a tapestry of routine and survival. She never leaves their tent without covering her head. A war widow, she must still honor her brother.

Today Halima senses something strange is about to take place. She feels it before it happens: a slight tingling like the chords of an oud strumming against her skin. On her way back from the communal water spigot she trips over a pile of bricks and almost falls. She's never before seen anything like these rectangular blood-red blocks. Photographs of Somalia show houses made of mud, the color of earth and with softer lines. She doesn't know where these strange cubes come from, who scattered them in her path. But she is lithe and quickly regains her balance.

A bit of the water she carries has splashed from her bucket but most of it is still in the pail. And when she turns to look back at what has almost cost her the precious cargo, there is nothing there. Could she have dreamed the bricks?

Halima can't stop thinking about what almost caused an accident that would surely have resulted in a barrage of recriminating words, or worse. And the next day, returning from the spigot, she notices the bricks again. Now they are no longer a small pile but a broken wall, some stretches reaching to her shoulders. She stops and sets her pail on the ground, straining to see what's on the other side.

Through the window of a real house, she catches sight of a woman tucked into a real bed. She has seen such things in pictures. The woman is sleeping but mumbles something as she turns from her back onto one side. Halima can't make out the words but can clearly see what's in the woman's subconscious, what she is dreaming. There is a brightly lit white hallway and a few men dressed in matching tan shirts and pants ambling along it as if they are ghosts. She almost reaches out to touch these people but something akin to an electrical charge causes her to draw her hand back. When she gets to their tent, she sets the pail of water down without a word, goes to her corner of the family's sleeping mat, curls up and closes her eyes. Her head hurts.

Bernie thinks this absurd captivity might finally be getting to him. Old political connections rise and fall but nothing changes. There is no chance of appeal, no reprieve.

Over the past several days, awake as well as asleep, he's caught sudden flashes of unfamiliar scenes. Places he doesn't recognize. A small girl carrying a pail of water on her head. It looks like one of those horrible refugee camps you read about, an expanse of shabby tents as far as the eye can see. Sometimes he catches a pungent stench of raw sewage. It almost makes him retch but he manages to contain the urge. His privileged sense of self is all he has left.

Then everything shifts and he is in the small bedroom of a nondescript brick apartment building, a place unlike any he's visited since his Brooklyn childhood. Long before wealth or status. He is stuck there, in close proximity with people who smell and wear the same clothes days on end. He thinks of asking to see the prison doctor, but the guy has always been so unsympathetic. Bernie is still astonished that no one here treats him with the respect he deserves.

Guadalupe has been having unusually vivid dreams. Not nightmares, not that frightening. More unsettling, really, the sort that refuse to leave when she wakes and come back to haunt her when she least expects them to. Last night was peopled with odd characters: disembodied faces she'd glimpsed along her journey from Guatemala up through Mexico and into the United States. Her grandparents. A childhood playmate murdered by the Mara Salvatrucha. A couple of threatening strangers. A woman who saved her life a few miles past the border town of Tapachula. One man she has never seen before ambles dejectedly through antiseptic brightly lit halls, some kind of institution. A young girl carries a bucket of water on her head.

Lupe, as she is always called here, had made a run for it when staying seemed likely to mean death. Her mother begged her not to go. A grown son wanted to come along but insisted on bringing his baby. The child's mother, too, had been a victim of the Mara. Lupe thought she would have a better chance on her own and slipped away one night, leaving only a note and her few possessions. "If I make it, I'll send for you," she wrote. "Stay safe."

And she did make it. There are times when it feels like the end of the road, but she's always managed to cajole or convince her way to the next challenge. She is a good judge of character, knows who to trust, who not.

Crossing the big river was the least of it. By the time she arrived on its bank she'd risked too much to fail. On a moonless night, alone and silent, she swam across and sat naked for several hours in a matorral, waiting for the desert breeze to dry her clothes. Then she began to walk, grateful for her luck. Grateful to the Virgin. Grateful too for the plastic bottles of fresh water left by kind strangers along the way. "Angels," her people call them. She knows about organized groups of such strangers. Her new country's government is cruel in its treatment of those who would breach its borders, but its people are embracing in ways she couldn't have imagined.

Now it's long days at the Seven-Eleven, picking up every bit of English she can, and long nights in the tiny room where her new friend Jackie lets her stay for free. "Just until you get on your feet," she says, and Lupe makes note of yet another funny English figure of speech. The difficulties of this new language, her longing for home and constant fear of the migra are like a physical weight pressing against Lupe's neck and shoulders, leaving her exhausted at the end of each day.

Sleep comes almost immediately. And with it these dreams. Tonight, the aimless older man and young girl are here again, more urgently visible than before. He moves like a ghost. She touches his elbow, looks into his face. Is she asking for help? Little good it does her. He doesn't notice, engrossed as he is in bitter rumination. Lupe thinks he sees only himself yet has no idea of who he is.

This is the fourth day Halima stops at the brick wall, which has grown taller than she is now, hiding a large part of the camp. Once again she sets down her water pail and stands on her toes, straining to get a glimpse of what's on the other side. Places where bricks are missing or gaps between them remain, affording several vantage points. Now this dreary man in his strange suit blocks her view. Timidly, she pokes at his shoulder, hoping he will step aside, but he doesn't respond. He exudes a disinterest rare in the camp, where people generally display the solidarity born of shared misfortune.

Bernie is disoriented. Too many days and nights and months and years in this place, he thinks. Too tired. Too frustrated. He'd have thought at least one or two family, friends or old business associates would visit. Even just once. He was so good to them all. But no one does. He sleeps a lot now. It helps pass the time.

But lately his dreams have taken him to unfamiliar and disturbing places, a vast expanse of tents crowded with dirty people somewhere in the Middle East, nothing like that luxury hotel where he once stayed in Abu Dhabi. The cramped toilet of a Seven-Eleven. Bernie can't remember ever having been in one of those stores, even as a child. A young girl wearing one of those ridiculous head coverings tugs at his arm. A middle-aged woman stares at him, her piercing eyes set in skin the color of the fur coat he gave Ruthie on their fiftieth anniversary, not silky soft but deeply weathered.

"I need to see my lawyer! I need to see my lawyer now!" Bernie clutches at the white steel bars on his cell door, bangs a book against the sturdy lock. His words echo the length of the block, ringing in the earphones of the guard on duty at the command post on the other side of the building. The guard puts down his morning coffee and stares at the monitor where he can see the prisoner straining and shouting. "Bernie's at it again," the guard says to no one in particular, since he is alone in the cubicle. He continues to enjoy his breakfast.

Lupe thinks about her dream. As a child she learned about dreams from her grandmother, a wise K'iche' woman who wore the huipil, wraparound skirt and red woven sash until the day she died. Ati't Chachal Be was a Day Keeper, knew medicinal herbs, taught her granddaughter to pay attention to what happened at night. "Your dreams will always tell you where to go," she said, and Lupe remembers her grandmother's teaching as she makes the perilous journey north.

Now, though, Lupe is often confused about the people she encounters and the feelings she gets from the scenes that fill her nights. The aging man and young girl appear often. Do either of them know where they are or what they need from her? Can she help?

Halima believes the brick wall is a map that will take her where she wants to go.

Bernie thinks he is losing his mind; this absurd punishment has taken its toll.

Lupe tries to converse with her visitors, inside her dream and out. She is sure she has something to tell them. Perhaps she is a vehicle for a message from her Ati't Chachal Be, duty bound to pass it on.

The dream itself has never had an exaggerated sense of its own importance. Nor does it play favorites. It doesn't distinguish between believers and disbelievers, the faithful and faithless, those who are searching for something and those content with their lot. It only knows its job is to provide a safe and welcoming space. The rest is up to those it keeps alive.

El Lugar

When I first went there, so many years ago, El Lugar was a smattering of one-room adobe houses in a hollow surrounded by low hills that changed color as the day unfolded, from the deep gray-blues and purples of early morning through the baked brown of midday to their crowning moment in late afternoon when their gentle shoulders glowed like the bright pink flesh of a watermelon. The houses were a uniform *café con leche*, the color of the earth in those parts.

The earth produced beans and chile so hot it would make you sweat, a few scattered *milpas* with their stunted ears of corn, small round squashes and some coffee plants in the broad shade of the occasional mango tree. A few thin horses, goats, chickens and the usual skinny dogs roamed freely. A truck that was part Ford, part Chevy, with a Dodge hood ornament was parked in the shade of an old tree. It looked like it had been there for a while.

No one now alive knows when or how El Lugar got its name. Not even old Ágata remembered, although she could tell stories of rebels who didn't know the 1910 revolution had ended and were still holed up in the hills when she was a girl. She would trace Villa's great belly in the air with one bony arm as she pulled her *rebozo* tight about her with the other. The *rebozo* was identical to those worn by all poor Mexican women: a close dark weave flecked with threads of white, its fringe sparse after so many years of being scrubbed against a stone washboard.

The villagers told me Doña Ágata spoke with ghosts. She would follow them around El Lugar, listening and nodding her head in deep conversation. Even laughing at times at a shared joke. Some of the older women—a generation younger than Ágata but still ancient—might ask her to inquire about Tío Agustín or Doña Sofía, she with the forest of warts on her face. Ágata brought back stories of the dead, the answers to troubling questions, condolences, reassurances, premonitions.

If it were true that Ágata was really 112, as she claimed, she would still have been a very young girl when the rebels came through that Chihuahua hill country. But her childhood memories would have been reinforced by the stories her elders told. I always regretted not having spent time with the woman; on my first visit in 1971 someone pointed her out to me but I was too concerned with my own problem to pay attention. A few years before, I was told, someone from a European country, I no longer remember which one, made the difficult journey to El Lugar with the sole purpose of speaking with Ágata. He said he was traveling the world, interviewing people who'd lived more than one hundred years.

When describing the European, the villagers made small gestures of someone writing in an invisible notebook with an invisible pen or pencil. Ágata received him with her toothless smile and a Nescafe jar of berry wine. She answered all his questions. But the lack of an official birth certificate prevented the visitor from including her in his study.

As to the village's name, someone must have asked and someone else referred to the small collection of houses as *El Lugar*, the place. And the name stuck. It was never replaced by the name of a battle or saint, an unusual rock formation or singular tree. Not even with that of a large landowner. There were no large landowners in those parts, at least not by the time I stumbled into that world.

What brought me to El Lugar? Curiosity and chance. Curiosity about what might be down that dirt road or over that hill. I was 18. I'd quit university mid-semester and headed south in my 1966 yellow Volkswagen Beetle, unsure of what I might find but eager to explore. I was driving through Mexico's state of Chihuahua, a desert landscape with mountains that beckoned on either side of the long straight highway. I'd heard about ancient ruins and petroglyphs, small villages where the inhabitants had scant contact with the outside world.

I was drawn as well by a web of ruins, no longer visible to the eye: the strangely shaped hill that surely hid a pyramid, bits and pieces of clay pots painted with geometric designs, you could reach down and pick up almost anywhere. I had the sense I could smell some previous life, its mesquite fires, the lichen clinging to stone or moist texture of adobe.

I had all the time in the world and enjoyed getting off the main road. I wanted to see places I suspected might speak more of previous centuries than the present. This particular road was more track than one that invited vehicles, but the Beetle was game. I only realized I had a flat as I approached the village: that ominous ka-thump, ka-thump, as the car slowed and lurched to one side. Worse, as soon as I sprang it loose from under the hood, I saw that the spare was also punctured.

I remember the village looked other-worldly but not forlorn. I saw the customary church, nothing flamboyant but freshly painted and clearly tended by many hands. Life enjoyed a different tempo. Old coffee and lard cans filled with flowers sat in front of some of the homes. There was a neatness, a sense of purpose. I didn't see a commercial establishment of any kind. Still, I assumed there must be a mechanic somewhere, or at least someone who could fix a flat. That was before I looked around and noticed there were almost no cars. A lone pickup truck with all four tires melted into the ground. That might have been a clue. Hardly the range of motor vehicles that warranted the road leading into the village. I soon learned traffic was mostly horse-drawn wagons or simply horses with riders. My Beetle and I were anomalies. As such, we immediately drew a small crowd, mostly curious youngsters.

The people of El Lugar didn't have much, but compassion and ingenuity were plentiful. Soon a weathered farmer appeared with a large wagon drawn by an unflappable team of oxen. Before I knew it, they had used two long wooden boards to construct a makeshift ramp, and half the village turned out to push the Beetle up onto the wagon bed. They explained they would take the car to a town about twenty kilometers distant, where they thought they could find someone able to repair the tire. It would take a while, they said. The oxen were sure-footed but slow.

I wondered, in my patchy Spanish, why the ox cart and not the truck. Between gestures and words, I was finally able to grasp someone's explanation that the pickup had been out of gas for years. How long had it been parked there: monument or point of reference? The villagers' help came so quickly, I hadn't thought to say they didn't need to haul the whole car. "We can remove the wheel. *Quitar la rueda . . . mira, se quite.*" I was reaching for enough high school Spanish to make myself understood. *Buenos dias* came easily, but the other phrases that surfaced were more on the order of *Me llamo Elaine* or *¿Dónde está la estación de trenes?* Utterly useless in this situation.

As I felt more and more embraced by these people who had come to my aid, I remembered the word for wheel and then the one for tire. And so, the Beetle descended the ramp the same way she'd gone up—accompanied by lots of shouting and laughter—and one of the villagers helped me detach the wheel and support the chassis by piling some rocks in its place. As I put my weight on the tire iron, leaning in to loosen the first lug, a couple of young boys mimicked my efforts in good-natured theater. An older woman shushed them with her eyes. The young men kept up a stream of continuous commentary about the car, the wheel, the tire and me, as if I wasn't right there. On the edge of respectful but with an undercurrent I couldn't quite make out.

A stocky young man with unusually long arms and prominent ears was tying the wheel to the saddle of his horse. I suggested he might want to take the spare as well. It would be a good thing for me to be able to continue my trip with five tires in decent shape. The long-armed man departed on horseback soon thereafter, a dusty wheel hanging from either side of his saddle. Where he was headed I didn't know. No one asked me for money to pay for fixing the tires. It was my first indication that money wasn't that important, or even common, in El Lugar.

I liked talking to El Lugar's youngest inhabitants. Magdalena who, in her teens had been sent to Cuauhtémoc for school, only to return because the peaceful village life "*me viene mejor.*" Her younger brother, Eat, was five. He didn't take his eyes from me. It took me a while before I realized that Eat was spelled IT. His parents had named him after a futuristic being with sleek features and a monotonous voice they'd heard about from someone who had a friend who owned a television set and was privy to the science fiction films then beginning to be popular. A Down Syndrome boy who might have been eleven although he seemed younger. His parents tended him with a kind of devotion and pride that brought tears to my eyes. This was the early seventies, and even in what we thought of as the more developed parts of the world, shame too often enveloped such children, especially in their own families.

Night came and there was no sign of the horseman. Or the wheels. No one seemed concerned. I was still sitting under one of the big mango trees when the parents of the Down Syndrome boy—I learned his name was Miguel—said I could come in to eat if I *tenía hambre*. If I had hunger. I suddenly realized I had a great deal of hunger; I hadn't eaten anything since morning.

Inside their single room there was no table spread with dinner, no dishes arranged at each place with knives and forks and spoons, no napkins, no chairs. Family members perched on a lopsided rocker, an overturned crate, the edge of the only bed. Doña Gloria ladled frijoles from a single pot, passing mismatched bowls around. I tasted some sort of root vegetable, maybe even a whiff of pork back. It was delicious.

Fresh tortillas kept coming off the *comal*. Doña Gloria produced them one after another with a rapid weaving motion of her knotted hands and passed them out steaming hot. If I close my eyes, I can still see the light of the fire playing on those hands, how they interacted as disembodied flashes of flesh and shadow, shadow and flesh. The crowded room smelled of sweat and *nixtamal*. The adults washed the meal down with a strong corn whiskey. The youngsters drank Fanta from a shared bottle, that suspiciously luminous orange soda so popular throughout the country.

It wasn't long before I felt drowsy, eyes closing despite my best intentions. Miguel walked me to a privy out in back. It was spotless inside. He waited a polite distance from the wooden structure before taking my hand and accompanying me back to the house. I was glad to take the heavy blanket Doña Gloria offered and curl up on a mat in the corner. I had no doubt I'd be reunited with the Beetle's wheels in the morning.

And I was. They arrived by horseback just after the sun came up, both tires patched and ready for service. Some of the young men and boys got the Beetle off the rocks while others held that side of her up and still others—including Miguel—followed my directions as to how to mount the wheel: "*Así, mira no más, cabe así.*" The same youngsters who had mimicked me the day before did so again, their brief dance as comical as it was pointed. One of the older women chased them off, laughing. I caught Doña Gloria beaming at her son. The Beetle was ready to go. Hugs all around and I told them this wasn't *adios*. "*Volveré,*" I said, "I'll be back." I believed it would be soon.

But you know how it is. Life takes over and the best laid plans, as my daddy used to say. I returned to the States, finished school, got a teaching job and then a husband. Two children before that marriage ended. I thought about El Lugar, dreamed of it from time to time, tried to write about it once, but twenty years passed before I was able to even think about driving that vast Chihuahua desert again.

When it happened, I wondered how many of the people I'd met there would still be around. What would the village look like? Had it had been spared modernity or invaded by a world where schools and medicines and cars came into use? Where plastic flowers replaced real ones in old coffee cans and money changed hands at a local convenience store?

The yellow Beetle was only memory now. I was driving a Toyota with good traction and high clearance, a much better bet on the backroads here. Getting my vehicle across the border was harder than it had been on my first trip, or maybe I had forgotten the paperwork. It took a couple of hours and a wad of pesos slipped to an official with a sham smile and polished knee-high boots. By the time I got across, the bright desert light was fading fast, so I drove slower, feeling my way. On the highway from Ciudad Juárez to Chihuahua City, I wondered if I would remember where to turn off. Dozens of dirt roads went into those purple hills. I stopped several times to ask.

At first no one knew about a village called El Lugar. My Spanish was a whole lot better now, so that wasn't the problem. My mention of the place was most often met with blank stares: "*El Lugar... no se, pues...*" And the person asked would look down at the hard-packed Chihuahua earth. I was wary of the one trucker who offered directions quickly, remembering that Mexico is a country where many prefer to make a route up rather than say they don't know. It's considered more courteous.

Around Kilometer 81, a man on horseback, his small son in the saddle before him, recognized the name. My question elicited a broad grin and the assurance that it wasn't far. "*Vas a llegar a una casa en ruinas,*" he said, "*ahí vas a entrar.*" I knew he didn't mean enter the house but the back country. Once on the dirt road I was sure I would find my destination. As I remembered, the road ended in El Lugar.

I didn't recognize the house in ruins. Perhaps it hadn't been in ruins on my previous trip. I exited the highway and the road began to feel familiar even if I didn't notice any distinctive features. Intermittent cliffs, a certain undulating vegetation, the color of the earth all seemed to be welcoming me. I breathed in the pungent scents of mesquite, rain-soaked adobe, nixtamal. At one point I thought I heard the strains of a reed flute.

El Lugar was still there and so were some of the people I remembered, twenty years older, graying or stooped, adults with the same slow gait and children pulling their play from old bike rims, sticks and their imaginations. Our first mistake when returning to a place we've been before is to look for its people as they were back then. Our deficient sense of time is slow to conceive of change.

Doña Gloria was the first to approach me, leaning in toward my car window almost as soon as I parked. I recognized her slightly off-center smile. One gleaming gold tooth shone where only a dark gap had existed before. Her hair was whiter but her eyes held the same distant gaze, as if looking at something no one else could see, although one of them was now almost entirely covered by a milky cataract. "*¡Mi Elaine!*," she whispered, her soft voice scratchier than I remembered. I noticed a large goiter beneath her jaw, peeking out from under the *rebozo* she wore just to her thinning hairline.

"*¿Miguel . . . ?*" I asked, looking around for the boy. She shook her head. Her voice thick with emotion, she told me how he'd sickened and died a few years back. "*Te quiso mucho,*" she confided, "He liked you a lot. *Ahora está con los espíritus,*" she sighed.

I felt tears welling up in my own eyes. But I was out of the car now, surrounded by bodies and voices, gestures of welcome, greetings eclipsing twenty years. The man with the long arms was older and bent but seemed finally to have grown into his extremities. He held out his hand and took mine, in something between a clasp and a shake. Some of the younger folk hugged me awkwardly.

When the crowd thinned I took my first look around. The church was still there of course, in pride of place, its barren interior bordered by a smattering of hand-carved wooden saints. I thought I saw fewer mango trees. And there was a small plaza with two green metal benches, already rusting along their curved arms.

Doña Gloria pointed out a miniature health center, told me a doctor comes their way once or twice a month. I saw there was now a school as well, *Escuela Primaria Gobernador Francisco Villa*. I thought of Magdalena, lonely at school in Cuauhtémoc. Now El Lugar's children were able to study in the village, no doubt making it easier for some of them to eventually leave this place for the wider world. I wondered about Magdalena until I saw her again, older and heavier with three youngsters tugging at her skirt.

My old friend ushered me into her home, talking all the time. It looked much the same as when I'd spent the night there so many years before. She pointed proudly to a small black and white TV. Electricity had finally made it to El Lugar, decades after empty promises by several administrations. She was fiddling with the on button, trying to tune into the only channel, when I noticed a bundle of bony limbs huddled in the corner. Doña Ágata!

I gasped despite myself, then turned to Doña Gloria: "*¿Cómo . . . ? ¡No es posible . . . !*"

At that, the ancient woman rose, smiled, gestured at me in passing and moved out the door into the late afternoon chill. I watched her pull her old *rebozo* about her still proud shoulders as she limped slowly toward the village plaza. She seemed transparent, incorporeal, and I thought I could see the angular lines of the school through the soft silhouette of her body. She stopped to talk to others, even tossed a wayward ball back to a young boy batting it at a tree stump with a length of two by four.

I turned back to Gloria: "When I was here before, you told me she was 112. I can't believe that . . ."

But Gloria cut me off. "*No muera,*" she said. "She doesn't die. We have good air here. Our people live forever. If you stay a day or two, you might run into Miguel. The spirits talk but don't try to touch them or slow their pace. They don't like that. *Ni un poquito.* Not one little bit."

She grabbed a lump of *nixtamal* and began palming it into a thin flat round ready to toss on the *comal.* She would feed me as she had so many years before and I would eat, wondering if Doña Ágata had been a whiff of longing, an apparition or simply a metaphor for a place that lives by other rules.

What I didn't let on to Doña Gloria, didn't even allow myself to think about at the time, was that as Doña Agata floated past me on her way out of the house she crooked one spindly finger, urging me to follow. I sat, frozen, unable to move. As I write this today, I wonder what would have happened if I had.

Carmen's Story

The girl sat on a flat rock at the river's edge, letting the water cool her feet.

Carmen repeats her opening sentence several times, until she thinks she's committed it to memory. This is her first experience trying to write a story entirely in her head, without a computer or even pencil and paper. She believes if she can do it, sentence by sentence until the story is part of her, she will be able to write again, to create. Even in these impossible conditions. That will be her victory.

The girl sat on a flat rock at the river's edge, letting the water cool her feet. The low hanging branch of a willow grazed her shoulder. The girl sat . . .

She says each sentence several times, slowly, trying to give them life in this dark cell where everything conspires against life, but most of all trying to memorize them, hold them within her. The worst are the interruptions, never knowing what to expect or when. She'd been hooded when she arrived, her bruised body dragged by people with a cruel grip under each arm. She may hear footsteps approaching along what she imagines must be a long passageway, only to discover a plate of barely edible food shoved beneath her cell door. Sometimes the footsteps mean someone is coming to take her to another interrogation.

The footsteps come mid-morning, judging from the sliver of light filtering through the transom high above her, or they come after dark. A day may go by without them. Or what feels like a day. Or two. And the guards are rarely the same. No way to establish consistency, even with the enemy. The only certainty is no certainty.

When she joined the Organization almost three years ago, there'd been lectures about what to expect if you were captured. The lies they would tell you about comrades confessing. The torture. The importance of refusing to give information for at least forty-eight hours, enough time for those on the outside to transfer people, wipe safehouses clean, destroy evidence. Carmen remembers a young man who'd spoken about the psychological torture, how they try to play with your memory, distort your sense of time. But it had all been so abstract. Until you experience it yourself, there is no way of understanding what it can do to you or how you will respond.

Carmen thinks she was able to hold out those first forty-eight hours, but she can't be sure. Time changes almost immediately upon arrival in this place. She tries to count to herself, slowly, in intervals that feel like seconds, translate those seconds into minutes and then hours. That strategy falls apart the first day. The numbers become meaningless as they dissolve in a sea of dissonant sound: the guards' muffled voices, far off conversations that seem to float on fetid air, rarely revealing more than a word or two, the occasional scream of another prisoner being interrogated or the moans of one recovering.

The girl sat on a flat rock at the river's edge, letting the water cool her feet. No. *The girl sat on a flat rock at the river's edge. The water cooled her feet.* Past tense or gerund, it doesn't really matter. Better to get the storyline now and worry about tenses later, when she will have escaped this terror and will once again have access to a home, a place to write, the calm that locks memory into something she can take in hand, count on, preserve. The idea that there is life after this comforts Carmen. If she can hold onto that, she will be alright she thinks.

Carmen is proud of how well she responds to her jailors' lies, the psychological pressure, even the torture—so far. When the older man with the gravelly voice says they have Antonio and he broke right away, answered every question, implicated her and others, she is able to picture her brother as he looked the day he recruited her, center his calm face in her mind, know it isn't true. But even as she rejects her torturer's claim, she wonders if it could be true. Maybe the torture was too much for him. Can't go there, she thinks. I have choice. I choose to believe he didn't speak. That's one of the tricks, to hold onto those few prerogatives left to her, hold onto them with every bit of strength she can muster, again and then again.

Even the physical torture allows for some degree of resistance. Slight, it's true, but something. Whatever they inflict, from the intense jolts of electrical current in her tenderest places to the terror of them forcing her head beneath filthy water, it has a beginning and an end. If she can experience the pain and fear as discreet units, she is sure she can win. Winning means making it through without breaking, without giving in. Death is the worst thing that lays in wait, and death itself now assumes a new identity, one of release, even peace.

But death doesn't come for Carmen. After what she imagines were those first forty-eight hours, she stops trying to establish how long she's been in this place. How many days, without a window, a consciousness of seasons or any measure of time. Reduction is her secret weapon: reducing what she thinks or feels to the smallest unit. Something she can bear. Memory. Preparation for what might come. This story that keeps her creativity alive.

Or her left foot. When they drag her from or to her cell, even when she moves freely within its damp walls, she tries to keep it from touching the floor. Her big toe buzzes with its memory of electrical burn, throbs with the infection she's sure is eating at her flesh. Visualizing a soothing poultice or even the effect of an antibiotic is inadequate but useful in the moment. Short-term deliverance helps when there's nothing else.

Carmen sits on the floor at the corner of her cell. She believes she is alone. Yes, she's sure of it. That itself is a luxury. No need to wonder if she must deal with an informer, someone placed with her to get information. Although there are times human contact, whatever its source, would be welcome. She leans into the wall that gradually loses its chill as what's left of her own body heat makes it less unbearable. She can feel the ridges of her spine, still in one piece, still responsive. Her shoulders and arms have recovered from the intensity of being dragged. She can bend her fingers and touch her face. Temples. Forehead. Lips. Hair, matted with dirt and sweat but still there, still growing. She allows herself to feel gratitude for each part of herself they haven't been able to destroy. Gratitude not to some mythical god but to her own power of resistance.

The girl sat on a flat rock at the river's edge, letting the water cool her feet. The low hanging branch of a willow grazed her shoulder. The sound of the water . . .

The sound of the water? She is rarely allowed to shower here. Maybe once every few weeks and always with a female guard watching. But Carmen remembers what cool water feels like on a hot summer day. The light touch of a willow branch, perhaps brushing her shoulder and then not, and then brushing it again as the wind jostles its leaves.

In describing the senses, she knows she is substituting what her senses must endure in this place with the pleasurable sensations her memory evokes from earlier moments in her life. But a story can't only be about the senses, she thinks. I need a plot. Something must happen to the girl and then the girl must engage her own will, decide to do one thing rather than another. Perhaps she should give her protagonist a disability. She wonders why this occurs to her. She sits with the word disability. Disabled as broken or disabled as different? Will what she is enduring now mean disability for her own future?

This is going to be the hard part. It's one thing to paint a picture of living nature in opposition to the overwhelming ugliness, control, and death in this prison, quite another to imagine a compelling storyline when resistance to what is being forced on her here takes every bit of energy and more. Sometimes she's tempted to abandon the story and write an imaginary letter home, let Benjamin and Carmencita and Antonio know she's alive, that they haven't broken her, let her mother know she isn't yet one of the statistics in this seemingly unending war.

Letters would be easier, speaking to her loved ones in the languages they share. But she knows they wouldn't reach their destinations. No visitors to sneak them out, no friendly guard. The story is hard precisely because it lives by its own rules, demands attention to a structure difficult to come by in this place. By choosing the more complex genre, Carmen knows she is embarking on a journey capable of removing her from despair. At least in her imagination.

The girl sat on a flat rock at the river's edge, letting the water cool her feet. The low hanging branch of a willow grazed her shoulder. But all was not peaceful. She sensed something or someone moving behind her, turned slightly to . . .

To what? No, that's not the right question. She knows what. It's not about what, but how. How to confront what she knows is coming. Whenever and in whatever way it comes. How to control her own response if she can't control their strategy or tactics.

What is the measure of a human being, Carmen asks herself, what defines human interaction? How do these guards sleep at night? Not the big guys who give the orders but the salaried lowlings who carry them out? Are they numb to the work? Empty of feeling? Do they tell themselves they're doing it for the nation, the common good, that we are criminals attacking their laws and peaceful order? Is that enough to quiet their consciences? And the women. There are women among the guards, those who watch her shower and she's sure there was one at her first interrogation. Carmen's generation of feminists wants to believe women are innately different. A sad mistake.

She tries to stay with her story, but her mind goes back to the moment she fell into their hands, that brief sequence of events that could have gone either way. Memoir, not fiction. Or a different sort of fiction. If only she'd. If only they'd. Or if only they hadn't. Absurd suppositions. It happened the way it happened. No changing that now.

Carmen remembers thinking she should leave the café. Waiting five minutes for a contact who doesn't show up is the limit. Five minutes, not six. What had induced her to break that rule, she who was always so careful about rules? She doesn't know. She can still see every detail of the two men approaching her table, as if in slow motion, their dress and manner leaving no doubt they are undercover cops. The expressions on their faces, her fumbled attempt to talk her way out of the situation, the barista who turns away, not wanting to witness them taking her out. Not wanting to be involved. Was there a struggle? Not the slightest.

And then quickly: the hood, the car, the drive through parts of the city she tries to document through sound alone. Their arrival inside a courtyard hidden from the street. Two men pushing her from the car, dragging her into the building. That first interrogation. And the ones that follow. She's curious to realize she's lost count. But not upset. One thing she's learned in here is that it's not such a good thing to dwell on the past, especially those parts that can't be changed. Focusing on the present is the best thing she can do.

But the present doesn't hold together. Pieces fall out of it, try to swim to other shores. Some she remembers, some aren't at all familiar. Carmen repeats the first two lines of her story, fixed in her memory now, but they don't make her feel like they used to. No sense of accomplishment. Not even of escape. Confused, she realizes she doesn't care about the girl sitting on the riverbank. The river itself, its millennial seam where rock and water meet, is no longer clear in her mind. The interrogations seem fewer and farther apart now, and when they come don't involve as much physical pain. Her interrogators seem almost bored. Her left toe is healing.

Time is the new torturer. Worse than any punishment of the flesh or the lies about her comrades she's learned to ignore. Meaningless words spewed from mouths that are not to be believed. Time is no longer reliable. It no longer comes in manageable increments. Forty-eight hours. A week. The number of evenly spaced scratches on her cell wall by a previous inmate who must have had some sort of sharp object capable of turning days into inch-long marks. Carmen counts them, then forgets the number she's tried to retain in her mind since the last time she counted.

Time stretches and then collapses in on itself without warning. Even the sliver of transom light has lost its rhythm, the voice with which it once measured her existence in this place. Food comes and is taken away. Sometimes she manages to swallow some of it. Sometimes she is too weak to try. She almost wishes they would come for her, take her to another interrogation session. But no one comes. They've forgotten about her and, rather than relief, Carmen feels abandonment. Time's odd behavior tells her this is her life now.

When the female guard opens her cell door, she is carrying a change of clothing. Again, the walk to the showers, the freezing water. But this time, no one tells her to hurry. And there is a sliver of soap and a towel with which to dry her aching skin, gently pat its sores. Instead of a clean set of greens, the guard hands Carmen the odd-looking street clothes: "Get dressed," she says, "you're being released."

Carmen looks at the woman's impassive face. Not a hint of how she might feel about the news she bears. She looks at the clothes: a summer skirt with a bright floral design, about as far as she can imagine from anything she would choose to wear, and a jacket that looks like the top half of a tailored suit, decades out of style and badly frayed. Where do they get this stuff, she wonders, as she dutifully removes her prison greens and pulls the ugly outfit up and around her. It hangs awkwardly on a body she hardly recognizes. Her cell door is still open, but she is not being taken back there. She follows the guard down the long hallway, seeing it for the first time.

There is no package with the clothing she wore the day they captured her. No return of her wedding ring or watch or the string of small turquoise beads the friend who'd given it to her had called *hishi*. The officer shuffling papers behind his large desk points here and there, indicating where she must sign her name. Not allowed to read it, she wonders if this is a confession. It would hardly matter now. Her hand seems to have a will of its own, but she manages a shaky signature. She notices the official doesn't refer to her by name. But as she exits his office he calls after her: "I hope you know you're one of the lucky ones."

Outside the prison, Carmen finds herself on Avenida 28 de julio. The same old trees bowing to each other on either side of the broad artery. She's known them since childhood. They seem both taller and less imposing than she remembers. She is astonished they can hide a prison on such a busy thoroughfare without anyone being aware.

No one is here to meet her. But I can walk home, she thinks, amazed that home is so close to this place where time has almost swallowed her. Across the park. Then a few short blocks to the west and one long one south until she comes to the four-story building with its pretty iron grillwork railing on either side of the stoop. She walks slowly, deliberately. Her contained eagerness erases any embarrassment she might feel about how she's dressed. Passersby who notice her stare briefly, then turn away.

Without a key, Carmen is forced to knock on her own apartment door. When Benjamin opens, he stands there for what seems like a very long time before taking her in his arms. His tears feel warm against her cheek, but her own eyes are dry. She's happy. Of course she is. But she's forgotten how that feels in this other world, the one she hasn't known for months. Or is it years? And he seems strange, different somehow. She can't put her finger on what it is.

No one mentions the skirt and jacket. She is eager to get into her own clothes, although put off by the fact that they hang so loosely on her now. The first time Carmen is confronted with a mirror, she is confused at her reflection. For moments she thinks she is looking at someone else. Recognition comes with a jolt: the bony face, mottled skin around her eyes, wispy hair, small mole at the corner of her mouth looking bigger than she remembers. It's hard not to feel sorry for the woman whose face she sees.

The changes in Carmencita tell her it must be years. Her daughter is taller and looks more mature, perhaps wiser. And her eyes hold a permanent look of fear. Or maybe it's just an alertness the mother hasn't seen before. She too holds Carmen in a long embrace, then steps back as if to make sure she is there before grabbing her close again. For the next several weeks she is reluctant to leave her side.

Antonio visits. He is relieved to see his sister, know she's come through. Carmen notices a distance between him and Benjamin but can't decipher its meaning.

Days become weeks. Carmen thinks time will surely settle now, assume its familiar dimension. It doesn't. Her unfinished story comes back to haunt her. She tries to remember how it went, wonders if she might finish it now. Didn't she used to have a computer? Benjamin must have put it somewhere. But the story feels transparent, without substance, too far away to feel real.

The Organization orders Carmen to see a trauma therapist. The therapist says her flashbacks and nightmares may diminish. Not will but may. A lot has happened in the twenty-seven months Carmen now knows she was locked up. A bloodless coup put an end to the dictatorship and meant amnesty for the prisoners who survived. But the new government is cautious. Carmen hears even her own comrades say it's the best way to move ahead. Clean slate and look to the future. A nation that works for everyone.

But who is this everyone? Carmen wants to be happy, to get with the program as she hears someone put it. But her own body tells her this isn't right. What about the prisoners whose screams still sound in her ears, those who didn't make it out alive? What about her? She can't force time to act as it should. The uncontrollable shaking and nightmares don't stop. When Benjamin admits he's been seeing a woman he met when he didn't know if Carmen would come home, she's surprised that she feels nothing at all. Not jealousy. Not recrimination. "Are you in love? You should go to her," she manages to say. "I understand."

Although Carmen doesn't really want an explanation, Benjamin wants to tell her why he gave up on her: "You just disappeared," he says. "You have no idea how long we searched, going from precinct to precinct, asking at the prisons, checking in with Human Rights Watch. No one would tell us anything. We even got a government official to try to find out if you were being held somewhere. He risked his job to help. Nothing. We had to assume you were dead."

Carmen listens to him without saying anything. She feels numb to these words that fall around her like spring rain, full of promises but inadequate against the drought. And she remembers the Organization's unwritten law about such situations: women are expected to remain faithful to their husbands in prison and be able to resume the relationship if and when they are released. They need our support, the comrades always said. Women, but not men, of course. None of those expectations mean anything to Carmen now.

Carmencita graduates from high school and enters the public university's school of social work. A way of helping people that doesn't require putting your life on the line. She takes responsibility for supporting her mother and father equally, often acts as a bridge between them. She understands they both went through hell, albeit of different sorts. When Carmen is diagnosed with stage four ovarian cancer, her daughter begs her to submit to the recommended treatments. "You've been through so much. Please don't give up now. You never know," she tells her mother. "You could be one of the lucky ones."

But Carmen remembers she has choice. The one thing no one can take from her. She opts not to do the chemo or radiation. "One of the lucky ones" has a different meaning for her now.

Two months later, her funeral is attended by hundreds: old family friends, estranged husband and grieving daughter, militants of their own political organization she wouldn't have known as such in life. They line the streets and follow the hearse to the cemetery, where Benjamin and Antonio lower the coffin into a fresh grave. It remains unmarked until two years later when Carmencita, now a mother herself, decides it deserves a stone: "Carmen García, 1959-2003. She resisted."

The Table

I was just beginning to prepare breakfast, when I noticed our table was placed differently from the day before. Instead of arranged along the wide front window, it faced into the room. Must have been my wife, I thought, she's always changing things around. A need to improve our living conditions, helped along by her OCD, makes this a constant.

"Great idea," I said, pointing to the table as I filled the little two-person coffee maker with our favorite dark French blend and lit the flame beneath it.

"What's a great idea?" she asked. Then she noticed the table's new position. "I didn't do that." She looked mystified.

We stood for a moment, looking at one another, at the table and then back at the perplexity I'm sure each of us expressed. Neither said another word for what seemed like an eternity. This wasn't the first nor would it be the last time a piece of furniture mysteriously shifted position in our home, a half-filled glass of water topped itself off, or the treadmill on which I exercised each morning began to move beneath my feet without my having touched the switch. Sometimes I would return to my standup desk to find it raised to its highest level when I'd left it only minutes before positioned down low in front of my chair. And then there are the inexplicable disappearances occurring throughout the many years we've been together: the big flashlight, some small but necessary kitchen implement, an expensive pair of leather gloves I'd inherited from a grandfather I despised, more than one book. Items both important and superfluous. These events happened with a regularity we'd come to expect. It was easier not to question them.

A current philosophical point of view, unknown to most laypeople but seriously studied by several prestigious scientists, posits that if we can develop a mathematical model of consciousness based on data obtained from brains, we can apply that model to other systems, for example computers or thermostats, to see what it says about their conscious experience. This point of view is called panpsychism. Following these pathways to their logical conclusions, the scientists in question believe they may discover that all manner of systems—even the universe itself—possess consciousness.

The events I've described, mysterious as they are, hardly fall into this category. They don't really denote consciousness, even considering the different sorts of consciousness that a variety of creatures and objects may possess. From an outsider's perspective I perceive an important difference between computers, thermostats or other inanimate objects and living beings. Thermostats are meant to receive information and convey it. Connected to heating and cooling units, they can be set to regulate a room's temperature. Computers, too, undergo change. They are of a particular age or generation, contain a certain amount of memory, a speed that may seem instantaneous to us but isn't. And so, they can store just so many zeros and ones and no more, follow our instructions rapidly or sluggishly as the case may be. Living beings would seem to be at the far end of a consciousness spectrum, with capabilities that develop and can be trained in complex ways, inanimate objects at the other end: static except for wear and tear or eventual breakdown.

Yet we poets and artists have our own definitions of consciousness. We know that the images of bison and other animals painted on the walls of a cave 40,000 years ago transmit a consciousness that may leave us gasping today. Not the photographs of such paintings but the work itself with all the power it contains. Standing where those artists stood millennia ago, we can feel the awe they experienced, the movement of their brushstrokes tracing life that awed or threatened, their passion as they drew on those walls. Transmission of consciousness? I'd say yes.

It isn't hard to imagine nature itself as conscious: a living landscape changing with the seasons, deserts shifting sand and shadow, mountains hiding crags and crevices behind their majestic faces, oceans in all their moods.

Most people assume that only humans are conscious beings. Some extend the condition to animals. You may be thinking about your dog or cat. Of course, you believe it experiences wariness, aggression, fear, loyalty, love. You know it has a certain sort of consciousness. I have no doubt all animals do. Elephants are famous for their long memories. Whales are known for journeying through feeding, mating, and birthing cycles over thousands of underwater miles. Migrating birds follow seasonal routes year after year. Monarch butterflies find their destiny in Mexico. And tiny desert shrimp breed in shallow water holes and, if their habitats dry up, remain in stasis for as many years as it takes for water to find them again; then, whatever part of their sixteen-day life cycle they have yet to complete, they do so without question. Consciousness or instinct? Perhaps an irrelevant question.

Again, this is not what I'm talking about.

It may be a hard leap for you to make but think about inanimate objects. Your car. A favorite shirt worn for many years. An old pair of shoes. A piece of furniture.

Our dining room table came into our lives when we lived in a house large enough to have a dining room. I found it a decade ago at a local furniture showroom. It stood strong and proud among couches conventionally upholstered in the wrong fabric or color, pale end-tables with their little spindly legs, bookcases in odd proportions, and overstuffed recliners, their inner mechanisms promising all manner of balm to soothe an aching body.

The table made no such promises. In the store it spoke to me in a compelling voice. It stood simple and unpretentious in its darkly finished Honduran pine, with a gently rounded circumference and inserts that allowed for six or even eight diners. Without the inserts it barely seats four but takes up almost no space, fitting perfectly in the tiny condo where we live now. At the old house, it needed those extra planks so it wouldn't look lost. Now smaller is better. The condo's entire living and eating areas, kitchen, and the large nook my artist wife turned into her painting studio contain fewer square feet than the dining room at the old place. We downsized for real.

The stunning idea that consciousness may exist in inanimate objects is relatively new. As a field it emerged from the hope some scientists have lately deposited in the exploration of mathematical algorithms. They claim consciousness is likely due to quantum vibrations in microtubules deep within brain neurons as opposed to the more traditional view that it resides in the connections between neurons. They believe they will discover an algorithm that proves and describes this consciousness they intuit. When we speak about scientific intuition, we mean something quite different from the equations or connective maps we poets see. Our maps depend upon imagination and memory, a legacy of moments joined in the magical time we inhabit for as long as there is someone alive who can evoke them.

The Honduran table tells me stories. I believe it possesses consciousness, although perhaps not of the sort that is discernible via an algorithm. The table speaks to me of an old growth forest. Rural guerrilla fighters might have moved silently among its trees during Central America's civil wars of the 1970s and '80s. Now it may battle international lumber companies eager to profit from its natural wealth. Resistance is doomed but proud.

More than once our table has whispered the tale of its transformation, from living wood to boards prepared at a local sawmill, then sold to a furniture maker in San Pedro Sula. How it went from life in the wild to pliant raw material and finally to an elegant object with a rich finish the color of the earth in which it once grew. I wait for the next chapters: sale to a US import company, journey north, brief rest in that showroom where it caught my eye, and then delivery to our home.

No algorithm needed. This communication is direct, immediate, exuberant. And from now on every scuff and scratch on its surface will add to its unfolding tale. I never know when it will speak, when it may interrupt my mundane routine with a further revelation of its secrets.

Can this be called the table's consciousness, or is it my perception? I can tell you there are times the table is quiet, almost austere, its classic lines and high polish communicating peaceful elegance. At other times it might be described as hospitable or friendly, beckoning us to gather around it and share what is offered on its simple wood.

I've always named the important objects in my life. My cars, for instance. Years ago, I called one and then its replacement Mónica after Mónica Ertl, a particularly innovative and courageous guerrilla fighter in sixties and seventies Bolivia. She was the daughter of Hans Ertl, a German photographer and Nazi immigrant. She loved his creativity. I have no idea how she dealt with his political heritage.

There was no doubt about where Mónica's own allegiance lay. She started the first women's health clinic in La Paz back when that was a novelty, hid militants in her home and joined the National Liberation Army that came to international attention in 1967 when its leader, Ernesto Che Guevara, was ambushed and murdered by government forces on orders from the CIA.

Because of her cultural background and fearlessness, as well as her impeccable marksmanship, Mónica was sent to Hamburg, Germany, to execute the man who had severed Guevara's hands, desecrating a body revered and loved by millions. Roberto Quintanilla Pereira had been named Bolivian consul in that city. His government thought it could save him from reprisal by sending him far from the scene of the crime. Posing as a student interested in visiting Bolivia, Mónica gained access to Quintanilla's inner office and deposited three silent bullets in the man's heart. Then she got rid of her wig, exited before anyone knew what happened, and made her way back to Bolivia. She would live another year before she was gunned down.

This is a story that merits repetition. Who can say it is devoid of consciousness? And where does its throbbing consciousness reside? In the gun? In the wig? In Mónica's risk or escape? In her passion and brilliance that live on in new generations of rebels who know they too may not survive to see justice in their country but that if it comes it will be because of their efforts? A half century after Che's defeat in the remote Yuro ravine, an Indian named Evo Morales was elected president of Bolivia and began making the changes Guevara dreamed.

I call my desktop computer Rosa, after Rosa Luxemburg. Consequently, my little travel laptop is Rosita. As you can see, I'm partial to my heroines and heroes, those women and men who have tried to bring justice into our world, independent of their success. And I anthropomorphize freely. When I speak the names of these objects, I am reminded of who inspired them.

We once had a car we called Biko, for South African freedom fighter Steven Biko. Our current vehicle is a Rav-4. We call it Herman Wallace after a Black Panther falsely accused and held for forty-two years at Louisiana's infamous Angola Prison, much of that time in solitary confinement. Wallace dreamed of a house of his own, not a cell but a house and drew haunting pictures of what it might look like. They released him days before died of cancer. When we talk about Herman, we tend to say things like: "He'll be waiting patiently for you to finish up at the market," or "I hardly had to touch the steering wheel; Herman knows the way by now."

Are those comments reflective of consciousness on the car's part or on ours? They are just a few of an infinite number of stories, like the one about our table's memory of old growth forests, Honduran woodcutters, a carpenter with an eye for utility and grace, and the commercialization that carried a piece of furniture from Central America to a shop in Albuquerque and then into our home.

When we talk about a conscious universe, people of diverse religious beliefs may think about God. Or a legion of undying souls. Or faith itself, which implies a certain consciousness. I am not talking about that convoluted interpretation of consciousness but something far more explicit, registered between objects and ourselves in ways we don't yet understand but will when science catches up with the phenomenon. Until we can access a more scientific understanding, I am content to imagine memory holds the connection.

On Tuesday, October 2nd 2018, I got up around six as usual and went into our small kitchen. I started cutting up fresh fruit to prepare the small salads with which I always begin breakfast. I lit the flame under the water for my wife's soft-boiled egg and sliced a few pieces of homemade bread. After setting the coffee pot on the burner, I turned to transfer saltshaker and pill boxes to the table.

That's when I froze. Without realizing the absurdity of my gesture, I looked around the room. The table was gone. Vanished. Disappeared completely, not even its shadow left as evidence. No chalked outline on the floor, signaling where it had been. My wife emerged from the bedroom then, still flicking sleep from her eyes. She stopped in her tracks.

We looked at one another in silence. Both of us began to experience difficulty breathing, as if the gasps and unanswerable questions to come had already clutched our lungs.

"Where . . .?" I finally said.

"Don't" was all she answered.

I didn't. Not out loud, at least. But I couldn't help wondering, even if the table was gone if its consciousness remained. And if mine would continue to reap its stories?

Ruth's Time

"You say you never smoked?" the specialist asked, his tone of voice belying disbelief. "Perhaps second-hand smoke?" Ruth thought he was determined to fault her for being sick. When the doctor finished telling Ruth that there was nothing more that he could do for her, he forced his face into what he hoped she would take as a sympathetic expression. "Do you have any questions?" he asked.

Ruth couldn't take her eyes from the highly buffed brass name plaque set in what looked like walnut or mahogany, also polished to a rich hue. The brass was so bright it looked like gold. Maybe gold plate. Despite such a prominent display, Ruth never could remember this doctor's name. She would pronounce it to herself, trying to apply some mnemonic device for easy recall, but it was no use; seconds later it had escaped her memory.

Now Ruth felt the room go very still. She checked to see how her body was taking the ultimatum. "Any questions?" he'd asked. She knew his question was rhetorical but what immediately came to her mind was: "How much time?" She didn't really believe this officious man with his impeccable manner knew the answer to that. Instead, she heard herself inquiring: "And if I manage to turn the clock's hands back?" Her words bounced off the walls in the pristine office.

Her own question surprised her. At 57, and with a respected position in biochemical research, Ruth wasn't given to fantasy. She enjoyed poetry and art, read widely, thought about issues outside her field, but looked at the world through scientific eyes. It was as if some stranger had uttered those words that had just emerged from her lips.

The doctor looked equally surprised, unexpectedly jolted from the little speech he'd rehearsed and used regularly. Ruth wondered if she'd struck an unusual chord with him, dislodged his calm demeanor by asking about something about which he wasn't an expert. Still, she waited, expectant.

"Well," he said after an awkward pause, "we'd all like to be able to do that if we could now, wouldn't we?" Ruth thought his comment patronizing, his smile completely out of synch with what she was facing. She noticed the doctor's lips seemed to be pasted on wrong, the lower where the upper should be and vice versa. It gave his face an incomplete look like those skulls with missing jawbones one sees in photographs of archeological sites.

It would depend, Ruth thought. You wouldn't want to turn the clock's hands back if you were lost in the wonder of a marvelous theatrical production, listening to your favorite symphony, walking along an idyllic beach at sunset, or in the arms of the person you love. No, then that would be the last thing you'd want. A list of delicious scenarios continued to unfold before her eyes. On the other hand, if you were giving birth you might want to push those hands forward to end the pain and begin your relationship with your newborn. But none of those situations seemed relevant right now. The discomfort of childbirth, after all, promised the joy of mothering. Not that she'd ever experienced childbirth herself. And walking along an idyllic beach . . . no one would want to turn the clock's hands back on that.

Ruth ran her fingers through the strands of her thick hair, pushing it off her forehead, something she tended to do when deep in thought. When she was younger, her hair had been her glory. She always wondered if the streaks of premature gray might feel different, perhaps coarser, than those that remained a shining black. In recent years she'd finally been persuaded to cut her long braid, but her hair was still the envy of her friends. She was glad she'd refused the chemo sessions, resulting in hair loss, having to shave one's head or finding interesting scarves to wear. And then learning how to wear those scarves; her friend Belle, who was Black, created hair wraps in minutes that always looked elegantly constructed. Ruth tried but couldn't make them look right.

The big decisions were threatening enough without having to juggle all these smaller ones. Now Ruth was being told she had months, maybe weeks or days to live. Why was she evoking all these alternatives or, worse, considering how her response might strike this man who sat before her: unfeeling judge and executioner?

This experience was entirely unfamiliar, one Ruth hadn't faced before. Being told that you are terminally ill imposes its own rhythms, unique tempo, an unknown quantity and quality of angst. Instantly time constricts. Does it really constrict or are you newly aware of its limitations? You might be hit by a car or struck by a bolt of lightning tomorrow, she told herself, but not knowing in advance makes all the difference. There would be no anticipation woven from grief, no anxiety about making your remaining time count before any such eventuality.

Making time count. Ruth contemplated the idea. She visualized time as a tall slender woman with long fingers sitting on a boulder carved in the shape of a saddle or seat. As the woman bent to gather small pebbles and take them in her hands, she let them fall onto a high desert landscape dotted with low brush and smelling of sage. She counted the pebbles as she let them drop. Ruth wanted to call out to the woman, tell her to savor each pebble against her skin, learn its feel and meaning, release it only when she knew it well. Although her lips formed the words, no sound came from her mouth. She realized the woman she saw was Madison.

The oncologist rose from the leather upholstered chair behind his desk. This meeting had gone well beyond the fifteen minutes allotted for such consultations. Averting his eyes from Ruth's, he straightened his white coat. Ruth focused on his tie, perfectly knotted in its subtle elegance. Perhaps a Brioni or a Stefano Ricci, she thought, recently having been stunned when she saw those advertised for two and three hundred dollars. For a tie! Where, a moment before, the doctor had been all authority laced with just the right amount of faux compassion, now he seemed in a hurry to leave his office. He had deployed his expert opinion. The patient would have to take it from here.

Ruth followed that receding back with her eyes. She imagined a bright red target on the white coat. Her gaze was an arrow, searching its mark. She sat for a few more moments in what now felt like a victim's chair, considering her next move. Then she rose, checked to see she had all her belongings and left this tastefully sterile room where everything had changed. She took care to close the office door gently. She ignored the receptionist's cheerful "Have a nice day."

Once outside the building and despite a faint scent of seasonal *bizcochitos*, the air seemed threateningly oppressive. She looked around for vendors of the miniature cookies but didn't see any. It was as if the tantalizing scent carried an unfulfilled promise. No, this couldn't be right. She stopped for a moment just to breathe in and out. Each breath was deeper than the one before. She was right: the air wasn't oppressive but filled with life: a slight breeze, whiffs of imagined sugar cookies and an unmistakable scent of real curry stew floating from an open window: aromas of early fall.

Ruth thought she should go right home, find a way of telling Madison what the doctor had said, get started on what she knew would be a very different chapter in their lives. But she wasn't ready, not quite yet. Neither did she have the energy for her favorite stroll along the river, but she might just walk a block or two, settle into one of those inviting benches, some of which bore plaques honoring someone in town who had died. The thought that one of those plaques might bear her own name in a not-so-distant future, held her attention but only briefly. She decided to try not to dwell on the doctor's ultimatum.

Leaning against the bench's latticed back, gazing into the ribbon of clear water as it rushed between its sandstone banks, Ruth realized that a good exit depended on her ability to consider the inevitable while not getting bogged down in a sense of loss. True, she would be losing everything. And everyone who loved her would be losing her. Madison. Lisa. Lori. She felt a brief sense of relief that both her parents were gone. Can I take them with me, she wondered? What can I leave behind? Abstract questions, not really requiring answers.

Ruth rose from the riverbank bench and headed slowly back toward the center of town where its pride and joy, the lovely old Spanish colonial city hall, was surrounded by well-kept landscaping. Joshua trees. Century plants. Cacti with their red and yellow blooms. A statue of some Catholic saint who had mistreated the indigenous population. Lately she'd heard talk of tearing that statue down, replacing it with one that respected everyone's dignity, but the plan had come to nothing. She looked up at the large clock on the building's north face. She was sure it had read twenty past three when she'd left the doctor's office. Now its hands clearly said two minutes before the hour. She stopped and stared. She thought the clock face was looking directly at her, imagined she caught a complicit wink?

Although it meant detouring a bit from her usual route home, Ruth walked slowly around to the east side of the tower. Its clock said quarter to three. Impossible, she thought, the four clocks were famous far beyond Riverside for their synchronization and accuracy to one-tenth of a second, something villagers never failed to tell visitors who remarked on the tower's architectural beauty. City Hall had been built at the time of the conquest and remodeled over the years as needed. The clocks had been added later but remained a symbol of civilized timekeeping aimed at the Cahuilla people, the area's original inhabitants who, being indigenous, were historically found wanting in their sense of how they understood time.

As Ruth forced herself to make her way around to where she could view the other two clocks, she was astonished to see that the next said twenty to three and the last two-thirty. As she stood there, staring at the tower's western face, she heard the familiar bell that linked all four strike two long peels followed by a shorter one that rang the half hour. It's really happening, she exclaimed, immediately grateful no one was near enough to hear.

Ruth had seen *The Curious Case of Benjamin Button*, the recent Hollywood film in which Brad Pitt was born a wrinkled old man who gradually got younger and younger throughout his strange life until he died a newborn who should have been able to look forward to many happy years. She thought about that film for a moment but couldn't remember what its point had been. Perhaps to capture audiences with the appeal of an intriguing but impossible story.

The positions assumed by the hands on these village clocks were equally impossible. Except that she was looking right at them. This wasn't Hollywood, but something was definitely going on.

What if time really was moving backward? Did this mean that Ruth might have longer than the doctor's dire prognosis? Maybe she didn't need to think about how she was going to break the news to Madison. At least not just yet. Or anyone else. I guess I'll have to see how I feel, she thought. And she pushed the strap of her large leather bag a bit higher on her shoulder, pulled her pea jacket close against a sudden invigorating gust of wind, and turned onto the street that led home.

By the time Ruth reached their apartment, Madison was just getting out of bed. She was surprised to see her wife dressed and looking as if she'd already been out. "Did you go for an early walk?" she asked. "I know you have your appointment with the doctor this afternoon. Please let me go with you. I've already asked Ellie and she says to take all the time I need."

Ruth took off her jacket, put her bag down and waited a moment before answering: "I don't know if I'm going to keep that appointment," she said finally, searching Madison's eyes for a reaction. Although she'd marked the meeting on their kitchen calendar with three bright red exclamation points, talked about it with dread but never thought about not showing up, now she wondered if subjecting herself to the doctor's imperious manner again was really necessary. Hadn't once been enough?

To Ruth's astonishment, Madison didn't seem surprised. She didn't try to convince the woman she loved to follow through, bring home the answer they both dreaded. Instead, she looked at her own watch, smiled and said: "Oh, it's earlier than I thought. I don't have to be at work until eleven today. Let's go have breakfast at The Door. I'm in the mood for one of those chocolate croissants. What do you say?"

Ruth hugged her wife then, held her beloved body close, reluctant to let go. She delighted in the other woman's shape, the temperature of her skin, the faint scent of fresh berries she always exuded. They'd had twenty-seven wonderful years together. Maybe they could look forward to more. Despite how crazy it sounded, if time was moving backward for Madison as well, this shift might be real. Ruth's body felt lighter and, despite the inoperable tumor she'd been told was growing in her right lung, she breathed more deeply than she had in months.

The two women went to their favorite neighborhood cafe. The croissants were fresh, the coffee perfect. Ruth looked up from their sidewalk table to the clock on the west side of the City Hall Tower. She tried to do so casually, all the while directing a stream of conversation at Madison. Ruth hoped her wife wouldn't notice. She had to see the time on that clock.

It said 9:46. Was this the same day? Ruth had been with the doctor in the early afternoon and now it was midmorning. Something wasn't right. But then, in another sense, it was more than right. "Gained half a day," she blurted, not realizing she'd said the words out loud. "What do you mean?" Madison asked, looking at her quizzically.

Ruth wasn't exactly hesitant to talk about the time reversal with her wife. She just didn't know how to begin. She really wanted to talk about Lisa and Lori, the twin daughters they expected home from college in a few weeks. One was at Oberlin hoping to major in history. The other was at Drexler with an as yet undeclared major. From the moment she and Madison had traveled to Guatemala to pick them up, they'd noticed each had her own personality and needs. Lisa was a happy baby, perennially calm and content. Lori was moodier, often fussing for no apparent reason. It had never worked to dress them alike, put them in the same classroom, expect to have the same problems or delights with those girls. Now, at 18 and with a semester of college behind them, they would no doubt arrive with their separate experiences, both happy to see Mama Ruth and Mommy Madison but both predictably distraught at the news that Ruth was ill.

Ruth and Madison had talked about this. How to broach the subject. How to help each girl deal with the implications. Their reactions would look different on the surface, but they knew both would suffer. And then Ruth choosing not to go through the usual treatments. Lisa would be supportive of that decision. Lori would beg Ruth to reconsider; she would go online and print out endless articles with all the latest opinions and statistics. Ruth knew their different responses would mask a shared fear and anticipation of loss.

Did this time thing mean she might not have to tell them her doctor's prognosis after all? Maybe she wouldn't even have to tell Madison?

"Is you watch broken again?" Madison interrupted Ruth's thoughts. "You keep looking at that clock when you have the time right there on your wrist. Does it need a new battery already? Seems I got you one just last week."

Ruth looked at her wrist. Her watch was going strong. And it now said 9:05. Something was happening with all the time pieces, public and private. As soon as she checked one, it was earlier. Sometimes by a few minutes. Sometimes by more than an hour. She began to think about pace, then, wonder if she could somehow regulate how fast time was moving in reverse and if she might grow younger as it did. What if she became an eighty-four-year-old child, like Benjamin Button? What if everyone she knew grew younger? Madison interrupted her wife's reverie by saying something about it getting late and didn't Ruth think they should be heading home?

Ruth didn't know what to think.

On the one hand, this backward movement of time was taking her ever farther from premature death. On the other, she wondered why she seemed to be the only one who noticed the strange reversal. Madison and everyone else acted as if nothing was amiss.

Lisa and Lori came home the following week. They'd taken the same flight from Cleveland. They were full of stories from their respective schools, happy to be together but clearly treating the family as a way station before they returned to where they now felt a new sense of belonging. Neither of them had asked about Ruth's health. They'd never been told she was ill.

Ruth gradually began to relax into this new reality. Since no one else seemed to notice anything odd, she didn't feel the need to explain. Even to Madison. Three months after that unnerving consultation, she dutifully went for her three-month scan. The doctor seemed surprised to see her when he called her in to give her the results. The same intimidating office, same officious name plate, different expensive tie. He looked at the folder in front of him, flipping its pages for what seemed like an eternity before looking up at her: "You won't believe this," he said, "but the tumor is gone. No sign of it at all. This is one of those things the medical profession rarely sees and can't explain. You are a very lucky woman."

Ruth smiled. She rather enjoyed his bewilderment. He'd certainly seemed more comfortable giving bad news than good. She wasn't about to say that she wasn't surprised, preferring to listen to the man unable to show off his expertise. When he launched into a speech that sounded like he was somehow taking credit for her recovery, Ruth stood and held out her hand.

After a while—was it really a while? —Ruth noticed that whenever she remembered the cancer, all the clocks in her life made noticeable little leaps backward. Each did so at its own pace, causing no small amount of disruption in her life. At first, she tried to synchronize them, but soon realized that wasn't possible. It would take a while for things to get back to normal, whatever that might be.

On the other hand, when Ruth forgot about her illness and its terminal prediction, time moved more evenly, going back a few minutes each day, leaving her to enjoy a fairly routine existence.

The girls graduated college. Lisa married a guy she'd known since grade school and soon made Ruth and Madison grandmothers. Lori came out as transgender the year after he finished school. That had been a process of adjustment although also one of relief. Their son's claim to his authentic self was a welcome response to years of unhappiness. They all stepped up in support. Lori became a memory, Larry the much happier human who took her place. It was interesting to have a man in the house but certainly no more of a shock to Ruth than her brush with mortality several years before.

When Madison stepped off a curb one day and was hit by a city bus coming much too fast around a corner, the clocks on all four sides of the Tower and the watch on Ruth's wrist went silent for a full twenty-four hours, as if in mourning. When Madison's broken body was pronounced dead upon arrival at the hospital, though, her own watch was still running. Its glass face was smashed but its hands kept making their little jogs backward, as if to plead not-yet-not-yet-not-yet. After telling Ruth how sorry she was for her loss, the nurse on duty mentioned how strange it was that Madison's watch hadn't stopped at the moment of impact. Then she looked away. Perhaps this wasn't the time for such an observation. She hadn't noticed that the watch was moving in the wrong direction.

Losing Madison was the worst thing that had ever happened to Ruth. She sometimes caught herself making little bargains with a God in whom she'd never believed: I'll take the tumor back. I'll gladly trade my life for hers. Why can't time have slowed for her before the accident? I'll give you . . . well, anything to have my woman back.

She knew none of those options were possible.

Ruth waits, now, for her own time to catch up with itself.

The Photograph

Although much of life comes down to love or its absence, this isn't a love story. It's better described as a ghost story. Still, to set the stage I'll begin by telling you about the two women in the stone house on the hill.

To most of those who knew them, and even to those who didn't, Marlin and Agatha were an unlikely couple. They couldn't have appeared more different in looks or temperament. Marlin had been a fixture on tiny Isla de las Tormentas since she was a child. She'd never really known her mother who died when she was two. She arrived with her father, who relished the deep-sea fishing, home schooled her, and made a life for them there. Everyone knew her: the tall, large-boned woman with olive skin, long dark hair, and an inobtrusive habit of coming to the aid of her neighbors.

Marlin's father died when she was in her early twenties, and she stayed on in their stone house overlooking dramatic leeward cliffs. She seemed to have a private income, enough to live on in any event, and spent her days looking in on villagers who needed help repairing a fence, sick children to whom she might administer a shot of penicillin, or dogs who could use her homemade flea remedy. The locals counted her as one of their own and called her Mar.

Agatha showed up a dozen or so years ago. The islanders, who had trouble pronouncing the TH, called her Agata. She was small with delicate features and unruly hair bleached by the sun. And she was either shy or a loner, friendly when spoken to but liked keeping to herself.

Agatha had decided on a Caribbean vacation one summer and unexpectedly chose the Dominican Republic rather than one of the larger, more popular Caribbean islands: Jamaica or the Virgin Islands, even though they spoke English on those. She flew to Santo Domingo and then just had the urge to keep going. Which was how she discovered Isla de las Tormentas. She couldn't remember how she'd heard about the place. An offshore province, it didn't appear on maps but was known to the local fishermen.

From the moment she arrived, Agatha was captivated by the highly polished cliffs lashed by the sea over millennia of frequent storms. Those storms had given the name to the otherworldly rise of land not much bigger than an atoll. Tormentas possessed a privileged landscape: stark cliffs, intimate sandy beaches, a lush interior valley, and volatile skies. Or maybe it was the fact that Tormentas was a place devoid of tourists.

Agatha's high-pressure copyediting job at Newsline had finally gotten to her: the late-night deadlines and having to fight for a raise or benefits. She wanted different, quiet, remote. What she didn't expect, couldn't have imagined, in fact, was that her second day on the tiny island she and Marlin would meet at the village's only café. Before they abandoned its pungent aroma of seafood stew, both women knew they'd found the person with whom they would share their life. The pheromones were powerful.

Agatha moved in with Marlin. Without naming it, the villagers easily accepted their relationship. They'd known and loved Marlin most of her life. Any choice she made had to be a good one. Agatha quit Newsline via the island's weekly mail service. Phone calls were impossible, any attempt at conversation interrupted by the thundering sound of sea on the wire. At first, she sometimes hitched a ride on the supply boat and spent a few hours at a Santo Domingo cybercafé, but she eventually got used to the isolation. Her parents and friends were astonished, but the conviction in her response to their questions or pleadings finally convinced them she'd made up her mind. Despite promises, none ever came to visit. Twelve years have passed now, and Agatha is as much of a fixture as Marlin on Isla de las Tormentas.

It was only last week that Agatha discovered the box. She was looking for something on a high shelf in the closet of the small room she'd appropriated as her studio. Just behind the rudimentary kitchen, it had a window that opened toward the water. That haunting island light flooded in from early morning to late afternoon. With a rough-hewn plank for a desk, the old laptop she'd brought with her so many years before, a makeshift rocker and a cot where she could sleep if she was up late writing and didn't want to wake Marlin, she had everything she needed. She'd somehow never explored that closet shelf before and was surprised to find a shoebox containing old photographs. She took it down, settled into the rocker and began examining its contents.

Agatha was careful to hold one photograph between her thumb and forefinger, allowing only its edges to come in contact with her flesh, sweat, any possible body salt or acid that could further damage it. Pinking shears had serrated the slim white border in the fashion of a bygone era, helping to camouflage the natural deterioration of the paper. For a moment she thought she should be wearing a pair of those white cotton gloves that archives and museums require when handling something so fragile. From the fading grays of the portrait's surface, eyes both riveting and oddly challenging stared directly into hers.

Hello Lidia Sandoval, Agatha thought, as she returned the woman's gaze. She knew that wasn't what she was called but rather her own penchant for naming; and that the subject of the photo couldn't be aware she was looking at her. In fact, Agatha had named her on a whim. She had no idea why she'd baptized her in that way, so alien except for its Latin syllables. A woman growing up on the island would more likely have been called Maria, Carmen, or Dolores.

The magic of photography freezes a moment in time—a look, gesture, defiant stance, or easy acquiescence—even as it eliminates an ongoing connection between the subject and all subsequent viewers of the image. The person snapping the shutter might think he or she is building a bridge when in fact they are raising a metaphorical gangplank, allowing the ship with its passenger to sail, and leaving all viewers standing on a distant shore. We can never know all that went before or comes after the instant when the lens opens and closes.

Lidia's dark hair was parted in the middle and pulled back, severely except for a few wayward strands rebelling in the vicinity of her ears. Her face was slightly weathered but still beautiful. She was wearing a simple peasant dress, typical of the homespun woven in these parts. Its high collar, bordered with a narrow strip of embroidery, reached to just below a prominent chin. The woman's image faded just above her breasts and below her mid upper arms, giving the impression that she was floating. Puffed sleeves and other elements of her outfit dated the picture to the final years of the nineteenth century. It was clear the portrait had been made by a professional photographer. Not a studio professional, more likely someone who roamed the islands making pictures for a price. There was no exotic backdrop or other formal prop. This was a woman alone who chose to have her picture taken and looked directly into the camera.

Agatha couldn't really say what attracted her to that portrait. Maybe the eyes. She had no idea who the woman was. Lidia lived in that box along with dozens of others, most of them recorded in amateurish snapshots. They seemed to trace back several generations. When Agatha excitedly brought her find to Marlin, her lover shuddered. Said if she had her way, they'd throw the box out along with everything in it. Said all that musty old stuff gave her the creeps. Who knew where it had been, who'd touched its grimy contents? What was it even doing in the house? All of which seemed logical coming from a woman who'd grown up on the sea and was always more comfortable outdoors than in. Marlin lived with the essentials, seemed to scrub everything down to its minimum expression. Even her name, odd for a woman and especially here, reflected her father's obsession with the ocean and its most combative fish.

But Agatha couldn't toss the box. She'd developed an intimate relationship with its inhabitants. Sometimes she'd pull it down from the closet shelf, then sit with it in her lap for a while, slowly examining each image. Lidia was the one who claimed most of her attention. There was something mysterious about the woman, something elusive yet compelling. The box's cover had the word PHOTOGRAPHS written in block letters, neat but obviously inscribed by someone who hadn't practiced writing much.

Another portrait was of an elderly couple in a formal pose, perhaps someone's grandparents. And there were various generations of children; sometimes Agatha could follow one of them growing older from picture to picture. A little girl, turned to look at the camera as she struggled up a jungle gym. Not a jungle gym like the steel ones of her own childhood but a clever arrangement of brightly painted carved wooden animals standing on each other's shoulders and providing delight to the children lured by its fanciful design. Tormentas was known for a kind of whimsical creativity.

The girl might have been five or six. She looked startled. Agatha struggled to read her face. Was it fear? The camera had caught her mid-movement. The hand that let go of the highest animal was blurred. Could it have been warning the intruder away? Agatha wondered who'd taken that picture, what connection he or she had with its subject. It also occurred to her that the child on the jungle gym might be the woman in the formal portrait. Yes, she thought, those could be the same eyes before they experienced more of the world.

A boy appeared in several snapshots. His face looked almost the same: as a toddler, teenager, and finally a young man with his arm around a woman who seemed around his age. Agatha thought the face familiar. She might have seen it, older but retaining some of its youthful features, in the village. There was another picture in which the same man posed in a military uniform; World War II judging by its style, an army private because he had neither stripes on his sleeve nor stars on his shoulders. Agatha knew a small contingent of Isla de las Tormenta's young men had fought on the side of the allies. He must have been one of them.

She found quite a few postcards in the box as well: the Eifel Tower and London Bridge, perhaps attesting to weekend leaves when the soldier was stationed somewhere in Europe. On the backs of those cards, in careful Palmer penmanship, were brief messages: *No es lo mismo sin ti* and *Contigo esto sería el paraíso*. Most had no address. They hadn't been sent through the mail. Were they written to the woman he'd come home to, given to her when he arrived? Touching and nostalgic, she thought. One exception, a postcard mailed from Paris, bore a one-and-a-half-franc stamp.

Agatha thought for a moment about how prices keep going up all over the world, postage and everything else. But here on Tormentas they stay the same. And if one lacks resources, one can always barter for what one needs. Similarly, there was little inorganic waste. People brought their own receptacles and bottles to the village and filled them with what they purchased. These were things she loved about the place.

Each time Agatha got the urge to revisit the shoebox, its contents suggested more elaborate stories. She was intrigued by a souvenir picture, taken by a professional tourist photographer, of two couples and a fifth person, an extra man, seated in a row on a flower bedecked wooden gondola. The row of we're-having-fun smiles showed even white teeth. An arch above their heads read: *Lupita*, the name of the local-style raft, written in flowers. She was sure one of the men was the guy in uniform, quite a bit older and a civilian now.

Just as the photographer snapped the shutter, the woman seated beside him turned to look at the odd man on her other side. Agatha tried to read her expression. Or maybe she was reading into the woman's glance a story she herself had narrowly escaped. She recognized the black and white photograph as having been taken at Xochimilco, a complex of canals on the outskirts of Mexico City left over from when the entire valley of Mexico had been a great lake. The photo was evidence that some islanders traveled from time to time.

It was as if the people in the photographs were revealing their lives, their secrets along with the most mundane events. But Agatha brought her curiosity and imagination to bear as well. She invented stories about how each of them had lived and died. She kept a notebook with her observations. Perhaps she would write them into a novel one day.

Some reached old age, she decided, others died young. She told herself the young soldier had made it through the war, returned to Isla de las Tormentas, married a local girl, and become a gardener. She didn't know why she assigned him that vocation. Maybe he had the face of someone who loved plants. Did he and his wife have children? She couldn't find a picture that conclusively answered that question. But she liked imagining that tending gardens had helped the man heal from whatever horrors he'd experienced during the war. Then she consoled herself further by deciding he'd worked in intelligence and hadn't been a victim or closeup witness to any of the anguish wars unleash. Agatha was fond of the people in that box and wanted them to have good lives.

As casually as Agatha invented stories about most of the faces she saw, the portrait of the woman she called Lidia held a special fascination. She spent hours with her, mesmerized. And the woman's expression appeared to focus on Agatha as well, as if she knew she was there—or here. Her slightly parted lips seemed about to tell her something. Agatha knew the woman's story was important but wasn't prepared for what happened next.

She heard the woman's voice for the first time late one night, hours after she and Marlin had gone to bed. The sound roused her, and she emerged from sleep with a start.

She looked at Marlin, but her lover hadn't stirred. Then she heard the voice again. She had no doubt whose it was or where it came from. It wasn't loud but could clearly be distinguished from the ever-present sound of the sea. And it seemed to be directed at her. She slid from the covers, then, grabbed her bathrobe from the chair, and followed the insistent call to the closet in her studio. She pulled the box down, trying to be as quiet as possible as she settled into her large rocker and lifted its cover.

It astonishes Agatha now that she can't remember exactly what that voice said the first time it spoke to her. She'd experienced it as a kind of wordless beckoning. All she knows is that it was enough to rouse her from bed and entice her to respond. And her subsequent conversations with Lidia hadn't exactly been easy to follow or understand. Often, she had to ask the woman in the picture to repeat herself. Sometimes Lidia was willing, at others she shrugged and fell silent.

Over the next few nights, in uneven bursts, the woman told Agatha that her name wasn't Lidia, but she didn't mind being called that. Now that she was no longer among the living, it was as good a name as any. She didn't volunteer her real name and Agatha didn't ask. She said she was born and grew up on the island but had traveled a bit: to Santa Domingo and once to Panama. She knew she loved women from her earliest stirrings, but believed she was alone in that aspect of her identity and that it would be useless, perhaps dangerous, to pursue her desire.

And so, she resigned herself to a life of loneliness. She became the postmistress of Isla de las Tormentas, receiving letters and packages from the boat that arrived weekly from Dominican Republic and delivering them to their recipients who stood before her polished wooden counter, smiled and thanked her, then departed after exchanging a few pleasantries. Most villagers thought her aloof. When she died of flu in her fifties, the requisite number of mourners accompanied her body to the cemetery on the hill, but none had really known her.

Agatha was struck by the difference between this woman's story and those she'd invented for the other occupants of the box. She acknowledged her naïveté in having contrived happy endings for them while Lidia had lived a life of privation and pain. She was particularly moved by the fact that she and Marlin could be together without condemnation, even in such a remote place as Isla de las Tormentas. Back in New York, where she came from, gender diversity was increasingly accepted even by a largely heterosexual society. Occasionally she'd get ahold of magazine articles that brought news of welcome progress. But the threat of backlash was always present.

Agatha and the woman she called Lidia conversed until there was nothing left to say. Words or some form of telepathy? She would never be sure. The woman in the photograph wanted her to know how fortunate she was. Once she got that message across, she fell silent. Their talks stopped. Agatha waited night after night for the voice that no longer came.

"I miss her," she told Marlin one afternoon, as they walked into town to have dinner at the café where they'd met what seemed like a lifetime ago. It was no longer the only eatery on the island, but they were loyal to its inviting atmosphere and the place it represented in their history.

"As long as we have each other," Marlin said, pulling Agatha close against the cold wind coming in from the sea.

Procreate

It was Tuesday, but a Tuesday like neither of them could remember. As if the week's most opaque day was suddenly vying for some much-needed attention. Stella was beginning to make their breakfast, something she did every morning but Sunday when Jessie would go out to their favorite café and come back with a sesame seed bagel for her wife and two steaming lattes.

"Can I show you what I did last night?" Jessie was holding her I-Pad across the counter that separated her workspace from the kitchen. Stella knew it was another digital painting, one of the many her wife had been making over the past several months. They'd come one after another, each exciting the artist as much as her partner of forty years. At first Jessie had been tentative about this new medium, taking time to experiment with brush strokes, lines, color panes, forms—all within the magic of digital technology. Like acrylics or gauche, it had its own pathway to expression. Once she became comfortable with the program's possibilities, she produced the paintings in series, delighting in her new voice.

"Of course." Stella turned away from the stove, wiping her hands on her Levi's. She looked in astonishment at the screen Jessie thrust in front of her. Yet another combination of color and line that spoke of her woman's astonishing talent and imagination. The way she sees the world, Stella thought. It's entirely her vision. "Oh, I love that," she said out loud, "it's got to go in the exhibition."

Jessie was preparing to show these digital paintings at Here We Are, the coffee shop across the street from where they lived. She would choose a dozen or so, take them to the printer who'd always come through for her, and get him to reproduce them as large as possible. Stan was worried about color accuracy, choice of paper, what he'd have to charge for each print. Jessie didn't know about any of that; she loved making these paintings, the details to be worked out later. They decided on 36 by 36 inches. She knew there would be differences between the luminosity one saw on a backlit screen and how an image would look on paper. That was all part of the process.

Jessie wasn't cut out for the business side of art. Since she'd retired from teaching middle school special ed students ten years ago, all she wanted to do was draw and paint and print, working in the tiny studio space she'd carved out of their living/dining room, doing what she'd had such a hard time believing she had a right to do. Growing up in an evangelical home, "artist" hadn't been on the list of encouraged or approved activities. Neither was free thinker or lesbian for that matter. Those old prohibitions were hard to shake. Stella encouraged her to be who she is, do what she was born to do. Sometimes it seemed like she had to unpack that encouragement again and then again. Old damage clings like mold.

These new digital paintings were a departure for Jessie. Radical, yet entirely hers. For years she'd been working small. Now, with Stan's help, she was going big. Her show would open in a month. Just enough time to get the paintings back from the printer, take them to the frame shop where David was as enthusiastic as Stan, and then hang the work. "Beautiful," Stella said, when Jessie brought the test strips home from the printer. "You should see them now," Jessie exclaimed after the framer had done his magic. Jessie was excited despite herself, despite worrying nothing would sell—the printing and framing had cost a lot—, despite those nagging slivers of doubt that could still make her wonder if she deserved giving in fully to this primal part of herself.

Jessie was back at her desk, the I-Pad sitting before her. She had an unsettled expression on her face. When she'd gone to open the device this morning, she'd discovered it was already on. She was sure she'd shut it down last night. But no, the screen was illuminated and *Procreate* was right there, staring back at her. The painting program with a name that evoked continuation, creation, birth. She thought she even caught a wry wink, must be imagining things. The artist slid back into her desk chair now and stared at the monitor. Maybe she'd mess around before breakfast, see what showed up. Just because she'd chosen the images for her show didn't mean she had to stop making more. She sat very still, then emitted a short gasp as she watched the device itself choose a brush and then hover over a color wheel on which hot reds and yellows melded seamlessly into cool purples and greens and blues. Before her startled eyes and stopped breath, a brush point she would never have chosen on her own proceeded to fill the digital canvas with unfamiliar lines and shapes.

"Wait for me!" she muttered, not realizing she'd said the words out loud.

Stella was putting the finishing touches on the small bowls of fresh fruit she liked cutting up for them each morning. The water in their miniature saucepan had just begun to boil and she scooped Jessie's egg up with the spoon she held in her left hand while with her right she set the stove's timer for six minutes, the perfect number for the soft-boiled texture she found revolting but her wife loved. Stella tended to look away when Jessie emptied the scraped contents of the shell into the ramekin and sopped them up with the half slice of gluten-free bread Stella had toasted just enough to take the refrigerator chill off but not so much that it burnt around the edges. This morning ritual was one that comforted them both. It set the mood for their days. They were of an age when you're done with eight-to-five and can devote yourself to the work you love: writing for Stella and visual art for Jessie.

But now the artist sat immobile, distant, almost somewhere else. She didn't take her eyes from her I-Pad monitor where something was happening that defied her ability to understand or explain.

The stove's timer sounded. Stella ignored it. Moving on automatic, she'd turned the coffee off. Next on her list of breakfast preparations would have been pouring just the right amount of dark liquid into the mugs of milk she'd heated in the microwave: a bit for Jessie, twice as much for herself. She saw the expression on her wife's face, though, and left the kitchen nook altogether. Something inexplicable was happening.

Jessie had removed one pair of dime store glasses and replaced it with another. Ever since her left eye had gone dark a few years back, she'd suffered strange alterations in her sight. The vision in that eye had returned, but differently. Sometimes she described it by saying her eyes didn't play well together. Their depth of field didn't match. Scary for an artist. Scary for anyone, really, but especially for an artist. She'd managed to navigate eyes that didn't play well together by changing glasses frequently. But no damaged vision or alternate glasses explained what was going on now. She was sitting frozen at her desk. Stella could tell that she was as astonished as she was confused.

"What's going on?"

Jessie didn't respond. She was fixated on the I-Pad.

Stella stood behind Jessie and looked over her shoulder at the screen. Things were happening of their own accord. Jessie's hands were nowhere near the device. She hadn't touched the drawing pen which was sitting inert in its cradle atop the monitor. Both women's eyes followed what looked to be *Procreate's* entirely independent movement: brush strokes, lines, shapes and areas of color laying themselves down with their own decision and energy.

"It's painting . . . by itself . . ." Jessie's words trailed off. She couldn't take her eyes from the I-Pad, where an occasional click or ding could be heard accompanying a complex series of movements as some unknown intelligence or energy was painting of its own volition. Lines linked to other lines, creating a developing perspective. Layers of color spread over other layers, sometimes straightedged and at others fading in and out, occasionally erasing themselves and going for a second try. The image emerging was interesting, perhaps exciting. But it wasn't Jessie's. No. It had nothing to do with her.

The human artist was caught between astonishment and fear.

"I'm not . . ." Jessie's voice seemed subdued, out of body.

"No, no, I can see . . ." Stella had released all thought of breakfast. The egg bouncing around in its little pan must be hard-boiled twice over by now. Neither woman noticed the stove's timer chiming its continuous attempt to get their attention.

Stella pulled up a chair. Both women continued to be riveted to the screen. A few more rapid swirls or deliberate lines appeared on what was quickly becoming a finished work. Then everything stopped. Several minutes passed. Jessie imagined a being inside the device, contemplating what she or he or it had produced. Stepping back. Closing one eye, appraising the painting. What was she thinking about: closing one eye? As if whatever was doing this had an eye! The little dot that was the latest generation cursor moved to save the image and placed it in an entirely new folder titled "My Work." Who the hell was My?

For a while everything seemed quiet on the digital art front. Both women remained with their eyes on the monitor for what seemed like an eternity, expectant, listening to their own breath. Neither of them spoke. Only when they began to smell burnt eggshell in a dry pan, did Stella move quickly to the kitchen, silence the timer and turn off the stove. On the egg's white calcium, a dark brown scorch fixed it to the pan's bottom. When she lifted the lever to eject it from the toaster, the half slice of toast was burnt to a crisp, inedible.

All that day Jessie and Stella were plagued by wonderment and confusion. Jessie would go periodically to her I-Pad only to discover one or two additional paintings in the "My Work" folder. They had clearly been done by the same hand, showing a unity of vision and style. They ate, somewhat distractedly. Stella did a bit of wash, then tried to work on a poem but couldn't keep her mind on the words. She almost feared finding someone else's texts in her computer and checked surreptitiously. Mostly what the women did was return to the I-Pad from time to time to take stock of the mystery work as it emerged.

They felt strangely conspiratorial, and at the same time comforted to have one another. It wasn't as if they could tell anyone *Procreate* was doing its own thing, producing paintings without any input from Jessie, paintings entirely different from those she made. Who would have believed them? Each woman had experienced moments in her life in which silence was ever so much more expedient than explanation. Trying to explain an event that verges on the supernatural invariably brings one of two responses: either you're lying or you're crazy. Asking Google didn't seem like a possibility either; the moment you inquired about anything like this you'd be labeled some sort of conspiracy theorist and could expect to find your inbox filled with messages and offers that wouldn't leave you alone.

That night their usual turning-in time of nine or ten came and went. Neither woman made a move toward the bedroom. Finally, around midnight, they abandoned the more than thirty images the unknown artist had left in "My Work." Sleep seemed urgent. As she closed her eyes, Stella was pondering the subject of artificial intelligence—about which she knew almost nothing.

Was it a woman? A man? Another gender? Some version of AI? The way they portrayed the latter on TV and film always seemed to include a figure that bore more than a passing resemblance to a human, perhaps with Data's non-expressive face and scalp flap beneath which his mechanism could be rebooted when necessary. We sympathized with his yearning for emotion. In recent science fiction films, the theme often involved human protagonists falling in love with AI beings; audiences waited anxiously for the crisis of incompatibility. So long as it was fantasy, it was all very entertaining, didn't threaten your real life.

Unlike those entertaining characters, this artist who lived in Jessie's I-Pad was invisible. She, he, or it assumed no physical form. At least not one they could see. It was messing with Jessie's mind, and with Stella's too for that matter. It was the art that mattered, painting after painting stored in a folder set up in the conventional way. In snatches of restless dream that night, Stella thought she might be touching on a possible explanation. The voice speaking to her in her sleep was disembodied. "She'll have to push against me," it said. "She'll have to assert herself, put herself out there in spite of all the old damage, inhibitions, doubting whether she deserves to think of herself as an artist."

Stella knew the voice was talking about Jessie, alluding to the ways in which her childhood still threatened her at every turn. She'd had to fight hard to be who she is, come out as an independent thinking human being, claim herself as an artist as well as so many other parts of her identity. It had been a constant battle to inhabit the space she needed, still was at times. Stella had watched the woman she loved move forward, slip back, then move forward again. No gain ever seemed absolute.

"But who are you?" she interrogated the dream voice in every way she knew how. "What are you doing in her I-Pad? How did you get there? What's this all about? You must realize how unsettling this whole thing is . . ."

Stella hesitated to tell Jessie about these conversations that continued night after night, sometimes unsatisfactory as an empty mirror, sometimes coming close enough to dialogue that she woke thinking if she'd only been able to stay longer, try harder, manage the right arrangement of words, she might have some sort of answer.

At first Jessie was put off by the mysterious force taking possession of one of her mediums. She didn't touch the I-Pad for several days, going back to the little notebooks where she liked to draw or the Gelli blocks she'd discovered made interesting prints. Then her longing for color got the better of her again and she approached the device, almost timidly at first, as if wary of what might have gone on in her absence. Invariably "My Work" would contain new paintings. Most now seemed facile or clichéd, moving her to respond with her own more interesting ones. She began using *Procreate* to paint again, producing images that were bolder and more stunning than before.

After a few days Stella finally mentioned the disembodied voice in her dream to Jessie. Their years together had allowed them to build a trust that enabled even the strangest of confidences. Jessie listened but didn't seem that convinced. The messages Stella managed to transmit seemed amorphous at best, adding to the mystery rather than pointing them toward any sort of explanation.

"The strangest thing," Stella said, "is that I don't see anyone. Not a woman, not a man, not even a facial feature. It's just that voice, keeps coming to me in my sleep, telling me things I only partially understand. It seems to have something to do with you claiming your space as an artist. Fully. Believing in yourself. Doing the work."

"But I am doing the work." Stella thought Jessie seemed irritated. Or maybe defensive. "By putting myself out there do you mean the whole marketing thing? Looking for a gallery? Promoting myself? Trying to sell?"

Stella was surprised at Jessie's response. She'd never pushed her wife to go the commercial route. In fact, she'd consistently told her they could live on their pensions and social security, what came in from her writing. That she should feel free to create for its own sake. "No," she said, withdrawing a bit. "I think it's just about understanding you're an artist, doing your work without retreating into self-doubt or worrying about any of the rest of it."

"I know I'm an artist," Jessie responded, angrily. Then she pulled Stella into her arms and held her for what seemed a lifetime. "Forgive me," she said, "this whole thing is just so stressful." The two women melted into one another, releasing the tension the phenomenon had introduced into their lives. After mutual assurances they were okay with one another, Jessie sat down in her small studio space, opened her I-Pad, clicked on *Procreate* and began to choose colors and move brushes. For the first time since this craziness started, she ignored "My Work" completely. Let it make the art it wants, she thought; I'll make mine.

Stella understood that her dream conversations reflected her own philosophical questions. They didn't really have anything to do with Jessie or the force that had taken possession of her I-Pad.

Jessie's show opened to rave reviews and hundreds of attendees who almost uniformly loved what hung on the walls. The large images, set off by narrow black frames and the two-inch white border the printer had left on all four sides were a commanding presence. Jessie received phone calls almost every day from people who wanted her to meet them at the coffee shop to talk about her work. Stella noticed that she smiled more than usual.

After a couple of months, Jessie gathered the courage to talk to others about the artist who'd borrowed her computer program and made a personal series of digital paintings. Phyllis and Stuart were friends, visual artists themselves. He a sculptor, she a watercolorist. Both used computer programs in their work. Could anyone else have experienced something like this, remaining equally silent for fear of what others might think?

The couple came over for coffee, and Stella was surprised when she heard her wife mention the mystery.

Stuart seemed at a loss for words. Phyllis immediately asked to look at the stranger's work. It sounded like she wanted proof, something palpable she could see with her own eyes. Jessie motioned her over to her desk, turned on the I-Pad and went directly to the files. She would open "My Work," she thought. Seeing would be believing.

But scan as she would, she couldn't find "My Work." It had disappeared from the device, taking the mystery artist's paintings with it. Minutes passed, while Jessie searched on her I-Pad, scrolling through the program as if cutting grass with an old-fashioned lawnmower and making sure every inch of lawn had been sheared. An awkward silence spread through the room, punctuated now and then by Jessie's "wait a minute" or "just let me . . ." or "okay now. . ." Jessie looked at Stella, who complied by assuring their guests this strange event had really happened, it wasn't their imagination. Phyllis and Stuart looked at one another, then at the floor. They picked at the strawberry rhubarb pie Stella had baked. Eventually they took their leave, their faces masks of faux understanding mixed with the urgent desire to flee what was clearly some sort of weird cry for attention.

Stella and Jessie stared at one another in silence, then burst out laughing. There were no answers, certainly not for anyone who hadn't experienced what they had. Stella found herself thinking about a progressive Catholic church she'd visited in El Salvador years before. The liberation theology priest had commissioned a mural with panels running the circumference of the nave. There were scenes from the Bible as well as those from the country's long struggle for liberation. Behind the altar abstract swirls of color represented the God they worshipped: an amorphous image as distant from the old gray bearded deity as could be imagined. When talking about the mural, the priest always emphasized the fact that no one knows what God looks like, so why make the presence male or female, old or young or human in any way. Traditionalists in the community never did accept the abstraction. The more adventurous loved it.

Stella wasn't a believer, but she'd been struck by that priest's willingness to allow the unknown to remain unknown. It translated into humility in her mind. No male patriarch, no Mediterranean Jesus absurdly portrayed with blue eyes and long blond curls. The abstract "portrait" had seemed more honest, somehow, a question rather than an answer.

Stella knew this wasn't about God, about believing or not believing. It wasn't about dreams or disembodied voices. She realized she was imposing her philosophical bent on a phenomenon that wasn't analogous. She began to wonder if a hacker had somehow gotten into *Procreate*, introducing a virus or worm that had produced the phenomenon they'd observed. Could such an invasion have manifested as an avatar capable of confronting the program user with its mysterious presence. And if it had happened to Jessie, why hadn't it happened to others? She wondered if artificial intelligence possesses consciousness, or if it is dependent upon the hacker's intentions?

Maybe that was our visiting artist, she thought, a question instead of an answer. A being who didn't need to assume a human dimension or even the arbitrary image of what we imagine AI looks like. One dictionary entry for AI described it as referring to "the simulation of human intelligence in machines that are programmed to think like humans and mimic their actions. It is used for data discovery, analysis, visualization and even prediction." Some say it democratizes analytics. The idea of AI democratizing anything made Stella uneasy; she was too suspicious of the racist, patriarchal and corporate forces responsible for its dissemination. Perhaps on some other plane of existence, in some other world so to speak, the mystery painter is making its way through its "My Work" folder, choosing what it wants to show and preparing for an exhibit that will be attended by others of its kind.

No philosophical explanation worked. Stella and Jessie knew they were dealing with science, and the nature of science is change. They resigned themselves to not knowing. Jessie kept on making art in every medium that drew her to its possibilities. Her doubts about self-worth still plagued her at times. That was who she was. Stella still talked her woman through her moments of self-doubt. That was who she was.

The Invitation

Brittany plans to spend the summer interning at The Globe. Between junior and senior year at Boston College's School of Journalism, students can sign up for an unpaid summer of experience on one of the area papers. First come, first served. She knows she's lucky to get The Globe. But the day before she is due to begin, everything changes. An old romantic interest she hasn't heard from in more than a year calls and, after the minimal "how've you been?" and "yeah, I know what you mean," asks if she wants to spend a month with him in Barcelona. "I'm paying," he adds, before she has a chance to say no.

She puts a name to the face. Brock is someone in whom she once had more than a passing interest. Now she brings up the good things rather than the bad and thinks what the hell.

She says yes.

Brittany puts down the phone, astonished at how quickly she's assured Brock it sounds perfect. She'll have to invent something she can tell The Globe's newsroom editor. She was so eager during their interview. No matter, she thinks now. Another journalism student will be glad to get my spot. She'll take the train to New York and be ready to leave with him in a week. A trip to Barcelona suddenly seems meant to be. Brittany stops packing only long enough to get online and google Gaudi, the Sagrada Familia, and the Gothic Quarter. A series of romantic-looking villages along the Catalunya coast beckon from her I-Pad screen.

Having taken a cab from Penn Station to Brock's fourth floor Greenwich Village apartment, Brittany is out of breath from hauling both her suitcases up the narrow stairs. She is further flustered when a woman wearing one of Brock's shirts buttoned wrong and nothing below mid-thigh opens the door. The two women look at each other in embarrassed confusion. Brittany can hear her former lover's voice from the bedroom: "Who's there, honey?"

The other woman, awkwardly introduced as Penny, quickly changes into her own clothes, and leaves without saying goodbye. Brittany can't remember if a soundtrack accompanies her retreat. Now Brock is doing a bad job of explaining Penny's presence—something about wrapping things up and last goodbyes and thinking she'd said she was arriving this afternoon—as he urges Brittany to sit at the Formica-topped kitchen table and brews her a cup of her favorite piñon coffee. See, he remembers. After each garbled utterance, he turns to her with those earnest eyes she recalls once made her forgive him almost anything, waiting for the absolution he's been used to since prep school quarterback fame.

"Anyway, you're here." That boyish grin. Yes, Brittany thinks, I am.

The intoxicating scent of the small white fruit of a desert tree roasted to perfection sooths Brittany's hurt pride and banishes her doubts. She told The Globe an out-of-town aunt had been taken ill and said goodbye to her Boston friends after excitedly revealing her sudden invitation. Returning in defeat would be harder than ignoring Brock's bad timing and telling him he could go off to Europe without her.

That night Brittany thinks she can still smell Penny on Brock's sheets. She might have played hard to get for a day or two, but boyfriend habits die hard. Instead, she mimics her old responses to his romantic overtures, fakes orgasm as she did when they briefly lived together and does her best to convince him it's all good. The afternoon she arrives he proudly flashes the Iberia tickets at her, pointing out that he splurged so they could fly Business Class. Brock was always one to speak in dollar signs.

Brock's offer is enticing. But an internship at The Globe isn't something to be taken lightly. Brittany feels tempted, but says no.

Her first day on the job, the newsroom editor tells them he's glad to have such a promising group of interns. He asks each of them if they have any special interests or fields of expertise. "Write about what you know," he says. "It may sound like a cliché, but believe me, it's the best advice anyone will ever give you."

Brittany can't think of an answer that might set her apart from the other bright young students, all women and all but one wearing uniform tan slacks and starched white shirts. The one from Idaho is in an outdated denim jumper over a pale pink blouse.

Theater? Gardening? Brittany surprises herself, then, by saying something about the crime beat, how her father was a cop and took her with him to the precinct on Saturdays when she was a child. She'd always been interested in what he did. The newsroom editor looks at her quizzically, then says she should feel free. The other three interns look at her with a mixture of jealousy and mild resentment, for beating them to something more interesting than fashion or summer socials.

Over the preceding months a stalker or peeping tom plagues Cambridge in the area around Harvard Square. A freshman in one of the women's dorms is the first to report catching sight of a guy looking in her first-floor window when she's undressing one night. Upon seeing him, she immediately draws her curtains but can still glimpse his silhouette. She says he lingered. Black or white? She can't be sure. But with a paunch. A few weeks later it's a middle-aged housewife who reports she was followed home. She manages to enter her house and lock her door before he can force his way in. When she looks out the window he's gone. No, she hadn't noticed any distinguishing features.

The woman who was raped while jogging around Fresh Pond early one morning in May also has a hard time providing the police with a physical description of her attacker. She felt more than saw him, thinks he might be Italian or from somewhere in the Middle East. Dark. Shadowy. A strong smell of garlic. She can't be sure of his build. She says she feels like she left her body during the ordeal, must have been concentrating on making it out alive. Several other rapes that happen within a two-month period might well have been committed by the same guy. None of the victims mentions anything as unique as a birthmark, a tattoo or unusual piece of clothing.

These are separate events. No news story suggests a connection. But so many events so close together and in such a short period of time? Brittany has a hunch. As a child she remembers her father telling her that hunches are important. "Ignore them and you may be sorry," he said, as if he knew his daughter would be solving her own crimes one day.

And so, Brittany's summer job begins with an aura of possibility. She visits her father's precinct, where a couple of the guys who remember him give her access to files, photographs, evidence. They get a kick out of helping Joe's baby girl. Not that they expect her to be able to come up with anything useful.

Brittany reads interminable police reports, stares at disturbing images of bruised thighs and enlargements of desperate fingernails concealing possible clues. She covers her dining room wall with pictures she hopes might suggest a pattern. She links some of the items with red linen thread she finds in the sideboard drawer. She can't remember when or why she bought it. The wall looks like something straight out of one of those TV crime shows in which the alcoholic or bi-polar detective defies his superior who's suspended him for flouting the rules, and he solves the crime. Brittany sees only a random display of clippings, each concealing a story she can't decipher.

The newsroom editor isn't demanding. Let these young women get the feel of a big city newspaper, he thinks. That's enough. If none of them produces an article all summer, at least he won't have to waste time rewriting bad copy. He isn't being paid to turn amateurs into professionals; this is all extra-curricular. No one babysat him when he started.

Brittany puts down the phone, surprised that she said yes so quickly.

From that moment on, she thinks of little but Barcelona. A place she's never been. During the few days at Brock's before they depart, she easily falls back into her old habit of making do with a less than ideal situation. When she isn't acquiescing to her ex-lover's frequent demands for sex, she passes the time watching the Rick Steves' Barcelona and Catalunya video she downloads from YouTube or thumbing through the Fodor's on Brock's bedside table. He's high-lighted entire pages with yellow magic marker. She's never been with a man she doesn't feel she has to make excuses for—even to herself. Her father, for all his old-boy reputation on the force, was a big kid her mother managed until he'd died suddenly of a burst aorta at the age of 57. Brittany has no greater expectations of her own relationships.

By the time they're settled into their Business Class seats on the trans-Atlantic flight, Penny is no longer a memory. Brittany doesn't have to work at convincing herself she'll have a great summer. The Bloody Marys the flight attendant deposits on their tray tables go a long way toward sustaining her anticipatory mood.

❈

Maybe she'll be sorry later, but Brittany says no.

It's Lynda with a y, the intern from a small Idaho farming community, who sends Brittany in a direction she hasn't thought of before. Her quiet colleague finishes a predictably effusive note about Boston's big Flower and Garden Show at the city's Seaport World Trade Center. The piece is filled with superlatives about the spectacular color of a particular rose and the velvety petals of another. Their editor praises her efforts and publishes it in the next day's home and garden section.

Brittany notices that he leans in a little too close when pointing out a few places where Lynda might have shortened her sentences. She thinks the Idaho transplant seems uncomfortable. Perhaps that's why she invites her over after work that afternoon: "Do you like Chinese?" she asks. "I can pick some up on my way home. Here's my address. It's not far from here."

Brittany thinks Lynda seems grateful for the invitation. Maybe she doesn't yet have many friends in the city. She arrives with a modest Merlot and a bouquet of spring flowers that look like she picked them herself. What to Brittany is a spontaneous invitation, provoked by the embarrassing sight of an overeager boss, is obviously more than that to Lynda. She must be lonely, Brittany tells herself.

Over vegetable spring rolls and stir-fried tofu with rice—she'd forgotten to ask if Lynda is a vegetarian—the two women talk about the office atmosphere but avoid sharing confidences about their boss. Brittany asks Lynda a few polite questions about her family and why she chose Boston College. She tries to interest herself in Lynda's answers. It's her guest who stands up and approaches the wall with its map of clippings, photos, thumbtacks, and red thread.

"I heard you're looking at these attacks," Lynda says. "What makes you think they're connected?"

"I don't know. Just a hunch. Anyway, it doesn't hurt to explore all angles. The police haven't solved any of these crimes and women are afraid. We seem to have all summer with no real pressure to produce. I thought I'd follow my instincts." Brittany pushes one of the two fortune cookies across the table and breaks the other in half, extracting its tiny hidden strip of paper and holding it at arm's length. Her reading glasses are in the kitchen.

"You'll be hungry again in one hour," she reads out loud. Both women laugh. No Eastern wisdom, this fortune is meant to be humorous. Brittany wonders who writes these predictions and how much they get paid. Despite her disbelief in such portants she thinks of the leftover pieces of cheesecake she has in her refrigerator. If they're hungry again in an hour, she can always bring them out.

Lynda hasn't broken her fortune cookie. She doesn't seem interested in the message it holds. She is staring at Brittany's evidence wall, obviously absorbed in what it has to say. "What makes you draw a connection between the Fresh Pond rapist and the stalker outside the Harvard student's window?" she asks. "Is it the dates?"

"Maybe. He must have been frustrated when she drew her curtains. And then the attack at the pond is just two days later."

"I've always wondered what motivates stalkers, rapists, men who are compelled to attack women." Lynda might have been talking to herself; her tone is even, almost emotionless.

Brittany doesn't respond right away. She wonders why she only really thinks about the physical evidence and not the more motivational aspects of these crimes. Maybe because they are just the extreme edge of how most men see women, she thinks, rapists simply being those who take their sense of conquest to unacceptable, criminal, levels.

But Lynda is talking again, still thinking out loud: "Riggio's isn't far from Fresh Pond. I've eaten there. Delicious food, but I've only gone with my sister when she came to town, never with a man. It's like they cook every dish with so much garlic. You smell of it for days."

Brittany makes a mental note to check out Riggio's.

She knows she's accepted Brock's invitation without giving it much thought. Sometimes you just have to take risks, she tells herself now.

They hop in a cab from Barcelona-El Prat to their hotel in the city center. Brittany wonders out loud if it wouldn't have been cheaper to use RENFE, the train that leaves every half hour and only takes twenty-five minutes, but the dismissal on Brock's face tells her he doesn't think in terms of saving money. The more expensive, the better. He's reserved a room he's several times described as luxurious at a place called Majestic Residence. "It has everything," he tells her, proudly, as if he built it himself. Brittany decides not to question any more of his choices. After all, this is his invitation. She will try to relax and accept the gift on his terms.

The next couple of weeks is a whirlwind of sightseeing and restaurants that advertise diverse continental menus. Brittany favors long slow walks on which they might get deliciously lost and then found, discovering hidden treasures crying to be explored. She wants to eat at small family places where they can savor such local dishes as cannelloni stuffed with stewed beef or some of the tapas for which the region is famous.

Brock insists on their not getting tired. He anticipates all-night sex every night. Brittany bears up under his unimaginative performance, trying to show an acceptable level of emotion. He's clearly still the beloved quarterback, at least in his own eyes. Each morning after breakfast at the hotel, he rushes them into a waiting taxi and they head for the destination of his choice. He checks off museums and churches like a birdwatcher making his way through a master list of species.

The day they take the tour to Montserrat, the famous

monastery an hour outside the city, Brock seems to have memorized its combination of Romanesque, Gothic and Renaissance features. He spouts all sorts of details about the Benedictine order and its devotion to the Virgin of Montserrat. Brittany enjoys the mountain air but doesn't love the hodge-podge architecture or the way the square blocks interrupt the natural beauty of the rocky cliffs behind them. Brock talks non-stop all the way back to their hotel. He seems intent on transmitting his excitement to Brittany, or maybe just sparking in her some appreciation of his vast knowledge.

They've been in Barcelona for three weeks. Brock always finds something new in the guidebook for them to see. Brittany longs to walk aimlessly in the fascinating city, eat in restaurants unlisted in Fodor's, strike up conversations with anyone who speaks English or is willing to put up with her limited high school Spanish. Brock always has a better plan. Eventually Brittany surprises him by announcing she feels like staying at the hotel. She needs some time to herself. He should go out. She doesn't mind, will find something to keep her busy. He looks at her in disbelief but finally has no alternative but to give in.

Brittany spends much of that day talking to one of the hotel maids. The woman, whose name is Gabriela, speaks some Spanish and even a little English she's picked up from guests over the years. Brittany asks her about her family. They are from a small village called Taüll in the Boí Valley. Brittany looks it up in her guidebook and sees photographs of old stone buildings nestled against a backdrop of mountains, some of which remain snow-capped most of the year. "Three and a half hours each way," Gabriela responds to Brittany's question. Seven hours round trip! Brittany tries to imagine the energy that must take.

Gabriela has eleven brothers and sisters. She is one of the oldest. Her own husband left her, and her three children stay with her widowed mother while she sleeps at a hostel in the city during the week. She only sees them a few hours on Sunday when she gets up early to make the long bus trip home and returns as late at night as she can so as to be ready for work again Monday morning.

Brittany rejoins Brock for dinner that evening. He talks without stopping about his day—a monument to local victims of the Spanish Civil War and a museum he's sure she will be sorry to have missed. He says he just happened to spend time with the museum's director, who was impressed by how much he knows, and they made plans to see one another again. "You'll love him," he tells Brittany, assuming she'll want to meet him too. She listens attentively, then tries to share her conversation with Gabriela. Brock makes a pretense of listening, scanning the menu as he does. She stops, waits for him to give her his full attention. "What's the matter," he demands, a bit grumpily she thinks, "I can listen and read at the same time. One of the hotel maids, you say?"

Brittany thinks about Brock's invitation from time to time but is glad she turned him down.

It is Lynda's comment that a few days later sends Brittany to Riggio's. She tells the owner she's working as a summer intern for The Globe, visiting area restaurants, interviewing the staff. She doesn't exactly say she's writing for the food section but leaves that impression. He tells her he has seven working there, including the kitchen help, bartender, hostess and the two waiters who attend the small dining room. He doesn't object to her talking to them as long as it doesn't interfere with their jobs.

Brittany has lunch at the restaurant a couple of times. She asks to be seated at different tables and manages to strike up friendly conversations with both waiters. She just wants to get a sense of who they are. Such impressions go a long way. The following week she shows up for a late dinner, hoping to be one of the last guests when the place closes. The chef comes out to inquire about how she enjoyed her meal, and she's equally friendly with him, even flirts a bit. They talk for almost ten minutes.

It takes her several more maneuvers, though, before she can figure out where each of them was on the date and at the time of the attack on the Fresh Pond jogger. When she's gotten responses from everyone but the chef, she decides to ask him outright. Despite her best efforts, she blows her cover and is forced to beat a hasty retreat. Now it's time to check out each alibi, see if they all pan out.

As often happens when someone follows a good lead, the perpetrator begins to slip up. Riggio's bartender claims he was at work on the morning in question, but Brittany knows the restaurant doesn't open until eleven. The jogger's rape took place much earlier, just past first light. And then, the bartender often comes in an hour or so later than the rest of the staff. Not many diners order more than a beer or wine with lunch, and Brittany has observed that the waiters themselves handle drinks that don't have to be mixed.

Brittany convinces one of her father's old buddies at the precinct to run the man's name. It turns out the bartender is a registered sex offender. He exposed himself some years back in Hartford. Brittany thought Connecticut and Massachusetts would share such records but for whatever reason the guy had no trouble getting the job at Riggio's. The sex offender piece gets the sergeant's attention. When they bring the bartender in for questioning, they get a DNA swab. It matches the DNA in the jogger's rape kit. The bartender confesses, though he claims he has nothing to do with the other crimes linked by red thread on Brittany's dining room wall.

The day Brittany's story is published, the newsroom editor opens a bottle of champagne. Paper cups all around. Brittany credits Lynda in her article. Lynda says she shouldn't have, it was only a chance comment after all. After reading the story she looks at Brittany: "You'll be hungry again in an hour," she says laughing. Hmmm, Brittany thinks, she's got a sense of humor. This might be the beginning of a real friendship.

It was an easy decision taking Brock up on his offer of such an exotic sounding trip. It isn't like this sort of invitation comes along every day.

But the rest of their time in Barcelona is awkward at best. Brittany begins making excuses when Brock comes onto her each night. They spend their last two days in the city separately. He manages to check off the final two monuments on his to-do list and meet with his museum director acquaintance. She accepts an invitation from Gabriela to visit her village. They invite Brock but he isn't interested.

It's at the old stone farmhouse where Brittany finally has a chance to taste the famous calçotada, those long spring onions grown during Catalunya's winters, cooked in the ashes of an open fire and then wrapped in paper and served alongside a bowl of romesco sauce. Gabriela's mother says something to her daughter and nudges her to translate for their guest. "She wants you to know that the red pepper sauce should have nuts," Gabriela tells Brittany in her halting Spanish. "She's sorry she didn't have any." Brittany looks at the older woman gratefully. "Tell her it's the best meal I've had," she replies, surprised that her eyes are unexpectedly wet.

On the flight home Brittany thinks of all the things she liked about this Barcelona adventure. She's been to many wonderful places, gotten a glimpse of another culture, had experiences she'll always remember. She buries what the trip cost her in sexual favors and humiliation.

She wonders what interning at The Globe would have been like.

Wind

The young girl hovers in a shallow cave. She doesn't think of herself as a girl. Or for that matter as a boy. Nor is age something that concerns her. She cannot imagine status or race or education. Water, food, shelter, danger: these are the things that gnaw at her, day after day, year after year. The idea of a year is also beyond her grasp. An animal she can pierce with her lance, devouring as much of its meat as possible before it rots: that is what's most often on her mind.

When the girl sleeps and dreams, she believes she is in a trance of disconnected images where she can sometimes fly. When she tries this in the world where her feet are planted on the earth, it doesn't work. She stumbles, then, unnerved. The girl doesn't have a name, thinks of herself only as part of a community of other beings. Now she's lost those other beings in the forest, has been looking for them in desperation.

We call the girl Denisovan. It's like saying she is Greek or Ethiopian, Mexican or Swedish. It's also like saying she is Indian, Black, Latinx or Asian. It's also like saying she is human. Our young girl lived in Africa, around 100,000 years ago, give or take. We have learned a great deal about her probable height, weight, bone structure. What she ate. The diseases that ravaged her. From unearthed skeletons, our science can recreate her bodily characteristics and the features of her face. She was chunky and strong, with a wide pelvis, broad fingertips, a large rib cage, robust jaw and low forehead with a prominent overhanging brow. She might have gone naked or covered herself in large leaves or scraps of animal skins.

And we can conjecture that the sounds she made were likely high shrieks rather than the grunts our Disney-inspired imaginations imitate. Her ability to communicate depended on expression and gesture. So, no great Denisovan poetry, no magnificent symphonies, no farming or architecture. Perhaps some of what we call art—drawings of animals and symbols on cave walls—although the earliest of these yet found date to around 60,000 years after the time in which she lived.

The girl's aloneness brings strange pangs to her chest, in a spot deep between her small breasts. First eagerness, then almost relief followed by despair. She cannot name these emotions but that doesn't render them any less profound. Recognizable language, descriptions that convey thoughts and feelings, won't spring from minds and mouths for hundreds of thousands of years. Writing is much more recent, radio and digital speech in the last fragment of a second on the human clock. All the girl knows at this moment is cold, heat, hunger, sleep and danger. And wind, a roaring so big it makes her shudder and press her body harder against the rock.

In any age, wind's sound is like having all of nature inside your head. You don't only hear it; you see, feel, smell and taste its sustained battle cry. And it makes you desperate, from your innermost self out. You can run but not hide. Or, if you do, that all-encompassing noise follows and lays claim around you, above and beneath and within. You can cover your ears but the spirit-shaking noise is already inside.

You think: how can air, transparent and unseen, be so loud? Air charging landscape and concrete, from the largest to the smallest target, bending trees, ripping their branches from their trunks, rippling along electrical wire causing it to crackle and spark, thundering as it lashes, shaking every reflex set against it, whether staunch or pliant. You don't stand a chance of escaping its power. With its driving force, wind abrades earth's skin, rattles every window in the tallest buildings, devours all resistance in its path. It accumulates all the breaths, sighs, wails, moans, screams, sputters and gurgles, gathering them into one great cacophony. You are nothing against it.

You of the absurd hope, the pillow you pull over your head is the flimsiest of barriers. You with the graying red hair, no doors you close or towels you roll up and place beneath them will keep the sound from consuming you. You who are used to always getting what you want, some things remain beyond your control. You of the nine-month womb, best to relax and let its deafening sound synchronize with your labor and the child you are about to deliver. And you, little one, you can run to your mother's arms but she may be as terrified as you. The wind to end all winds is no longer an outside force but part of you now, its ear alert to the beat of time.

Our unnamed Denisovan girl has felt the tongues of gentle breezes licking her face. She has savored their tickling dance. When that air turns vicious, she wonders who has turned against her and why. She does not yet resort to prayer but believes there is a power beyond her management or control. She tries to imagine how she can calm its ire.

I met the Denisovan girl one night in a vivid and ongoing dream. So vivid, it was simply another reality, as compelling as the one I live when awake. Ongoing because it returned, night after night and repeated itself within a single night. I wouldn't have called her Denisovan then, more likely Neanderthal, the catchall label I'd heard people use for ancient humans. The dream came in fragments, gripping me with both hands until a blanket that had slipped to the floor or the urge to urinate brought me to wakefulness. After meeting whichever of those needs, I barely had time to ponder where I'd been. And I fell back into the dream once more. It continued right where it had left off.

"It was so real," I told Delia over breakfast the next morning, even as I tried to describe it wondering which was more real, the place I'd gone in the night or this familiar morning routine. Delia stopped eating and gave me her full attention. We'd been together too long and trusted each other too completely for her not take me seriously.

In the dream I'd come from work and was ambling along a quiet path that cut through the grassy fields of Central Park. When not in a hurry I liked taking this longer route home from work. My design job at the advertising agency had been demanding of late. I didn't like bringing the tension home and the park was always a great place to let it go.

I noticed how many of the leaves had dropped from their branches, the inevitable result of this early fall frost. A sparser foliage opened expanses where I could see farther, negative spaces where my eyes wandered. It was through one of these uncluttered windows that I spotted the girl, hugging one of the boulders about 200 feet away. A lone figure and completely out of place against that ancient Manhattan Schist. I stopped and stared.

At first I wasn't sure what I was looking at. Or who. The girl seemed to be concerned with anything but my presence, or even with her surroundings in some strange way. And, if I could believe my eyes, she was naked. I left the path and headed in her direction. The girl didn't seem to see me coming. And no one else around me in the park seemed to have noticed her.

As I drew closer, I felt a strange tingling on my skin. A sudden wind came up, then, rapidly becoming a roar. It exploded without warning. The sky turned a greenish gray. I was torn between retracing my steps and trying to take shelter somewhere or advancing toward the object of my attention.

You know how there are dreams in which you are conscious that you are dreaming. The awareness is like a seventh sense; it doesn't disrupt the dream itself, nor does it necessarily wake you. Perhaps its motivation is to remove a layer of separation or fear, just enough to keep you there. Or maybe it signals a possible exit. I've often experienced this seventh sense, but never felt I had an option. The dream's reality held me fast in space and time. This was happening.

That wind. It whipped my hair, opened my jacket, snapped the strap of my favorite briefcase and tore it from my shoulder. I watched, helpless, as the briefcase bounced against a bench, its brass buckle opened and papers scattered across the grass, whipped by gusts racing along at ground level. Could I risk going after them? A moot question in a dream.

I saw the girl was battling the same wind from a much more precarious position. It lashed her bare skin and set her teeth rattling. Shrieks issued from her mouth, dissolving into low moans. I realized I had seen the girl before, in previous dreams. And not just once. That night I feared for her safety. In the midst of my fourth or fifth encounter with an identical scene, I turned suddenly, made my difficult way back to the path, managed to exit the park at 79th Street and hail a taxi near the Museum of Natural History. Everything dissolved then and I can't remember what happened after that. When I woke, I was trembling.

But I knew that night or the next I would be there again and the girl would be waiting. Bedtime acquired a fresh dimension of both wariness and anticipation. Familiarity with an undercurrent of fear. Like going to meet an old friend but laced with foreboding or premonition.

I talked about my dream all the time. Not with folks at work; that would have been professional suicide, but with Delia. After our fourth or fifth conversation, she began asking for more specifics about the girl. That was when I went to Wikipedia looking for images of early humans, data about size, bone structure, where partial skeletons had been discovered, when it was believed that speech originated and how.

That was how I settled on Denisovan as an apt description of the girl's stage of development, her moment on our journey of becoming fully human. Of course, I had still only seen her from a distance. But her desperate silhouette against the dark schist was by now imprinted on my eyes. It was the wind's ferocity that finally interrupted my musings. In an instant I'd had to remove my attention from the girl and prioritize my own safety. That night I wondered if that had been the end of it, if I would see the girl again. I needn't have worried. Several nights later, she returned. It was as if our meeting was prearranged.

I was no expert on the genealogical tree whose branches support our anthropological assumptions about how we've gone from primates to modern-day humans. I'd never acquainted myself with Homo Heidelbergensis,

Homo Erectus, Neanderthal, Denisovan or any of the other designations. The only other time I could remember thinking about our distant ancestors had been years before when a colleague in the design department had gotten flack for drawing *Vogue*-like African American models posing in wild animal skins alongside starving African children. The indignation those images produced in the politically aware community caused the agency to cancel the ads.

After about a week of the nightly encounters, an astonishing thing happened. It raised the dream to another level. This time I'd come within about 50 feet of the girl. I could see her much more clearly, hear her shrieks. She turned her head slightly, then, and I could have sworn she looked straight at me. Our eyes locked across millennia. The girl's face paled. I thought I saw her shudder, one explosive tremor followed by a look of terror. Then she raised her right hand in what could have been a gesture of some sort. Was she waving at me? Perhaps beckoning?

The girl's gesture gave me a jolt. Before I could respond with a gesture of my own, I woke from the dream, feeling I'd been cast out of it despite every effort to stay. All that day I felt out of sorts, irritable for no apparent reason. I was even grumpy with Delia. I couldn't wait to get to sleep that night and, to my wife's surprise, retired by myself a little past seven.

I remember closing my eyes, determined to engage with the girl, not let her escape my overtures. I didn't have my brief case now. Perhaps I wasn't on my way home from work. No, I was frankly here in pursuit of the girl. When I saw her, I slowed my pace, not wanting to frighten her off. I approached her calmly, gently, and held both my hands out, hoping to elicit contact.

"My name is Molly," I said, which in retrospect might not have been the best opener. "I know, the wind can be treacherous this time of year."

The girl appeared frozen. She seemed to be staring at my mouth but it was clear my words weren't telling her anything. Unintelligible sounds issued from her lips but they were more contained than I remembered, less frantic shrieks than little blurting grunts.

I kept speaking and the girl kept listening. Gradually I thought we might be talking, not at but with one another. By some extraordinary leap in time, some compression of the long journey to where we find ourselves today, the girl and I could be having a conversation.

"I've seen you before," I began, "but you didn't see me. And I don't think anyone else sees you. You don't have to worry. We can go to my place and I can get you some clothes . . ."

"My people gone," the girl said. Or maybe she didn't say the words but I understood what she was telling me.

"There are others like you here somewhere?"

I felt I was understanding the girl but she wasn't understanding me, which gave me a sense of what the stuttering expansion of intelligence through time was like. Frustrating, to say the least.

"Lost my people. Big wind. My people." The words seemed to form in the girl's eyes rather than on her tongue, traveling straight from her eyes to my mind.

"Yeah, the wind was terrible the other day. It ripped my briefcase away." I realized I was getting off topic. What did the girl know of briefcases or the importance of their contents? She was naked, after all, and undoubtedly cold. And the wind was gusting stronger.

"How can I stop the wind?" the girl asked, her eyes

imploring. "How can I still the air?"

It was one of those times when experience and understanding come together in an unexpected moment of clarity. What they called a perfect storm. The girl was looking to harness nature, what we've attempted from the beginning of our time on earth.

I wanted to speak to her so she would understand, but civilization got in my way. I heard myself going on about the quaint windmills dotting a Dutch landscape, the farmer Sancho Panza and his lance, Dorothy carried off by a tornado to the magical land of Oz, hurricanes with their 200-plus-mile-an-hour winds that toss trucks into the air and destroy homes. Of course, the girl knew nothing of windmills, Don Quixote's sidekick, Dorothy, trucks or homes. Still, I wanted to tell her that the fastest wind ever recorded was clocked at 253 miles per hour on April 10, 1996 on Barrow Island, Australia. But what could clocked or recorded or Australia mean to her?

I thought of the ancient Greeks, how they explained wind coming from the cardinal directions as a deity with a split personality, ascribing a different name to each. Boreas was god of the north wind, Notus of the south, Zephyrus of the west and Eurus of the east. Boreas was also the biting cold wind of winter. Notus was in charge of the raging storms of late summer and fall. Zehyrus brought the light breezes of early summer and Eurus was just plain bad luck. In an effort to confuse, his wind was often accompanied by a soft rain.

I don't know why, but I also remember feeling an urgent need to explain that, because of the earth's rotation, air does not move in a straight line. That the earth's rotation pushes the air to the right, a phenomenon called the Coriolis Effect. That because of this, the air flows clockwise around high-pressure areas in the Northern Hemisphere and counterclockwise around low-pressure areas, and that the reverse is true in the Southern Hemisphere. But then I would have to explain hemispheres and clocks.

I even wanted to tell the girl that a Russian hacking operation against US security and political campaigns was known as SolarWind. I wondered why our intelligence community had given it such a poetic name. But then I would have had to explain hacking and security and politics, all concepts unknown to her.

Just shut up, I told myself. Little good that did.

I wanted to tell her that messing with nature can be complicated. I wanted to explain that we can build dams hoping to channel the power of great rivers, only to redirect their energy in ways that cause other problems. That we manage forests, causing devastating fires that consume whole towns. I wanted to expound on the virtues of wind farms, explain that wind itself is neither good nor bad but a force to be feared or used, depending on our ingenuity. I looked at her face and knew these were conversations for another time.

I was beside the girl now. I took her hand. She didn't pull away. I was contemplating how to get her out of the park and safely to our apartment. Would she come willingly? What about the others she kept referring to as her people? Would I be helping if I separated her from any hope of finding them?

And then the dream just dissolved around me. As I opened my eyes, I realized I had left it. Or it had abandoned me. For a few brief moments I tried to get back, refused to accept the finality of this forced separation. But the park, the trees with their almost naked branches, the schist boulders and the girl were all gone. Even the wind had calmed. I could no longer hear its breath.

What good was my spotty store of knowledge, all those legends and facts and stories about wind, the memories woven into the fabric of our cultural identity, if that fragile connection with the girl in my dream could disappear without warning, never to return?

I believe we made a connection and believe I'll see the girl again, some night when I least expect it. I sleep now with a different desire, a different sense of expectation. Delia tells me it's like having a third person in our bed.

Like walking the streets of my city hoping to run into an old friend I haven't seen in years, I keep hoping. And as is too often true in life as we know it, I have to remind myself that the girl may look different now from when she visited my dreams. That's the hardest thing: making allowances for the changes wrought by time.

I am most alert when the wind blows hard.

Sam's Self

Mirrors were hard. Especially those that magnify every hair and skin pore. They reflect all that taunts, shames, and makes you uncomfortable. You can suck your belly in, but the abs are there or not. You are only as tall or short, fat or thin, as close or far from your dream image as the person staring back at you. Sam's smooth, slightly tanned skin was always too pretty, his wavy blond hair too girlish no matter how short he cut it, his hips too broad. However intently he tried to imagine an Adam's apple, there was only a featureless neck where it was supposed to be.

Sam can't remember a time when he didn't feel like a boy. When he was old enough, he refused girl's clothing, toys, anything else forced upon him by adults who tried hard to steer him in the direction of the fraud. "Just give it a try," they said, as if it was about obedience or will.

His younger sister Linda called him Sam because Samantha confounded her incipient power of pronunciation, and the shorter name stuck. Sam liked it because it made him feel more like himself. Later, when she was older, whenever their parents said something that revealed their struggle to accept Sam's male identity, Linda would quietly remind them of Sam's self. She never failed him.

At Parkhurst grade school Sam always wanted to join the boys at recess. They usually sneered at his overtures, calling him Sissy and telling him: "Go play with the girls where you belong." In their upscale commuter community, that was the worst name they were likely to repeat after hearing it on their parents' lips. Later in life he would experience much worse: weirdo, tranny, cuntboy or sometimes just that nameless menacing sneer that promised a danger to which he learned always to remain alert.

As Sam got older, when the neighborhood boys lacked a ninth for their team's Saturday baseball game or wanted a heavy hitter more than they minded having a misfit or a girl, they might extend a grudging invitation. Sam knew they were thinking of themselves, not of him. He didn't really mind, he told himself. It was a small enough price to pay to be able to play with the guys.

The year Sam was in seventh grade, his mother got him a Mets jacket for Christmas. He could feel his heart beating hard as he tore the ribbon and paper from the package. The whole family must have heard the thump thump in his chest. As he unwrapped the jacket and gleefully put it on, his father's face told him everything he already knew about what his claim to his identity was doing to the old man. "It's what he wanted," Madge mumbled, trying to absorb her husband's silence with her words, half explanation half excuse. Sam thought he saw a glimmer of fear in his mother's eyes.

"The least you could have done was get him Yankee gear," Sam Senior said as he got up off the living room floor and headed for the kitchen. "My father wouldn't have had a Mets jacket in his closet," he added, returning with a half-downed Coors in his hand. By feigning dismay about anything other than his daughter claiming to be a boy, he felt he had an argument with which other's couldn't find fault. He seemed to have lost interest in unwrapping gifts, even when Madge pushed the small square box with the coveted made-in-Taiwan Rolex his way.

Christmas at Sam's meant sharing memories of past holidays, vacations, and other moments of family togetherness. Linda talked about her first Barbie, the miniature cook set with the real oven that heated up but was guaranteed not to burn (appropriate for ages 5 to 7), the time her parents bought her an ice-skating skirt: black velvet with bright pink lining and a line of gold braid at the hem. Linda twirled around the living room as if she were wearing that skirt. She mimicked herself and laughed when recalling bizarre or silly episodes. She was most charming when placing herself at the center of a story that most people would have found embarrassing. Sam could never think of anything he remembered or wanted to share. Humiliation was best repressed, pushed down and out of mind.

Sam's mother was by far the more receptive parent. His father made an excuse to leave the room whenever Sam or anyone else alluded to the boy's identity—or even just mentioned the subject of gender. Once he barged into his son's room when the boy was binding his small breasts. Sam stopped mid-task. He couldn't ignore the mixture of disgust and rage on his father's face. Sam Senior turned away. It was as if, despite his wife's pleadings for compassion and Sam's unfailing determination, the father understood a bridge had been crossed. There was no going back. He left the room without saying a word, hardly spoke to Sam or anyone else in the family for several days.

Madge did her homework. Studied pamphlets, read books, listened to stories of other parents whose daughters or sons had transitioned and they'd had to choose between losing them forever or somehow adjusting to this new reality. Unknown to her husband, she even attended a support group for a few weeks. At first it helped to be with other parents facing similar situations. Then she began to feel awkward at those meetings where mothers talked about losing a son but gaining a daughter, or vice versa. Some cried, then swore theirs were tears of understanding, acceptance. The occasional father sat stony-faced beside his wife, and the group leader was always so effusive, going on about "all God's children."

When Sam was 16, he began to talk seriously with his mother about starting hormone blockers and getting testosterone shots. He'd been binding his growing breasts for a couple of years. When Madge cleaned his room, she found a stick of Primal Pit Paste male deodorant and a tube of shaving cream in his top bureau drawer. The razor hadn't seemed that odd; after all, girls Sam's age shaved their legs and underarms. Now she thought no, this isn't a phase. She's not going to grow out of it. He, she corrected herself.

Sam never failed to correct anyone who referred to him as she or called him Samantha. He never had to rebuke Linda. She took to her brother's transition naturally, always pulling him close, comforting him when she saw he needed that. She told him she'd always known who he was inside, even did some correcting of her own when classmates or—worse—teachers insisted on calling her brother her.

Sam Senior preferred to ignore the whole situation, still hoping it would go away. If it came up in conversation, which it rarely did, he would leave the room. He always had an excuse for why he couldn't attend parent/teacher meetings at Sam's school, afraid he'd have to talk about this thing he couldn't acknowledge. Once in a while, especially when they found themselves alone, he would put his arm around Sam's shoulder, try to communicate that he still loved him "no matter what." But this "what" was too big, too overwhelming. Father and son ended up falling back into that silence that made them both feel empty inside.

Madge finally took Sam to a doctor who asked the boy a list of questions, writing down his answers on a yellow pad. "When did you know you are a boy? How does it make you feel when you have to wear girl's clothing? Have you ever tried to harm yourself? Considered suicide?" He waited for Sam to respond to each question, encouraged him to say more. Sam felt relaxed with this doctor, like the man understood him. Madge hadn't expected such professional ease with the subject. She wondered what she'd expected. Maybe she'd hoped the doctor would be able to change her son's mind, fix things somehow.

Mother and son left that doctor's office with a plan: weekly counseling sessions, then hormone blockers and a promise of beginning the testosterone shots the following year if the psychologist agreed. Then, when he was old enough, something called gender-confirming surgery—kids Sam was beginning to know called it "top surgery." Sam drank it all in. He left the doctor's office feeling lighter, as if he'd shed years of anxiety. That night he tacked a National Geographic calendar to the wall of his room with entries in different colors. The squares that marked dates with the psychologist or when he might begin to take the hormone blockers were full of smiley faces and exclamation points. In the mirror, his skin didn't look quite so smooth, his hair quite so girlish.

Despite herself, Madge continued to hang onto a single phrase the doctor had uttered: "You have to be sure," he'd said, looking at Sam, at his mother and then at the boy again. "After a certain point, there's no going back." That night Madge wanted to tell her husband about their visit, unload her new understandings and old fears, but she'd barely broached the subject when Sam Senior rolled over and turned off the lamp on his side of the bed. She knew he wasn't asleep. Still, she too fell into the silence that increasingly characterized their relationship.

That night Sam met the see-through boy for the first time. He thought of him like that because his body seemed translucent. Sam could see the silhouette of an unfamiliar landscape through his chest where a tight strip of homespun compressed burgeoning breasts. At first the boy didn't speak to Sam, just smiled in a friendly way as if trying to put him at ease. Then he motioned for Sam to sit beside him on a low stone wall. Sam could see the shape of the stones through the boy's groin. Where were they? Nothing in that landscape looked familiar. Or did it? Surreptitiously, he tried to distinguish a bulge in the boy's britches, finding only the smooth female contour.

Sam wondered at his use of the words "homespun" and "britches," unspoken but nonetheless present. They weren't terms he'd heard or was accustomed to saying. They smacked of another era, pictures from his eighth-grade American history book, of men with ruffled shirt collars, long flared jackets, tight pants or sculpted stockings and pointed shoes with prominent buckles. It was then that he got it that his new friend was from another time. The ruffled collar caught Sam's attention. It seemed so feminine. Sam wondered how a man could stand all that bunched up fabric beneath his chin.

That first night the two young men spent several hours together, getting to know one another. Seated side by side on the low wall, they talked about all sorts of things. Fears. Longings. Feeling as if every part of you was wrong, that even your skin didn't fit. It took Sam a while to realize they weren't using words, that their thoughts simply spilled from one mind to the other, flowing back and forth between them.

There was no barrier to their communication, such was the need Sam felt for a willing ear. Most of all, someone whose experience he could somehow make his own. When Phoenix, for that was the see-through boy's name, whispered tales of discarding tight corsets and awkward bustles, Sam felt he was burying forever the yellow pinafore his grandmother had gotten him for his sixth birthday, the one with the little lace collar. How he'd hated that girlie garment! To his grandmother's disappointment and mother's dismay, he'd never once put it on.

The next morning Sam awoke in an unusually good mood. Gone was the angst he almost always felt as he dressed for school, juggling what would be acceptable with what he could endure. That night he fell asleep in the middle of his algebra assignment, eager to get back to Phoenix and the comfort of their silent communion.

The boy was waiting on the low stone wall. Sam hurried to his side, all vestiges of shyness gone. His relief at not having to explain himself, forthrightly or in code, was almost more than he could bear. He could feel the tears welling up in his eyes. "They keep waiting for me to grow out of who I am," he told the boy with a sustained riveting look, "as if that would be a good thing."

"Not good for you," Phoenix acknowledged, squeezing Sam's hand.

That night the two kindred spirits talked for hours, maybe years. In Sam's dream, time assumed a different rhythm and shape. Phoenix told him a story about getting his first walking cane, mahogany with a silver handle, a falcon's head ornate in all its manly status. Sam took the story and made it his. The cane became a hiking stick he'd never owned. Now it was a part of his personal memory.

When his parents or Linda spoke about moments when they'd been somewhere or done something, seen such-and-such or so-and-so, Sam had memories of his own to share. He offered them joyously but even Linda looked bewildered. His mother turned her face, trying to hide her confusion. His father stared at the person he still considered his first daughter with something like defeat in his eyes. Sam was disappointed but tried not to let his family's disdain ruin his sense of self. He cherished these new memories.

In any case, now Sam depended less on his parents or sister for affirmation. He'd found a community, small it's true and made up of outsiders like himself, but people with whom he felt he belonged. Occasionally he still met up with Phoenix at night, but now he had flesh and blood friends he could hang with. They revealed secret doubts and deep certainties, talked about the side effects of the hormone blockers, exchanged ways of tempering the aggressive outbursts produced by the testosterone, looked forward to the time when surgery would make their unfamiliar bodies whole. They shared plans for how they would get the money, confided fear of the pain involved, wondered if simply presenting as men might not be enough. They promised always to be there for each other. And they talked about what else they were going to do with their lives, about careers and travel and women and the Mets' prospects for the coming season and the torque on Ford's new Raptor F-250.

When Sam tried to join a group called The Young Promise Keepers and was excluded when they discovered he "wasn't a real man," he was depressed for days. It wasn't what he'd expected of those youths who seemed so righteous, so consumed with digging deep for their essence as men. That night he found himself once again with Phoenix; they hadn't gotten together for more than a year. Sam didn't have to explain his disappointment to his friend. Before he could start, Phoenix was telling him about how he'd felt when he was rebuffed by the Charter Colonists. Even owning land hadn't been enough. "There will always be folks who put you down to build themselves up," Phoenix said, touching Sam's shoulder with a special tenderness. "It's that fear of difference. But your century is so much better than mine."

This was the first time Phoenix had made reference to the fact that they lived in different centuries. Rather than finding it comforting, the revelation put Sam in the grip of a new anxiety. He knew people like himself, born into the wrong body, suffered death and worse when his friend lived. He knew they continued to confront similar dangers now, even if life had gotten appreciably better in so many ways: new possibilities for acquiring a body that matched his identity, the slow journey to legal acknowledgment, support groups, even friends. He thought of transgender people of color, at the top of the list of those being abused, raped, murdered. He thought of a friend who called himself non-binary and wanted people to call him they. Sam's own needs seemed simple by comparison. All he asked, after all, was that people see him for who he is.

Sam's mother and Linda were solidly on his side. Even his father seemed to be warming to the son he never expected to have. Not often and not a lot, but enough so their blowups were less frequent. It didn't take long after that for Sam to understand that if he stayed clear of groups seeped in religious dogma or otherwise linked to status of one sort or another, he could avoid being caught off guard.

A good job in IT right out of college soon enabled Sam to save the money for the first of several operations. On his 22nd birthday, his mother slipped him a large check. He didn't have to ask if it was from both his parents; he wondered where his mother had gotten the money. Linda took a few weeks off school to accompany him to the clinic in Hartsdale. He recuperated at the home of a friend who'd already completed his physical transition. Sam's post-operative pain was tempered by the exuberant feeling he was closer to wholeness. When it was time for the next surgery, he was better prepared and had a whole list of friends who signed up to accompany him, care for him, nurse him through.

And now Sam had recovered some of his own real memories, firmly in place. That time at the lake when he, not his dad, had dived in to rescue the kid who'd fallen from the boat and was surfacing frantically, screaming and gasping for air. A grateful community judged that act immune to glances and inuendoes. The first time he read *Orlando* by Virginia Woolf all the way through to the end. The spring afternoon in seventh grade when he'd batted an astonishing .250 and the team looked at him differently for almost a month. His first gay pride march. One rare morning when his father yelled up for him to come down to breakfast: "Son, I made your favorite eggs and green chile sausage."

When Sam was 24, Sam Senior died suddenly of a massive heart attack. The doctor said it was brought on by stress. His mother called her son at his office. She was strangely calm but her voice seemed thin, almost ghostly. Sam heard grief streaked with an emotion he couldn't distinguish. He drove to the hospital, helped with the routine formalities, refrained from indulging in talk about the relationship they'd never managed to achieve or his father hadn't wanted with him. Had he ever really wanted to know his son? Sam wasn't sure and now he would never know. Madge fell into her son's arms. Linda cried like Sam had never seen her cry before.

Sam was one of the pall bearers at his father's funeral. Everyone seemed to accept that. Despite his materialist inclination, Sam caught himself wondering if there was anything at all after death. If there might still be a chance for his dad to come to terms with him. He quickly banished such thoughts. It had been hard enough to deal with the relationship when his father was alive.

It was after this that Sam began to understand that memories make a life. Those given to you and those you create. They are your story. Not just the present but the past. Not just the past but the future, which can only exist when there is a past.

How Norman Stopped Being Anxious

It started in fourth grade, when their teacher called the first roll of the year. She said "Norman" and looked out at the sea of students sitting before her in their lopsided regulation desks. The desks were annoying. Norman liked symmetry and that extra surface splayed out beneath his right arm and hand broke the rule. Norman liked rules. Besides, he was left-handed.

"Norman," the teacher repeated. He raised his hand, avoiding her searching glance. Behind him, Sandy Smith hissed: "Normal," and then quickly added "Not!" A dozen or so of the other students snickered. Norman paid attention to how many joined in. Definitely less than half. Not as bad as he'd feared. "The glass half full," as his mother would say: another one of those expressions Norman took literally and had trouble understanding.

Miss Abercrombie didn't come to his defense. Upon entering the room, she had written her name on the board: MISS ABERCROMBIE, in big block letters. As if anyone could forget a name like that. Now she simply called out the next student's name and the next. Each one elicited a raised hand. Except for two, whose owners were absent. How could you get away with being absent on the first day of class?, Norman wondered. He himself would have preferred to stay home. Or disappear into the field behind his house, sit with the rocks and trees and gently dancing grasses. He knew that wasn't possible. It would be breaking the rules, something his Dad always said: "wasn't in the cards."

The first time Norman heard his father say that, he wondered how rules could be in cards. He tried and couldn't find any. He went through every one of the 52 in the pack they kept in the middle drawer of the dining room sideboard. Pictures of red hearts, red diamonds, black spades and black clubs. Suits of four each. Pictures of a king and a queen. And a large letter J. Norman read that the suits represented the four classes of Medieval society. The hearts stood for the clergy, the spades for the nobility or military, the diamonds for the merchants and clubs for the peasants. He wondered if the rules had to do with that.

When his father said that sort of thing, his mother gave her husband one of her looks. Norman thought her deep gray eyes might bore holes in his father's face. She'd hold the look for eight to ten seconds—he counted them to himself, barely moving his lips—then glance quickly at their son and back at her husband. Sometimes Dad changed right away to a more literal form of speech, one that it was easier for Norman to understand. Sometimes he'd just get up and leave the room.

Once he slammed the door on his way out. Norman wondered if he would return or if he and his mother would live alone from then on. He was five at the time and frightened. But his father always came back. When he did, he put his arms around Norman and pulled him close. Norman thought he might suffocate but he was also relieved. He felt his father's tears on the back of his neck. They were like the drops of water that fell from the bathroom faucet even after you turned it off.

When one of Norman's aunts bought him a Spiderman outfit, he wouldn't touch it, refused to try it on. But after a week or so he did and then he wouldn't take it off. When it had to be washed, he sometimes wouldn't get dressed at all. He would sit motionless in his underwear on the edge of his bed until his mother washed and quick-dried the red and blue suit and returned it to him. He especially loved the cape, which he continued to wear every day even after he outgrew the rest of the getup. He fiddled in front of the mirror until he was sure it hung down exactly the same on both sides.

His dark hair was unruly. It seemed to grow in all directions. Norman parted it precisely in the middle. Once he used Elmer's glue to slick it down. After his mother had to rub his scalp for more than an hour to get it all out, he switched to water.

Norman's mother talked to doctors, then other specialists. She joined groups of parents with children like Norman. She read books. Norman would sometimes hear his parents whispering to one another after he'd gone to bed. They were usually talking about him. His mother's voice sounded pleading, his father grunted from time to time or was silent.

But just when his mother thought she understood her son a little better, Norman defied the norm. The norm in this situation that seemed to have no norm. Yes, he was shy, but only with authority figures or people he didn't know. He was okay with everyone else. True, he was uncomfortable when relatives hugged him, even though his parents told him they were only trying to show him that they loved him. But he could hug when he saw that someone needed the gesture. He comforted himself by noticing and counting, remembered the rules, took them all to heart. He learned to knit, loved making stiches that were perfectly even. If he dropped one, he didn't take that row out and do it over but started the project again, from the beginning.

Norman knew he was different from other kids. His mother explained his difference as special, a gift. Norman hadn't wanted a gift. He'd never asked for one. He would have preferred to have been like everyone else but he didn't know how. His father said: "Different, yes, which means you're going to have to make more of an effort, work harder." Norman thought it strange to be given a gift that meant working harder. He always worked hard.

When Norman was four or five he didn't have to worry so much about other kids, teachers, school. Or the rules getting so complicated. He'd spend his days in the field behind his house, exploring, imagining. Imagining had its positives and negatives. He pictured a world where no one made fun of him. That was a phrase he didn't understand either: making fun. It was never fun for him.

Sometimes imaginary friends came around, sat down beside him on the old oak tree stump, spoke unambiguously about the world as it is. It didn't feel so good when one imaginary friend interrupted another, both of them talking at the same time. Norman liked it when everyone took their turn, followed the rules.

But then Norman was six and the idea of school was introduced. He overheard his mother and father arguing one night, as they often did: "Beaverbrook would be the best," his mother was saying, "he'll get the attention he needs there." "You know we can't afford a private school," his father said, "and the sooner he gets used to the real world, the better."

Norman wondered if there was a real and an unreal world, and if so how you could tell the difference.

School was a challenge. Norman heard that word a lot. It was something that was going to take an effort. He was supposed to make that effort. It would prepare him for the real world.

Norman knew both his parents loved him, despite their different ways of showing it. He knew that Miss Abercrombie did not, despite her smiles and pats on the back that made him recoil no matter how hard he tried not to. When his mother took him to meet her at the big public school in town, she sat far back in her chair, looked away from them when she spoke, fidgeted with her hair, crossed and uncrossed her legs 23 times in the time they were together. Norman was sure. He'd counted.

"You know we can't be responsible for how the other students will react to your son," was the single phrase Norman remembered Miss Abercrombie had repeated several times during that meeting. His mother had seemed sad when she'd asked his teacher-to-be: "Why not?" Miss Abercrombie didn't answer.

"Well, how'd it go?" his father asked his mother when he got home from work that afternoon. "About like you'd expect," his mother replied. Norman wondered what his father expected. He didn't even know what he expected, but he wet his bed the night before his first day of class. Anxious, he thought. Bed-wetting was about being anxious. Mother had explained that to him, again and again. "It's not your fault, Sweetheart, you're just anxious." Norman didn't understand how to stop being anxious.

And then that class. When Miss Abercrombie wrote her name on the board, Norman noticed the line dipped slightly to the right beginning with the second M. She hadn't judged the space correctly. Norman would have measured it in his head before beginning to write.

Norman registered his classmates' faces, their eyes. Most looked away. Only a few looked directly at him. They were learning about the country's 50 states, were supposed to say the capital of each. Norman knew them all, but the teacher didn't call on him even when he raised his hand. Finally, there was recess, when he got to sit alone on a low wall watching the other children gather in small groups, shout and whisper, sometimes pointing his way. Then a bell rang, one of the new rules he would have to learn, announcing a return to the classroom, and an afternoon as interminable as the morning had been.

"How was your first day?," his mother asked, when she picked him up that afternoon. He opened the station wagon door, climbed in beside her and fastened his seat belt before answering. He knew that was the order to be followed. He hadn't forgotten the home rules, even in his effort to learn the new ones for school. "About as you'd expect," he said, remembering that was a response that seemed to fit in conversations.

Norman's heart feeling didn't match his answers to his parents' questions. That night he wet his bed again.

And the days succeeded days, weeks followed weeks. Each school day required a bigger effort to ignore the loneliness and humiliation, stay present until the bell rang, pretend Miss Abercrombie was nice and resist the boredom of being taught things he already knew. On Saturday and Sunday, Norman's favorite days of the week, he got to stay out in his field again, play with his imaginary friends, be himself. He never wet his bed on Friday or Saturday nights.

Then it was the end of that first school year. Summer came and went, and all too soon the next school year began. Norman made an illustrated calendar he kept beneath his mattress. He would spend hours looking at it at night. It told him how many days he would have to endure this "necessary experience" (his mother's words), when it would be over. Allowing for holidays and vacations, he came up with the number 2,160. He didn't include college because he believed, hoped, it would be more interesting. He also drew tiny pictures in the margins: open mouths, piercing eyes, Miss Abercrombie's cleavage.

Fourth grade followed third. He went to a new school for sixth. It was called a middle school and had a different name. General MacArthur instead of Riverside. Now his teacher was Mr. Green. Some of the kids were crueler but one became a friend. Richard was small for his age. One of his legs was shorter than the other, making for a slightly lopsided gait. And he talked funny. Norman quickly saw that he, too, was different, although his gift didn't seem to have an upside. Both mothers rejoiced in the friendship.

Richard had approached Norman on the second day of sixth grade, sat by him at lunch, asked about his new red and gold Nikes, offered him half his chicken salad sandwich. Norman tried to find a way to refuse without offending. He didn't want to tell his friend that he never ate chicken mixed with any other food. Especially if they were both the same color.

Norman was wary at first. He knew from experience that flesh and blood friends could be dangerous. They might be what his mother called false friends, who would abandon him for no reason he could figure out. They weren't like imaginary ones. But he was willing to give Richard a chance. "Give him a chance," his father said, "you won't know until you give him a chance." Norman wondered what it was that he wouldn't know. But he resolved to follow his father's advice.

One day at the beginning of seventh grade Richard greeted Norman with his customary "Howya doing, dude?" and Norman heard himself reply: *"Comment allez-vou?"*

Richard stared at his friend. Norman answered his own question then: *"Je ne me sense pas bien."* The summer before, bored as he always was, he'd decided to teach himself French. He'd ordered the Rosetta Stone tapes and played them every night on his computer. In less than a month he'd mastered the language. Norman's mother and father thought it was a good thing their son had gotten himself a hobby. From then on, Norman sometimes spoke to Richard in a foreign language, whichever he happened to be learning at the time. Richard didn't seem to mind.

Soon Norman became obsessed with languages. *"Kako si Nisam dobro?"* he inquired of his parents one night, after spending a few hours at the convenience store four blocks away. *"Kako si Nisam dobro? Kako si Nisam dobro?"* he insisted, ignoring his parents' blank stares. The convenience store manager was Bosnian, Mr. Aganović. He'd come over after losing his family in a terrible war. Some people called it a genocide. Norman looked up the word. It sounded right to him. Norman's parents grasped the general situation from the nightly news. But Norman was interested in the details, gleaned them from overseas papers like The Guardian that seemed more interested in world affairs. When Norman asked Mr. Aganović the same question, the old man smiled but shook his head: *"Ne ide mi dobro,"* he said. Norman patted him on the shoulder, a gesture that took some effort because he didn't really enjoy touching people he didn't know that well.

Once Norman had acquired a working knowledge of Bosnian, he became restless again. He began hanging out at the gas station on the corner of Holloway and Highway 12. There he followed Alang around, a compact young man from Laos whose parents had immigrated years before when, Norman knew, the defeated US army abandoned its supporters in that southeast Asian nation. Alang was born and grew up here but heard Hmong at home and spoke it as easily as English. Sometimes, while pumping gas or cleaning a windshield, he would sing in the language. Norman loved the sound. *"Ioj nyob li cas?"* he inquired of his own parents one night upon returning from the gas station.

Soon it was *"Come va?"* (Italian) and *"Sut wyt t?i"* (Welsh). No one knew where he picked up *"Bawo ni o se wa?"* (Yoruba) or *"Dei te pēhea koe?"* (Maori). There weren't that many foreign-speaking inhabitants in Oak Park. And Rosetta Stone's list was limited. Norman found the structure of each new language as easy as its vocabulary. And he had a good ear, no problem with pronunciation. He wrote a letter to Rosetta asking when they were going to add Hopi to their list.

Norman's mother began to realize that this passion for languages had gradually replaced her son's obsession with rules and counting. He hadn't knitted anything in years and no longer wet his bed. He seemed happier, better adjusted. Public school had been hard but he was getting through it. She noticed a line of dark fuzz along Norman's upper lip. It looked out of place against his too-white skin. He's becoming a man, she smiled to herself, realizing she'd never been sure that would happen. Norman's dad was still disappointed that his son was so thin and gangly. He waited in vain for the boy's muscles to appear.

Norman's mother bought him the latest Rosetta Stone for his 13th birthday. Yoruba in 25 lessons. He thanked her but said he already knew the language. *"Bawo ni o se wa?"*

Coincidentally, Norman's 19th birthday was the same day he graduated from Ohio State with a Masters in linguistics. His parents and Richard watched him walk across the stage to receive his diploma. Phyllis was there too, but

Norman hadn't introduced her to his family yet. He wanted to be sure first.

Norman silently counted the steps going up to the podium and coming down, making a mental note that the latter were seven more than the former. He forced himself to look out at the audience, smile and hold the empty envelope up like the other graduates did, even though he couldn't help wondering why an institution as organized as a university was supposed to be couldn't get it together to put each student's diploma in their envelope instead of sending it later by mail.

Norman's proud parents took him and Richard and Phyllis to the most expensive restaurant in Oak Park to celebrate. Yes, his mother had noticed the connection between her son and the young woman despite his attempts to hide it. They sat around the two tables pushed together, beaming at one another.

When it was his turn to order, Norman looked directly into the waiter's eyes: "A filet mignon medium rare without the bacon, an extra baked potato but hold the sour cream, peas instead of creamed spinach but please don't let them touch the steak. Oh, and leave the tomatoes out of the salad."

He waited with his hands folded in his lap for the waiter to finish writing his instructions down.

Not What it Looks Like

"It's not what it looks like!"

Henry blurts the words as he struggles to cover himself and the young woman beside him. He searches Carol's face, calculating the effort he'll have to make to convince his wife to believe him before she believes her own eyes. The young woman looks like she wants to leave her skin. She isn't looking at anyone, not her thesis advisor or his befuddled wife, not even her own blurry reflection in the dresser mirror across the room.

Carol's reaction unfolds in slow motion. Not what it looks like? It looks like her husband has been ravaging his student. Swan, the one he often tells her is stupid or naïve when they run into her at a campus event or her name comes up in casual conversation. Dinner talk, floating back and forth, in which he complains about the intellectual level of students these days and, she is sure she remembers, of this one in particular. "Well," she would always reassure her husband—comfort or just idle conversation, she no longer knows which—"they can't all be that bad. And you know what a fine teacher you are. I'm sure you'll see an improvement by the end of the semester . . ."

She has opened their bedroom door this mid-morning expecting to enter an empty chamber. Henry had kissed her goodbye after breakfast, the brief perfunctory kiss she'd come to expect after four decades of marriage. Said he was going to the college, might be late for lunch. Carol was halfway to her book club when she realized she'd left her copy of *Eat Pray Love* on her bedtable, the hand-woven bookmark signaling her place just a few pages before the end. She hadn't managed to finish it before sleep overcame her last night. She'd read enough, though, was sure she'd have something to contribute. Especially if they didn't call on her first; she hates having to be the one to start those discussions. Carol's habit of always being early allowed her time to go back to the house, grab the book and still be one of the first to arrive. The last thing she expects is the scene before her.

The furniture seems to be where it's always been. Matching dressers on either side of the small love seat, armchair by the window, narrow bench at the foot of the bed, the latter now strewn with unfamiliar garments: a lacy bra several sizes larger than her own, crumpled Levi's, a t-shirt with something written on it. Carol tries to read the words on the shirt but can only make out two of several Greek letters. Must be a sorority. The colors are the same as always: mid-morning light bathing a muted scheme of pink and green. The shapes are the same: long reach of the oak tree branch just outside the window, rococo curves on the Louis XV-style furniture they'd chosen together so many years ago. Yes, this is her bedroom, the familiar space she wakes to each morning.

Henry interrupts her reverie, still sputtering: "It's really not . . . Just let me explain," He is stumbling over his words. His voice seems an octave higher than usual, almost imploring—an attitude Carol doesn't recognize in him. Nor does she understand his urgency. She's hasn't said a word, is willing to give him all the time he needs. No exasperation, no tears, not even surprise. But his flustered exclamations fade now, into a swamp of academic pretense, robust dictates, opinions so educated each one must have its own Ph.D.

"It's not what it looks like." Well, okay. If it's not what it looks like, what is it?

Their bedroom becomes the sunny pathway then, through a formal garden, slightly foreign in flavor, smelling of roasting chestnuts. They are forty years younger, brand new at being together, strolling along on their honeymoon in Paris. A marble statue of a water nymph stops them with its grace. A young Henry touches the white stone where it drapes over the polished thigh, rippling in soft folds down her leg to just above her foot. The same nymph in a slightly different pose is repeated six times around the circumference of the fountain, the lilting sound of which seems to complete a romantic scene staged for them alone. "She reminds me of you," he tells his smiling wife.

Carol remembers that after they exited that garden she suggested they visit a small museum with a collection of Monets, his famous haystacks or waterlilies, she can't remember which. Their Micheline says Monet was famous for painting a favorite scene many times over, at different times of day, different seasons, different lights. The idea intrigues her. The guidebook says it's a short metro ride and the works fill a whole basement gallery. She is proud to have discovered this treasure.

But Henry says no. They've seen enough Monets for one day, maybe for the whole damned trip. He will take her to a nearby beer parlor where the great 19th century French poets Verlaine and Rimbaud gathered in their day. He is lecturing her about their importance. His tone tells her this is what they are going to do as he continues to propel her across the broad avenue, his hand firmly steering her elbow, talking excitedly about their next stop.

Carol still stands in the doorway, leaning lightly against its frame. Swan—young people have such strange names these days—has scrambled from the bed, dragging about her the quilt Carol's sister made for them before she died and leaving Henry to cover himself with the sheet. Her husband seems intent upon hiding his penis, that member she knows so well with its slightly awkward tilt to the right. She can't imagine why he seems so reticent after all these years of marriage.

Maybe it's Swan's presence. That must be it. Not what it looks like? If you say so, dear. Carol finds herself wondering what the sheet covering her husband must smell like this morning. Some mix of her body and the student's, she guesses. A real challenge for Extra Strength Tide. Her thoughts stray to the load of wash awaiting her in the basement. Probably need to divide white from color today.

But the scene shifts and she is the woman in that bed, her belly swollen and trembling as she concentrates on giving birth to Henry Jr., her husband on one side sweating as if he is the one doing the work, the midwife on the other instructing Carol when to breathe and when to push, telling her what a wonderful job she is doing.

Praise isn't something Carol hears often. She remembers all three of her children's births more for those welcome expressions of approval than for the pain, or even the differences in each delivery. Such encouraging words for a job that does itself, if you think about it. Oh, she tried to get through those births with grace, of course she did, but she suspects they would have come out the same whatever she did. That's one of the things about the way Henry has always treated her: liberal with his praise for whatever comes naturally, automatically if you will. Her big efforts are the ones he ignores, her successes rarely acknowledged.

Not what it looks like? The room is a long-ago meadow then, a childhood memory. Carol must be four or five. Her father and mother have taken her to this place, somewhere in the country, for a lazy summer picnic. She is behind them on the backseat of their old blue Ford, her feet dangling above the floorboard. The yellowish tan upholstery smells faintly like a radiator, its rough feel scratchy against her tender skin. They stop at her father's favorite place, unload the car, walk in silence to the shade of the tree he chooses. Mother and Father enacting the same presentation as always, eating the same sandwiches, cream cheese and strawberry jam with the crusts cut off.

After Mother lifts the two-part wooden lid and puts the uneaten remnants of their lunch back into the wicker basket, she brushes the remaining crumbs onto the grass and stretches out on the blanket they share, pulls her floppy straw hat over her eyes and settles into her customary afternoon nap.

This is the moment when Carol begins to feel uneasy. She knows what is about to happen. It's happened before, she thinks now, in those ominous darts of reality snagging memory and pulling it to the surface. As Mother's gentle snoring tells them she is asleep, her father's hand slips casually between her young legs. Creeps higher, the fingers of one hand touching her now with increased urgency. Entering her without words, only the agitated breathing she's come to fear. Fingers of the other raised to his lips in that gesture that says "Silence. No telling." A sour scent she associates ever since with a mixture of her father's aftershave and dying dandelions. Nothing violent, just occasional slivers of pain and a great cloud of shame. "Our little secret."

Not what it looks like. Of course not.

"You're not hearing me." Henry's insistence returns her to the present, where Swan is fully dressed, and her husband still believes an explanation matters. Words. Sometimes in rising wheedling tones, sometimes commanding. Who gets to have the last one? Who wins the debate? Words have a different hierarchy, Carol has learned, depending on who uses them and how. She smiles. She's probably always known this, she thinks, but articulating it even to herself brings an unfamiliar satisfaction.

Carol knows she has walked in on her husband having sex with one of his students. In their bedroom, their bed. She is the one who isn't supposed to be here. Her fault. She should be at her book club, after all. Surely Henry should have been able to count on that. A laughing string of shoulds. An apology rises in her throat, makes its way almost to her lips before she pushes it back down. That protestation, superfluous now.

They are in the hospital room at Stoneybrook General and she is fussing to make Henry comfortable. He's just been wheeled from recovery after the double bypass that is declared a rousing success by the surgeon who removes his cap and mask and smiles at her now, reassuringly. "He's in great shape for his age," the doctor says, "he'll be good as new before you know it." And then, looking directly at Carol for the first time: "Any questions?"

He doesn't wait for those she may have, but makes an immediate exit, leaving her to gaze at the web of tubes and monitors, listen to the unfamiliar sounds of the machinery attached to her husband's body. One of those modern symphonies for which no one prepares you. Carol sinks into the straight-backed chair to the left of her husband's bed. She is glad Henry Jr. and Bailey will be arriving soon.

"What it looks like." Anything at all. Truth or Dare. Truth or lie. Whatever Henry needs it to be in order to move on to the next story, next woman, next game. What

Carol needs it to be is for her life to make sense. Not a marriage bed with betrayal writ large between the sheets. A sunny field where danger lurks. A stroll through that Paris park where she is the naïve young bride who believes a perfect life lies ahead. The births of their children, each one Henry's proud accomplishment more than hers. A hospital room where her husband lays helpless and she is the healthy one, although he still commands attention and she is still the appendage. Years of college events, where she stands at Henry's side, wears what he has picked out for her, what accentuates those qualities he hopes his colleagues will envy. Years through which she practices radiating adoring looks and repeating stories in which he is the hero. Years of her book club where the other women share their own stories of attentive husbands, perfect marriages.

Henry is dressed now. He sidesteps his wife, still standing in the doorway, makes his determined way downstairs, opens the cut glass decanter on the dining room sideboard and pours himself two fingers of scotch. Then he settles himself in his favorite armchair and waits for Carol to join him. She can't stay in their bedroom forever. Swan has fled the premises, is probably back in her dorm room by now. He will have to figure out how to handle her when the time comes. Shouldn't be much of a problem.

Now he hears Carol in the kitchen. Must be making herself a cup of that African bush tea she's taken to drinking since their safari in Kenya the year before. He is still feeling a bit off balance when she carries the steaming cup into the room, sets it on the end table and herself in the rocker at the far end of the room. When she fails to start with her usual questions or complaints but only smiles affably, he decides it's up to him to address the unspoken issue. "You've got to understand," he begins.

Carol cuts him off. "Oh, Sweetheart," she says, "I do understand. Just like you said, it wasn't what it looked like. Don't worry about me; I'm not even here."

It's a perfect place for a summer picnic, a stroll through the City of Lights, a home delivery, a hospital room. Or in the basement separating dirty laundry, washing the sheets and towels with a bit of bleach for that sparkling brand new look.

Do You Want Music?

"Do you want music, today?" Susan asks, when she sees Helen pulling on her sneakers, taking care the laces aren't so long that they'll get caught in the treadmill's moving parts. Helen has a fear of freak accidents, sometimes thinks about the oft-repeated story of Isadora Duncan's flowing scarf catching in the rear hubcap of her open motorcar, strangling her to death. That thought, in turn, invariably sends her to that other Isadora Duncan tale, the one in which Isadora writes to Bertrand Russell suggesting they conceive a child together. "Just imagine," the dancer is rumored to have said, "it would have my beauty and your brains." Russell was unpersuaded. "Yes, but it could just as easily have my beauty and your brains," he responded.

If Helen says yes to the music, Susan connects her I-Pad to a small speaker and cues up one of a dozen of her wife's favorites. She takes great joy in doing these things for the woman she loves. Some days it's Johnny Cash, some it's the soundtrack to "Three Billboards Outside Ebbing, Missouri." Maybe "The Trio"—those beautiful women's harmonies—or Bach's Brandenburg Concertos. Bartok takes Helen back to her childhood and the sound of her father's cello. Any female vocalist evokes her years of coming into herself.

She remembers as a young girl, learning to touch-type to the beat of a catchy melody called "The Syncopated Clock." Music for exercising reminds her of that, but why not choose something less monotonous? Not being musical herself, it's taken Helen a while to figure out any rhythm will do. Increasingly, there are also days she prefers silence, a time of uninterrupted thinking in which she can sink into herself, work something she is writing out in her head. The crux of a short story, perhaps. Or a poem.

The treadmill has a monitor that displays how fast Helen walks, how long, how many calories are burned according to a person's weight and other variables superfluous to this moment in her life. The interface all but blinds her if she gazes at it too long. Sometimes she closes her eyes, sometimes she stares out the window or at the soothingly lowered blinds—easier on her aging vision. Her old workhorse of a Trotter lasted almost 30 years. It moved with them when they moved, from the house in the foothills to the one in town and finally, a year ago, when they downsized to this tiny apartment. The movers had to take it apart to get it through the narrow hall and into their pocket-sized bedroom.

Not long after that it stopped working. They'd get it up and running again, only to have it blow a fuse. These half measures finally told them they needed to invest in something new. Trotters were no longer sold for home use so they had to replace old faithful with this flaming Landice 7: more bells and whistles than Helen wanted or knew how to use. At this point a dependable treadmill was a necessity, a promise there'd be life ahead.

In this small home, the women have carved out meaningfully delineated spaces: studios where Susan does her art and Helen writes, a living area where they can eat at a dining room table of Honduran pine or before a television screen that is both obscured in a corner and the largest they've had, a stacked washer and dryer hidden in a small hall closet, and a bedroom where only precise spatial ingenuity makes it possible for bed and treadmill to coexist. What holds it all together is the art: paintings and photographs, ancient and contemporary, much of the latter made by friends. African and southern Pacific sculptures, Mexican folk art, Native American kachinas. The eclectic collection imbues the place with the richness they crave. When they moved in, people remarked on the fact that they'd hung the art before deciding how the furniture would fit. "How did you know where it would go?" they asked. "We just did," they said, laughing. Living without the art would be like eating what one needs to survive but never enjoying that favorite dish or surprising delicacy. They need to be immersed in that cultural richness.

Helen tries to exercise mid-morning, after breakfast has settled. She usually manages to do two miles four or five times a week. Not that long ago she could do that much every day. It's definitely getting harder. She's acquired a new empathy for her mother who quit accompanying her to a local gym when she was in her mid-nineties. At the time she remembers trying to convince her to keep going a while longer. "It will prolong your life," she urged. But Mother had made up her mind. Helen gets it now that she's approaching the age her mother was when they had this conversation. It wasn't the length of life that concerned the older woman but enjoying it. Not an unreasonable goal.

The treadmill is a last resort. A way of keeping fit when walking on uneven pavement has become too challenging, neighborhood dogs too insistent or really cold weather no longer something she wants to endure. As a young girl, Helen wasn't big on exercise. Friends took to saying about her: "Sure, she loves to walk—from the front door to the car." As a student she hated gym class, was invariably picked last for any team and that humiliation is something that's never entirely left her. She used her period as an excuse several times a month and became skilled at forging doctor's notes. It wasn't until midlife, when she and Susan got together, that her more active lover encouraged her to get outdoors, biking and hiking.

The biking was nice. It was something they could enjoy together. Helen hadn't been on a bicycle since she was a pre-teen and delivered newspapers around her family's upper middle-class neighborhood on her red Mohawk. She wasn't sure she still knew how to ride. But Susan was patient, never forcing the issue. The first morning they made it a couple of blocks. Before long they were doing 25-, even 40-mile rides. Flying through the bright New Mexico air, breathing in the sage and other desert scents. Helen preferred riding alone with Susan; when too many others crowded close, like at the beginning of a tour, she feared they would crash into her, cause her to lose her balance. Once she had an accident that laid her up for three long months. When she mended, she quickly returned to the sport. But it wasn't fun anymore.

Years ago, the two women even tried a brief parenthesis of rock climbing, going to a specialized gym every afternoon for several months. The lean muscular young male regulars were bemused but encouraging and kind. Helen delighted in learning to push off and pull up, that feeling of reaching for the impossible, knowing she wouldn't get there, but loving the adrenalin surge. Hanging off the precipice at the top, swinging gently in her harness, she was invincible.

But when Helen discovered hiking it changed her. And she'd had a good two decades in which she made hikes that introduced her to new landscapes and a whole different way of living in her body. There was La Luz, the storied route that ascended from the trailhead at 6,000 feet to the crest of Sandia Mountain just east of her city. The guidebooks said an average hiker made the climb in three and a half hours. It took her a year, advancing a little more with each attempt, until she reached the top. Five hours was her best time, but who was counting? She'd rarely felt so exhilarated. Moving up from desert through thick pine forest and finally past the rockslide into the snow, she was in a world of her own, oblivious of other hikers, a wonderous place. Helen made that hike a couple dozen times before she no longer could.

There had been other fulfilling efforts. Her first ascent of something that could be called a mountain, on the outskirts of Tucson. Two hardy friends took her up, Helen huffing, puffing and complaining all the way. Climbing a narrow trail that clung to a steep mountainside in order to reach an ancient granary and in the process learning it was possible to overcome a lifetime of vertigo. That had been another first, achieved with the help of a Grand Canyon river guide who could see she needed the challenge. The five-mile stroll at the bottom of Mexico's Copper Canyon, from the village of Batopilas to the Lost Cathedral of Satevó. Numerous sprints down Bright Angel Trail from Grand Canyon's South Rim; the farthest she'd gotten was Plateau Point and back, a 12-mile best for her then. Standing directly above Hermit Rapid, the thunder shaking her to the core, a thrill that never got old.

And then the toughest test of them all, packing into Kiet Seel, an Ancestral Puebloan ruin on Navajo land in northern Arizona. She'd done that hike with the help of a good friend. Mark was from South Africa, with a lifetime of experience in the bush. He was also a strong six foot two inches, a double marathoner, and carried 70 pounds to her 20. Along the way he stored water bottles behind rocks and beneath trees, relocating them easily on their way out.

They both gasped when they reached the ruin and saw they'd have to climb a 70-foot ladder to enter its secrets. Mark, it turned out, had a fear of heights as well, and for Helen it was another challenge to her vertigo. She remembers gripping the wooden poles of that ladder so tightly she had splinters in both palms by the time they got to the top.

Kiet Seel is situated at the end of a long canyon, nine miles in and nine out. In between they set up their tent at the small campground, shivered through a night that seemed unusually cold, warmed themselves briefly with the solar panels in the spotless toilet, and feasted on sandwiches Helen had made for the trip. They'd had the privilege of exploring an abandoned habitat few others see, ancient utensils and tools providing a sense of what life there was like.

All those hikes are memories now. Age has brought Helen poor balance and a fear of falling. Too many stories about an elderly person breaking a hip and that being that: the end of the line. And so, the treadmill is her fallback solution. She can grip the handles without worrying that a misplaced step will take her down. She can get through the 40 minutes or so without fear of disaster.

"I'm going to the gym," Susan calls out, leaving Helen to her morning ritual. "I'll be back in a little while. Do you need me to pick up anything on my way?"

"No, love, have a good workout."

Susan prefers the weight room, pool and sauna, a particular sort of socializing that happens when you frequent a place for years. Friendly people who know your name, listen to your stories, tell you theirs. The woman who tries in vain to convert you to Jesus, likes you too much to think of you not being saved. The guy whose political opinions

are so offensive he must be confronted, and you decide it's
your job to do the confronting. The guy who tells you more
than you want to know about his gall bladder. The woman
who generously exits the pool so you can have her spot in
this pandemic-era of one swimmer to a lane. People coming and going, enjoying a sort of friendship that demands
no real commitment but offers a patina of human interaction. Some succeed at losing weight or getting in shape.
Some fail to show up one day and then the next and you
know they are gone for good. "Uh um, D-A-I-D," quips
Helen, an irreverent bit of private humor that allows for
acknowledgement of the inevitable.

It was hard on Susan when her gymnasium had to
close because of COVID. It reopened with caveats a few
months back, and she says she feels safe there. "You know
they're constantly rubbing down the equipment, making
sure it's clean."

Helen trusts Susan's judgment. But she prefers working out at home. Sometimes in a worn oversize T-shirt
advertising some cause or struggle of her youth. Ban the
Bomb. Make Love Not War. Women's Liberation. Viva
the Cuban Revolution. Divest from Apartheid. Remember
the Chicago Seven. Women's Rights are Human Rights.
Or more recent struggles: Make the Dreamers Legal. I am
Trayvon Martin. Justice for George Floyd. Trans People are
People Too. Sometimes all she wears is one of those shirts
and a pair of underpants. The advantages of working out
in the intimacy of their home.

Helen hears the front door open and close. She'd
asked for the soundtrack from "Three Billboards" today
and closes her eyes as the music swells. Some of the songs
bring back scenes in the film. Frances McDormand's
superb acting. The intense moment when the young

advertising salesman and the racist cop who threw him out a second-floor window find themselves in the same hospital room. The cop has burns over most of his body from when our frustrated heroine bombarded the police station with Molotov cocktails; it was after hours and she thought no one was inside. Our human condition, raw and complex. The operatic aria soars. Helen never tires of this music.

She starts to walk, uninspired at first. A tenth of a mile. Then a quarter. At the half-mile point she begins to sweat. She can always count on that happening around then. Bursts of dry heat escape her body, turning to liquid and pooling at the mottled pale pink of her hairline, bathing her forehead, running down her cheeks and spreading to soak the front of the shirt that bears the message about making love not war. A good motto for any era. She feels the droplets descend her inner thighs, hears them splatter on the conveyer belt. That wash emanating from her pores makes her feel cleansed of life's small struggles, renewed. Now she's into the routine. The rest should be easy.

An hour and a half later, Susan returns. As she inserts her key in the lock and starts to turn the door handle, she experiences an overwhelming dread. Something's wrong, she doesn't know why she knows, but she knows. She shouts Helen's name. There's no response. Ordinarily she would remove her mask, wash her hands and take off her coat before going to kiss her wife hello. Now she sprints for the bedroom, fear rising in her breast, constricting her throat.

She sees Helen's foot first. It's on the floor, pointed away from the treadmill in the narrow space between it and the bed. Immediately, she sees the rest of her body. It is splayed, crooked, her head turned to one side. One leg remains on the conveyor belt and continues to move forward and back, forward and back. Her face is peaceful, eyes closed, what might even be described as a faint smile on her slightly lopsided lips. There is blood, not a lot but enough. The music is still playing.

Susan kneels before the woman she loves, tries to find a pulse, knows she won't. Something happened here, but what? Did death cause Helen to be thrown from the machine—which continues its steady pace of three miles per hour—or some sort of sudden accident throw her off, causing her to die. The part of Susan's mind that still functions is telling her to dial 911. That same part of her mind says there's no hurry.

Susan gathers Helen's inert body in her arms, rocks back and forth and begins to sob.

Helen too experiences a sense of loss that moves from her body to Susan's, reaching to touch her lover's velveteen skin, and returning empty-handed. The gesture ping-pongs like a lame animal. This feeling is desperate and fleeting, dense and light at the same time. Colors descend like rain. A scent of dying gardenias gives way to that of pure desert: the waxy blooms of the century plant, the deep red claret cup flower, creosote, juniper, sage, a history of sand. Her beloved landscape. On her tongue, the taste of fresh coconut, a New York bagel with cream cheese and the sharp brine of Kalamata olives. Music is cacophony now but not unpleasant. Temperature is beside itself. Memory lifts her in its arms.

When such love exists, rarely do both partners depart at once. One must leave, the other remain. Which is the harder task? It's the question that has no answer.

Now Helen is looking down on Susan holding her. Now she is looking down on herself hiking the Inca Trail, flying above its rough stone steps, her feet only intermittently touching the ground.

In the Peruvian highlands, Helen is descending into the ancient city of Machu Picchu by way of the Gate of the Sun. For years she's wanted to make this trek, lamented the fact that it's one experience she won't have before she dies. Too frail, the ravages of age and respiratory insufficiency impediments to that dream—and others. Now, to her utter joy she finds herself gulping the thin copal air of the Urubamba Valley, striding with unrivaled power along the trail, listening to the faint tone of a distant Andean flute, catching sight of the early morning light on perfectly fitted stone walls. Her children are with her, her grandchildren and great grandchildren. Susan too. She is sure nothing could be more perfect.

Far below, Susan must begin the rest of her life.

Little Margaret

She was sitting at the edge of my bed, legs dangling halfway to the floor, feet turned awkwardly inward, the left a bit more than the right. Her body was tensed and she leaned slightly forward, gripping the edge of the mattress with chubby fingers. I sensed her presence before I opened my eyes.

I discovered her as I was struggling to wake. I was stretching, rubbing my face, scratching a bit, flicking sleep from the corners of my eyes, picking a scab or two. Maybe I was still enmeshed in that dream in which I'd been trying endlessly to arrange rows of books according to their size, reaccommodating them as I found a place for each, attempting to line it up carefully only to watch it tumble between the shelf and the wall, clatter to the floor and have to be retrieved and put back where it belonged.

In my dream I had to remember the contents of each of those books, how the words wove together to complete the whole, what was said there and how. Titles from childhood passed before my eyes: *Nancy Drew*, *The Hardy Boys*, *Black Beauty*. Even a battered copy of *Ballad of the Be-Ba-Boes* my mother had bequeathed me, its embossed Maxfield Parrish cover worn and ragged. *I Married Adventure*, Osa Johnson's crooked story that thrilled me before I understood its colonialist nature. And *Daughter of Earth*, Agnes Smedley's hardscrabble tale of becoming a woman in a world of men. Marx's *Capital* never stopped chiding me for skimming its denser pages. De Beauvoir's *Second Sex* reverberated like the highest wire on a tightly strung guitar, telling me over and over what my body knew. I had to put all the pieces together, give pride of place to those that mattered, discard those that didn't. Not a nightmare, just endless breathless labor.

On the other side of the windowpane, dark oddly shaped clouds roiled above the mountain, then settled like granny caps on its highest ridges. It was a gray morning, daylight straining to take possession of the land. It had begun to rain, and large drops sounded hard against the glass. It was spring, but I got a whiff of the faint scent of late snow.

The girl's small body obstructed my smooth transition from sleep to wakefulness. My impatient gesture was met with a look of quiet reproachment just as I was about to throw aside the winter quilt. She didn't have to say a word.

Right away I knew I was looking at my younger self. Those wide-open blue eyes, the ragged hairline descending in braids on either side of a careful center part to embrace plump cheeks, the splash of freckles across the bridge of her nose. It was like gazing into a regressive mirror. She was wearing one of those print smocks with the shirred bodice and little white Peter Pan collar. My Grandma Jo bought matching versions for me and my younger sister. I hated my grandmother and always resisted wearing mine. Matching ribbons adorned the end of each braid.

I was naked. I'd been sleeping this way for years. Winter, summer, spring, fall. I make my own heat and love the feel of clean sheets against my skin. A nightgown would be superfluous. I've always been comfortable spending the night this way and am unembarrassed by it now. After all, who knew me better than she did?

She removed her shiny black patent leather Mary Janes and placed them neatly beside one another on the floor. I stared at them, remembering how they'd pinched my toes. How the shoe salesman smiled as he pressed what he said was the space between my foot and the end of the shoe, assuring my mother there was plenty of room for growth. My feet always knew better.

With a gesture that said I needn't get out of bed she hopped up and sat beside me.

I settled closer to her then and reached for her small hand.

"How did you get here?" I asked, confused.

"The same way you did," she replied, "it just took me longer. I was detained so often along the way; stopping to look, listen, learn or not. I was curious about everything." Her voice was a bit nasal in tone, high and thin but forceful for her small size.

"You mean it didn't take as long," I went into corrective mode without stopping to think it might be offensive, "because here you are already and you don't look older than four or five."

"I'm six," she said, "I might be small for my age but the important thing is the way you grow inside, what you carry with you, what you make of it."

I was stunned listening to such adult language on a child's lips. Even a child whose journey through time had caught me so off guard. "Why are you talking like that?" I asked. "How do you already know how to formulate ideas as if you were an adult?"

Her quizzical expression told me she wasn't going to bother answering that one.

Then I heard myself asking her name. "Why Margaret, of course," she responded, clearly surprised I had to ask.

I was embarrassed. "Of course," I said, "I should have known."

"Well, you were just trying to make conversation," little Margaret continued," obviously trying to put me at ease. I noticed she was very literal, answering each of my astonished questions or comments with detailed specifics. No allowance for simile, metaphor or banter. I wondered if she were somewhere on the spectrum.

"We're all on the spectrum," she said then, as if reading my mind, "some just more than others." I was sure I hadn't posed the question out loud. "The truth is," she continued, "all of life is just one broad spectrum. Each of us fits where we fit. Our cultures tend to define difference conservatively, afraid of confronting change. It's always hard to leave your comfort zone."

"What's with the theorizing?" I asked. "Aren't you a little young for that?"

I thought I saw a flash of something then, regret or shame, and tried to backtrack.

I was getting cold, sitting there without anything covering me so early in the morning chill, so I invited her into the bed with me. "We'll be more comfortable," I said. She entered willingly, curling alongside me from shoulder to hip, and I pulled her close, feeling almost as if I was extending a protective wing over her small body. I took up more room but she was the dominant figure: guest and astonishment. And I realized I didn't want to hear further generalities, wise as they may be. I was eager to fill in my own blanks.

"Tell me how it felt when Grandpa did those horrible things to me. I know you were an infant, but maybe you remember . . . "

"We both remember," she interrupted, gently. "It's just

that you've lost the words and I haven't yet learned them."

I began to shiver then, not from cold but from a current of fear coursing through my suddenly anxious body. I wanted and didn't want to hear more. I pulled her tighter and could smell her sweet breath. I hoped the decay of my age wouldn't scare her off. I wasn't really worried about this young girl seeing her own future on my skin, remembering how incapable the young are at imagining themselves experiencing the changes that come with the years: it won't happen to me, they believe, against the evidence all around them.

"You hated his demeanor," she reminded me, "that habit he had of simply taking what he wanted. But sometimes you also liked how it felt. That was the problem, that contradiction that tore through you like a messy wound, a confusion festering to this day. Grandma Jo was worse. Watching from that ominous distance, always watching. No pleasure from her, just punishment. And the expression of satisfaction she got the more uncomfortable a person was. Even as young as you were, you must have expected more from a woman."

I couldn't contain my tears. They fell from my eyes, washing down my face and filling my nose, making it harder to breathe against the pillows and tangled sheets.

"Cry," little Margaret urged, "it'll do you good. But remember, you were the one who asked."

"What do you mean?" I was confused again. "There is no me and you. We're the same. If anyone knows that you do. How is it that at six you're the one with the big picture? Why do you know so much more than me? Come to think of it, why did you come?"

"No, no, no," she hurried to explain, "you are the one who understands. Your words fill in the gaps, allow me to tell our story. Don't you get it? The feelings are fresh on the surface of my skin, but you've written them for the world to know. Sometimes when you move out into the larger arena you lose touch with your own pain. Feeling and reason. Together we make a whole."

As I tried to stop the tears, I began to distinguish a series of doors, some still firmly locked, others beginning to crack open, revealing their ugly secrets. A few were tall and imposing, heavy with medieval ornamentation, ostentatious in weight and inaccessibility, all those steps leading up to them. Others seemed makeshift, flimsy, easy to breach. I headed for those first. And in the timelessness of this encounter, I found they hid terrifying truths. What would I find if I opened them all?

"Take your time," little Margaret urged. "You don't have to go through the others now."

"Have you come alone?" I suddenly heard myself ask.

"I'm never alone," she said, "I have lots of friends. Surely you remember us at ten when lying became a tool. At twenty when we found our first living breathing model, not in a book but standing before us, beckoning. At twenty-two surrounded by artists who sacrificed comfort for the discipline of creativity. At twenty-four when we gave birth for the first time: that inexplicable joy. And a year later when we discovered our real place in the world. At thirty-three, surrounded by those who sacrificed comfort for justice and fear was a sharpened blade. At forty-seven when we came home to landscape, language, familiarity, at fifty when we discovered what love could be. At fifty-three when courage was finally able to rest a while. At fifty-eight when we finally had what we needed to do our real work. Now and in the past and future, as we come around again and again."

"Don't you get tired of traveling in such a homogeneous group?"

"No." Her small voice was almost inaudible now. "Too busy imagining myself as other."

"What happens when we have the answers?" I wanted to know.

"No chance," she laughed, "there will always be more questions." And I noticed the familiar gap between her two front teeth.

"Remind me of my lapses, wrong turns, some of the men with whom I shouldn't have been intimate, every gesture empty of truth, moments of frustration when I lashed out against those I loved or turned away when commitment called, all those times I said yes when I should have said no or no when yes was the better option, followed some fabricated road that promised destination but only ended in a place without temperature."

"Oh yes," she said, "like sentences that are all nouns, not a verb to be had." But they're of no importance. Weren't then, aren't now. Why dwell on ghosts?"

I sensed our conversation was coming to an end. I didn't want that to happen. "Do you ever think of me? I asked, searching her young face.

"Of course," she laughed. "But I think you've got it backwards. I can only imagine you. You remember me. Oh, I wonder what things will be like for me when I grow up, especially who I will marry, how many children I will have, those questions they pile upon us. You remember the expectations. Sometimes I think I will be a writer, but I don't know what that will feel like. It never occurs to me I will love a woman. I know you think of me. Memory isn't one-directional, after all."

"Isn't it? I don't think so, but I've never been sure." I

couldn't let her go, not yet. "Why have you come?" I asked, "why now? What are you looking for?"

Little Margaret looked surprised. "But you called me," she said, "I would never have made the first move."

And with that she wiggled from my side, scrambled over my naked body and slid to the floor, the quilt still wrapped about her.

"Where are you going," I called, already experiencing a loneliness I hadn't known.

"Back where I belong. You can always find me in your memory."

And I watched my six-year-old-self disappear beyond a distant horizon, unanswered questions clinging to my lips.

How Things Have Always Been

Roy Milam felt the tension leave his body. He tried to take a couple of deep breaths. They stuck halfway down, a painful knot he couldn't swallow. He'd done it, come through. He was proud of having maintained a regulation stoicism throughout the trial, an attitude worthy of a man in Blue. He'd never once looked at the boy's parents or the jurors charged with deciding his fate. Historically he knew he'd most likely be acquitted but you couldn't be sure these days; the country was whipped into such a frenzy for what it called justice. And more and more people seemed to have gone over to the other side.

Acquitted!

I got off!

Back to how things belong to be.

Roy had worried he might lose his reputation, maybe even his badge. He was third generation: his father and grandfather before him had been cops. There'd never been any doubt about what he would do out of high school. If there'd been an urgent war, he would have answered the call. So, when he heard *not guilty on all counts*, relief filled him. It took over, flowed through his body, releasing the tension in his muscles, easing the hesitation in his step. Now he could get back to work again, get on with the job of being a cop.

I got off! I got off!

In this northern metropolis, where civil shock could still rattle the bones of a pervasively racist white community and African Americans no longer felt anything but numbness, rage and loss, Jerome Jackson was dead. And Roy Milam was free.

Back to normal now.

The way things should be.

Even with his top-notch legal team seated with him at the table, Roy had felt isolated during the trial. Masks on the witnesses, the jury, even the judge.

This damned virus, keeping everyone apart.

So many jerks going along with the program.

A few rows behind him, Roy caught a quick glimpse of his wife's eyes above her mask, her tears overflowing and depositing flecks of mascara along the upper edge of the face covering she been forced to wear to be allowed in the building. The woman he'd loved since high school had aged noticeably these past few months: her light hair looked ashy, and he could see new lines at the corners of her mouth. He tried to get to her, but his lawyer and fellow officers were on him now, ignoring the COVID protocols, grabbing his hands, reaching for his shoulders, slapping him on the back, showering congratulations.

Roy knew half the occupants of the courtroom weren't happy with the verdict and avoided looking their way.

Too bad, they had their day in court.

His thoughts briefly raced ahead to Hardy's where beer would be flowing tonight.

Now Roy and his head lawyer were slowly making their way from the august building with its faux Greek columns and polished brass doors. A couple hundred people were out there, most holding signs remembering and honoring Jerome, a few supporting the forces of law and order. Roy searched the crowd. He wanted to see his grandfather's face, knew that wasn't possible. Gramps had been gone for years but Ray still looked to him for approval.

He'd be proud.

Halfway down the broad marble steps, Roy almost stopped cold when he saw Jerome himself, the kid who'd died beneath his knee, coming directly toward him.

Impossible.

What the fuck?

The ghost kept coming, a slight figure in pressed Levi's and a dark green sweatshirt with a Black Lives Matter logo on the front. He zig-zagged against the press of people descending, a dance as ethereal as it was determined. Again, Roy tried to take as deep a breath as he could under the circumstances. He'd been warned the stress might get to him but never expected this. He got a strong whiff of the kid's smell, Shea body oil he later learned was from Ghana. His nappy hair almost grazed his face. When he was all but upon him. Roy made an awkward little step to one side to avoid collision. He tripped in spite of himself, missed a step and almost fell. His lawyer caught him before he could go down.

Avoiding the ghost wasn't possible. The kid was with him now, beside him, brushing against the sleeve of his jacket, keeping right up. His arms were thinner than Roy remembered, his build less muscular. He didn't like to think about how easy it would have been to put the cuffs on him without throwing him to the ground.

Too late now.

What we're trained to do.

Get them before they get us.

Roy snuck a look around and was stunned that no one else seemed to notice the boy. Amidst congratulatory shouts and whistles, high fives and reporters shoving their mics and cameras in his face, no one looked aware.

Can I be the only one?

Whichever way the verdict went, Roy knew his lawyer would stand before a mic and acknowledge the outcome of the trial: express satisfaction or vow to appeal. Then it would be Roy's turn. He'd been thinking about that moment, wanted to say something memorable for the press, make at least one quotable statement that included a proper sense of regret for having been forced to restrain the young man while making it clear that his actions had been justified.

Accountability?

I'm accountable to the job.

This'll be for you, Gramps!

Roy wanted to send the message that the verdict had been correct, impress that on the public. It was what he'd thought most about if he won. But the kid invaded his triumphant courthouse exit, rattling his concentration. It looked like he wasn't going to get the chance.

"How are you feeling, now that it's all over for you?" the kid asked in that same death rattle voice Roy hadn't been able to erase from his head since the whole thing went down. The policeman—stocky of build, with his shock of light brown hair combed over a broad forehead, rosy complexion, pale blue eyes and an eager forward bent when he walked—felt the old rage rising in him.

Better not to show him I hear.

Jerome still remembered the terror and desperation. One moment feeling like he owned the sidewalk, walking along thinking of Ginny, the girl he'd just met the week before but was already wondering about how to impress. The next moment surrounded by shouts, orders to get down, get down on the ground. Then that knee on his throat. The confusion, the terror. Sight and hearing dimming.

Pops! Where are you, Pops!
Mama! Mama!

Once the choking sensation and the pain that invaded his body had ended, Jerome had been engulfed by a gentler sensation. Painless then, and somehow freed from the sudden horror of the assault, he'd looked down upon his lifeless body as if from an unbreachable distance. Blurred image of a woman holding up a cell phone. People shouting, enraged, desperate. The long bodiless wait beneath a plastic sheet. The ambulance. The autopsy. His mother, broken by grief, falling onto a son who no longer breathed.

"Would you say justice was done today?" the guy from *The Sentinel* addressed his question to Roy's lawyer, who had his hand on the cop's other arm. He was pulling at the elbow of Roy's suit jacket, the discreet dark gray business suit he'd recommended his client wear to trial. The suit was about looking like your father, brother, the guy next door. He knew he couldn't wear his uniform, and anything casual would have sent the wrong message.

"Yes. The jury has spoken. We're satisfied that justice was done," the lawyer managed to shout back without missing a step or loosening his hold. Jerome turned full-face toward Roy then: "Depends on whose justice," he whispered, looking unflinchingly into his murderer's eyes.

From that moment on, no matter where he was the dead kid didn't leave Roy's side. More than a presence, he was almost like a Siamese twin, stuck to the cop all day every day and in bed with him at night. Sitting on the edge of the tub when he shaved. Standing in the corner of the bathroom when he took a piss. Following him out into the backyard, down to the basement, to the garage when he worked on Roy Jr.'s bike. Even to church the one Sunday he and Lisa had attended mass since the trial ended. That

Shea oil smell invading his home. Days became weeks, then a month.

No one else saw the boy, heard him, was aware of his presence. But he was so real to Roy that he couldn't make love to his wife, not with the kid in their bed. It was impossible for him to enjoy a meal with him seated across the table. When he pitched a few to his older son, the kid was there, watching, sometimes even jumping to reach for the ball. When he tried to help his daughter with her homework, he was looking to see if he knew the answers.

I'm supposed to feel guilty about spending time with my children?

Roy couldn't even take a dump or a shower in peace. The kid followed him where he went. And when he tried talking to his wife or children or anyone else, there he was, staring him down, almost daring him to take refuge in his old bravado or even just live his life.

Jerome wondered if Roy imagined he liked sticking so close.

Probably never gives it a thought.

Doesn't give a shit about me.

No remorse.

But death is the great equalizer, a place where anything is possible. Where a person can become a symbol for those who have never known him in life while remaining an intimate memory to family and friends. Jerome could be anyone now, go anywhere, do anything. For him this time at the home of the man who murdered him was pure sacrifice, certainly not something he enjoyed.

For weeks Jerome hounded his killer with pointed questions. Roy was sure they were meant to make him feel like he'd done something wrong. One day he heard himself asking: "What's this all about? Okay, so I got you on the ground fast. I didn't give you a chance to explain. That's what we're trained to do, how the system works. So maybe I kept my knee on you a little longer than I should have. How was I supposed to know you had chronic respiratory problems? If it hadn't been me, you'd have gotten yours soon enough some other way. Our expert at trial testified it was your asthma killed you. I know your kind. No use pretending you're so innocent . . ."

"But I am innocent," Jerome's calm demeanor challenged Roy. "I didn't rob that convenience store, wasn't anywhere near the place. Just walking along, not a care in the world. Had no gun in my pocket, just a phone. I was trying to call my mama. Wanted to tell her what was going down, might have had a chance to say goodbye. Black mothers, you know, they live waiting for that call, fearing it. My mama had to watch me die on TV. Did you know that?"

Jerome saw his Pops' gnarled face, then, his bloodshot eyes, kind smile and wise expression. He was beaming at him from the sidelines, giving him that extra dose of encouragement.

I'm doing my best, Pops.

Roy felt his blood rising all over again. "You little prick, the trial's over and done, decision's been made. You think you can put me through it again? Fuck that . . ." His words stumbled over themselves, threatening to take him down with them. He was sweating and breathing hard.

"Now look here," Jerome interrupted, "I'm the one who's dead. You were fucked up for a few months. Get over it. I'm the one not going to see my family again. I'm the one won't grow up."

Grow up.

The words got Roy's attention like an itch he couldn't scratch, gave him something he didn't expect to have to be pushing about in his head. He looked forward to Roy Jr., Sunny and Lisette growing up, having lives of their own, getting married, giving him grandchildren.

Their kind multiples like rabbits.

Still, Roy knew a Black mother must want to see her son make it through high school, maybe get one of those athletic scholarships they're always talking about.

Even animals protect their young.

When he heard Jerome say: "I'm the one won't grow up," Roy felt the air leave his own lungs.

There'd been considerable community protest following the outcome of the trial. Thousands in the streets every day, white as well as black. Sometimes Roy didn't know where he stood, what he was supposed to feel, so many of his own people questioning how things had gone down. On the rare occasion he ventured out of his house, a stranger might rush him. He never knew whether it was to congratulate or condemn him.

Always talking about accountability.

I'll give you accountability.

A march that turned violent when the cops were forced to fire rubber bullets. Some looting downtown. The force had to detail a lot of good officers to control the situation. The city's crime statistics the mayor was so proud of releasing every month had risen as a result. A nephew who'd always looked up to Roy didn't come around anymore.

When will people learn they're putting themselves in danger?

Just making our job harder.

Roy's commanding officer suggested he take a couple of weeks off, lay low, enjoy his family and get his head together. More than a suggestion, it was an order. Roy stayed home, okay with it at first. He was tired and also afraid, although he wouldn't admit the latter. Then he began to feel restless.

Lisa warned him the press was still in the cul-de-sac in front of their house for a good hour or so every morning, until they left singly or in small groups, tired of waiting for him to come out. "Don't give them the pleasure," she said.

Lisette came home from school crying one day. All three of his children admitted that some of the kids at St. Mary's gave them dirty looks. When Roy went to talk to the principal, she told him it was complicated.

Complicated? Of course, it's complicated!

"Don't know why they have to take it out on us," his daughter said, "what did we ever do to them?"

Roy felt something was different with his own children. They didn't look at him with the same respect. He became more and more disoriented, unsure of those things he'd always been able to count on.

Come at me, fucker, but leave my family alone.

Roy would have said this to Jerome's face if he talked to dead people.

I'm no racist.

Black officers down at the station.

No, he wasn't a racist and resented it when the press or those stupid signs the protestors carried played weird games with his name, singling him out.

What makes any of them think they know me?

Blacks who understand their place are fine with me, always have been.

He remembered a few in his class at St. Patrick's. Hadn't known any of them that well, not really.

But whose fault was that? It's up to both sides, isn't it?

A Black man had done some handiwork around Roy's childhood home. He remembered the guy teaching him how to hit a nail with the hammer so it would go in straight. He suddenly flashed on his father's expression when he saw them together and his admonishment to leave the guy alone, let him work in peace. He saw his mother bringing the man water and later slipping the unwashed glass into the garbage.

"Okay," Jerome said one night as he watched Roy brush his teeth. "So, you don't think you're racist. Tell me how come words like nigger and coon just roll of your tongue, easy as spit? You don't hear me calling you honky or ofay or cracker."

Roy rinsed his mouth and spit into the sink. He was so damned sick of this: "I don't use the N word. Hardly ever. When have you heard me use the N word? Plus, what are you doing here at all? You have no right coming into my home, coming at me with all your questions. It's long past time you let me be."

It's not just about the cuss words, thought Jerome, wondering why he'd bothered to bring them up. It's that entitlement, always in your face.

Dignity doesn't die with the body. Jerome Jackson felt no anger towards his murderer, only a genuine desire to help him understand, to help him see himself for who he is, if that's possible.

"Time," the kid said one morning, his tone suddenly wistful. "What do you know about time? This has been one bad time for my family, for my mama, for my kid sister who needs her brother, for my little brother. My mama is crazy wondering if he'll be next. You took my time. I don't have time, not anymore."

Again, it was the way the kid said the words. They

reverberated in Roy even after he stopped talking. *Grow up* and *time.* They sounded different to him now, like he'd never really heard them before. He tried to put those words out of his head, but they came back at him, persistent, like a fly he kept aiming at swatting but couldn't kill.

Of course, those people aren't like us. Don't value life. If they did, they wouldn't be dying like they do, every week you hear about another one on the news.

Still, the idea of a person running out of time was one Roy couldn't shake. The possibility of his own death had gnawed at him since he'd joined the force. His mother blessed him now, whenever they parted, with a look of worry he hadn't seen in her before. Lisa told him she couldn't stop thinking about getting that telephone call she feared.

Although she couldn't get him to talk about it, Lisa knew something was up with her husband. He hadn't been himself since the trial. She'd tried staying out of his way, hoping he'd work it out on his own. She'd tried bringing it up casually, as an afterthought tacked onto any other conversation. She'd even tried confronting him directly, which turned out to be a mistake. The slap he'd given her then still stung.

Lisa urged Roy to see someone, but her husband sure as hell wasn't going to go to a shrink. He'd be the butt of his buddies' jokes, on the force and off. No, he would deal with this dead kid once and for all, banish him from his life. He'd been making trouble far too long.

Noise-cancelling ear pods helped, and loud music. Lisa's reassuring smiles. And one beer after another, beginning around noon. But even when he drowned out Jerome's words, the kid's face was there, his eyes like bullets, his gasping breath loud against the sudden quieting of the street. And then the cold silence of his death.

It didn't occur to Roy that the kid might be sick of him.

Jerome had courage. He knew he needed it from the time he was a child.

Listen. Watch. Be ready.

He could usually sense trouble, smell it before it hit him in the face. And he knew he could sometimes stand up to someone until his danger radar reached a certain level. But everything had its limits.

Roy's house smelled of hate, rigid and cold like Jerome's grade school classroom at Parkdale. Stale sweat and too much bleach. Jerome's parents had chosen the mostly white elementary school, hoping their son would get the education they wanted him to have. When he came home listless and disinterested every day, they'd finally switched him to Martin Luther King Junior before he went on to Jefferson.

Roy's family reeked of white supremacy: an evil Jerome had known about for as long as he could remember. Invisible because accepted as the status quo. A constant danger to those it targets. His father had sat him down at ten and given him the conversation.

I'm not getting anywhere here, Jerome told himself one day, and decided to call it quits. Better to go back to Mama's where he could lay his head against her warm bosom, give and get comfort. Better to visit with his sister Tamira, who still needed a big brother. Better to model what he knew about life to little Jamar. He missed his friends in the neighborhood. He'd given it his all, but enough was enough.

The morning after Jerome's departure, Roy woke with the sense that something had shifted, was different. It took a few moments for him to realize the kid was gone. Maybe he was downstairs, waiting for him at the breakfast table. He finished dressing, still uneasy, and went to the kitchen. But no, it was just Lisa and the kids about to head for the school bus. His wife had poured his coffee and put the familiar plate with bacon, eggs and two slices of toast at his end of the table, covered with a clean white cloth.

Roy looked around, his eyes searching out every corner of the room. He couldn't believe he was free of the kid at last. That night he told Lisa to wash their sheets and towels, scrub down the bathrooms, clean the bedroom. "But I did all that day before yesterday," she said, surprised he was talking about household tasks. She'd never known him to take an interest before. "Just do it," Roy said.

Roy began to relax after that. Every day he felt more like his old self. The guys at the precinct told him he was looking good. "You better believe it," he said, something of his old confidence returning.

Still, his life wasn't quite the same as before the kid's long stay. Sometimes he would wake in the middle of the night in a cold sweat. He'd have gotten a faint whiff of the smell the boy left beneath the sheets. Or sitting down to eat, he'd catch sight of a slight dark figure on the other side of the window. Sometimes he thought his kids looked at him funny, their eyes briefly replaced by the kid's soulful gaze. Or Lisa started an argument about nothing at all.

What stuck with him were *grow up* and *time*. The way the boy had pronounced those words entered his dreams and lodged themselves in his head even when he was awake. The way clocks looked at him now, accusingly, as if they expected him to explain himself. Especially the large red numbers on the digital clock by his bed and the ceramic sailboat clock on their kitchen wall. Roy felt haunted. He stopped wearing the watch the guys on the force had given him just before this whole fucking mess went down.

That kid left something behind, that's for sure.

At his own house, Jerome was Jerome Jackson again. Not the kid or the boy. He could hang out in his room with his Kobe Bryant poster, the Air Jordan Ones his father had taken from his body and placed neatly on the floor at the foot of his bed, the little chrome statuette he'd earned for winning his class spelling bee in fourth grade.

Jerome's house smelled of fresh laundry, Pop's cigars, his mama's lotion, sweet tea, and the ribs she'd bar-b-queued for his sixteenth birthday. None of that white folks' pasty food with its plastic taste: mashed potatoes with white gravy, vegetarian make believe meat, Weight Watcher's little individual prepared dinners, pie that was more crust than fruit. His room looked the same, although he knew none of it was real. The first thing he did was put his arms around Mama, nestle into her and stay there for as long as he could.

Mrs. Jackson cried tears of joy when she felt her son's breath against her face, wept although she knew it was only a blessed illusion. The child, who'd been his father's pride and mother's hope, was gone for good. This moment of closeness was as good as it was going to get.

Gotta protect Jamar. Can't let them get him too.

Jerome's mother sighed then: "I knew you'd come back to me, Baby," she cried. "Oh, thank you sweet Jesus! Thank you, Lord!"

Casa Alegre

When Miriam arrived at Casa Alegre, she usually sat for a while in the garden before heading to her mother's room. The pathways wound among a variety of cacti and other desert plants, some in brilliant bloom. They calmed and strengthened her for the visit to come. Ocotillo flowers flamed red along slender branches that fanned out and up, their fiery trill of blooms shimmering with the slightest breeze. Stately saguaros, like strange beings, extended embracing limbs; in May they might display a waxy bloom or two. The gnarled boughs of the mesquite trees reminded her of the weathered flesh of some of the place's residents, the lace of their leaves like floating clouds of memory.

Casa Alegre—Happy House. Miriam thought the name ironic. As if a place where the old and infirm went to die could really be happy. Those who worked there tried their best. The garden and brightly appointed common areas helped. But this was a place of loneliness and waiting. Loss of memory, faculties, agency. Adult diapers. Humiliating dependency. Waiting to die with all that loss overwhelmed whatever was left of each unique being. Some cared for bits of their former lives as if they were precious trophies, breakable if dropped. Others seemed utterly disconnected from who they'd been.

And then there was that invasive odor, a mix of strong disinfectant with some overly sweet perfume, that always blasted Miriam on her arrival, making her slightly nauseous. She wondered how her mother could bear it. It was probably easier once one was old enough that one's sense of smell had faded almost to nothing.

After her restorative breather among the ocotillo and saguaro, Miriam gathered herself and the bag of macaroons—her mother's favorite—and entered the sprawling building. Fake California Mission with its orange tile roof and broad verandas. It was made to resemble a home rather than a warehouse for fading men and women, some of whom could invariably be seen belted into wheelchairs parked along the halls, staring motionless into their own private pasts.

Many of the attendants were young women from the Caribbean: Barbados, Trinidad and Tobago, Nassau. Miriam wondered who had recruited them and whom they'd had to abandon to lonely deaths at home so they could come to work in this land of plenty from where they sent monthly remittances that made a difference. Those coffee-colored women moved lightly in their pastel scrubs, spoke in low almost musical tones, always patient, always helpful. If they carried medications or other signs of physical need, they hid them beneath a clean white cloth.

Miriam tapped lightly on the door to her mother's room but didn't wait for Verna's permission to enter. The only one of her children who lived close enough to visit, the gesture was mostly just to say she honored the privacy of her space, which of course wasn't private at all. Verna was seated at her desk, her arthritic hands, almost entirely covered with dark liver spots and resembling the claws of a large bird, rested on the ivory-colored squares of her computer keyboard, her eyes somewhere beyond the daughter's horizon. Verna was still, almost statue-like. She didn't speak, didn't even acknowledge her daughter's presence, although Miriam knew she was aware. "Hello Mom," she shouted several decibels louder than her usual pitch, "what are you working on?"

"Hard . . . places . . ." Verna caressed the words as if they were old friends. "This story . . . talking back, still talking back . . ." Sometimes Miriam had the impression her mother expected her to be able to read between the lines, understand her silences as well as her sporadic words.

Miriam hadn't asked to read anything of Verna's for more than a year now, almost since she'd been forced to move her mother here. And Verna hadn't offered. The daughter was afraid it might not make sense and she wouldn't know how to respond. Her mother could always see right through her lies.

The older woman had offered no resistance to the move, as if she simply expected this would be the next chapter of her life. And now she, who'd always been so eager to share her work with her beloved Briar, was reluctant to do so with anyone else. Her partner of 57 years had been her most reliable critic, but the younger woman died before the older, one of those unexpected disasters that takes everyone by surprise. Verna mourned her in every part of her being.

The only non-institutional addition to Verna's tastefully appointed room was one of Briar's large acrylics, hanging where she could see it from her bed. It's shapes and colors sang her to sleep. Verna's hesitation now is part of the veil that has dropped between her and others. Even her daughter. It divided the outside world from this strangely patterned existence.

On the computer monitor, partially clouded by light streaming in the window, Miriam glimpsed the word *living* and the word *stone*. "You really should move your desk," she repeated what she'd told her mother on previous visits. "Or close those drapes so the light doesn't hit the screen." Verna just smiled. Miriam wondered if her mother even looked at the monitor. At home she'd never had her window open or raised the blinds in her small studio. She often said she preferred working in a womb-like environment.

Now all those lifelong habits were either indelibly embedded or flaking off and drifting away, broken elements of a rapidly changing life. Miriam sometimes envisioned her mother on a placid little island in the middle of a raging sea, impervious to her surroundings, deep in an identity she'd constructed piece by piece throughout her many years. Next month Verna would be 104.

On a recent visit, the director of Casa Alegre had stopped Miriam on her way to see her mother. He wanted to talk about celebrating Verna's birthday: "She stays to herself, but you know she's highly regarded by the other residents. And she's one of the oldest we have, especially now that Mrs. Greenleaf is gone. Did you know she lived to 106? So, we want to give your mother a party. Would you like to be involved in planning it?"

Miriam appreciated the gesture. She didn't want to insult this eager, sometimes slightly officious, man. But she knew a party was the last thing her mother wanted, especially not one where she would be required to wear a silly paper hat, listen to an off-key rendition of "Happy Birthday" and eat a piece of cake equal to her sugar intake for the year.

"You know," she told the director, "I don't think that's really necessary. I appreciate the gesture, I really do, and I know my mother would too if she were thirty years younger. At this point in her life, she rather enjoys being left alone. She seems most at peace when she's in her room writing, remembering . . . whatever it is she does all day. And she hasn't really made many friends here." She caught the director's look of consternation. "No, I don't mean people aren't friendly. It's just not in her nature to be that social."

Not in her nature to be social. Miriam remembered her mother, then, as exuberantly social. In her own distant childhood, she'd resented sharing her with lovers, revolutionaries, literary and artistic figures, even other children. Hosting delicious dinners—how she'd loved to cook and bake—, active, an organizer, often doing five things at once. Not anymore. Not here. Perhaps this place provided the necessary rest after such a life.

Miriam herself would be eighty in less than a year. Old enough to understand some of her mother's idiosyncrasies, longings, needs. It hadn't always been this way. For years the two women had carried on a silent battle of resentments, sometimes sparring with one another in a dance that side-stepped the core of their tensions. This was history, and history is always complicated. Both women seemed relieved that their communication had gotten easier, even if some issues would never be resolved.

On her next visit, when Miriam mentioned the possibility of a party just to gage Verna's response, her mother looked at her puzzled: "You mean with the other inmates?" she asked. She always referred to them as inmates, never residents, the closest she came to saying she felt she was in prison. Her expression turned to one almost resembling fear. "No," Miriam assured her, "I told them you wouldn't want that. No worries."

Verna planned her days with deliberate care. After all these years, she still woke each morning between four and four-thirty, when the world felt like velvet. She'd turn her fragile body slowly so as not to do it harm. She marveled at how her elbows and knees still moved on their ancient hinges. For a few moments she'd indulge in the luxury of Briar's skin on hers, her beloved's temperature and touch, breathe in her scent. Then she would raise herself to a sitting position and do the simple stretches the physical therapist recommended, making little circles with her ankles, stretching and curling her fingers, counting out each set of ten and imagining herself on some mountain trail, perhaps descending Grand Canyon or wading through deep sand to the pictograph panel at Horseshoe. *Those glorious times. How lucky we were . . .*

Then Verna would dress in the Levi's and indigenous huipil that had been her lifelong attire, even though they hung scarecrow-like on her now. Pushing her walker slowly, she'd make sure she got to the dining room before the morning crowd. She knew Carina would have put out a bagel or croissant, a dish of fresh fruit and enough strong black coffee to fill her demitasse cup, and she'd carefully place those breakfast items on the tray table of her walker and slowly make her way back to her room. After a couple of months of trying to get Verna to socialize, the staff wisely realized she was implacably, unmovably, stubborn, wasn't about to be parted from her routine.

Verna lived in her world of memories: images of red rock canyons, vast desert landscapes, ancient ruins. Sounds of Andean flutes, Caribbean drums, a Brandenburg concerto, Dolly Parton's high clear voice. Although Miriam had tried to show her how to play music on her computer, Vera preferred an old unused tape deck someone had left in the common room and she had taken to hers. She would listen accompanied by Briar, always Briar. A photograph of the two women half a century earlier stood in a silver frame on her bedside table. They were seated together on the low stone wall at Grand Canyon's south rim. They looked complete in their world. Such joy.

Pictures of Verna's children, grandchildren and great grandchildren who lived in several different countries were scattered around the room. Was it Miriam or Jaimie who came to visit each month? Did she have great great grandchildren now? Verna couldn't remember. As one generation succeeded another, they blurred in her mind, but she knew that each member of her great extended family belonged to her, issued from her center like strong threads woven into their own diverse cloth. She loved them all.

After breakfast, Verna would settle into the comfortable chair positioned at just the right height before her writing desk, find the button that turned her computer on and wait for it to come to life. It was her friend, the only one she really counted on now. She felt immensely fortunate. Time had taken her beloved woman. Distance separated her from most of her children and their children.

Her country and the world still fought battles she thought should have been resolved decades ago: the ignorance of bigotry, the disappearance of resources as vital as air and water, endless migrations, problems of human wellbeing. Verna no longer watched the news. No matter how many invitations she'd had to endure, she never joined the other inhabitants of this place in front of the huge television screen in the common room. Still, she was aware of what was happening out in the world. A cycle that just kept repeating itself.

Her writing: that was inside. Safe and secure. A place that always welcomed her.

Verna preferred the intimacy of her room. Her space where memory came to her and she didn't fear interruption or annoying commentary, fluff phrases intended as conversation, empty of meaning. Carina or one of the others knew enough to enter quietly, help her with the essentials, respect her privacy. Miriam's visits were the exception to Verna's wish to be alone. She didn't mind. They were the bridge that kept her connected with what she remembered but could no longer assemble.

Verna had written many books during her productive years. Poetry. Essay. Short Stories. She'd also been a social activist, sometimes in situations of danger. Some had called her brave. That always puzzled her. She'd done what was necessary, no more. And the results hadn't been what she'd hoped. Verna had lived for long periods in other countries and raised four children. From a generation in which women were educated to be wives and mothers or, in extreme cases were made to feel they must choose between domesticity and a career, she'd defiantly "done it all." That was her intimate pride. Her work had been recognized, although not as much as it would have been had she taken a more conservative route. She'd never won any of the big prizes.

Now she'd been relegated to this strange place. Doable but strange. As long as she had her things around her. She was one of the lucky ones; family money and the help of friends made it possible for her to continue to live well, although alone. Miriam understood her mother still had something to teach her about refusing to die when expected, about continuing to work, although the daughter was no longer sure what the mother's work meant. All she really knew was that each new batch of macaroons replaced those she'd brought before, now reduced to crumbs in the little Puebla style dish on Verna's writing desk.

"I wanted to be a cryptanalyst," Verna said on one visit, looking directly at Miriam and getting the whole sentence out, something she wasn't often able to do these days. "But never good at math . . ." her voice trailed off. Or: "I wanted to pilot a plane." Miriam thought a response to these declarations was in order: "Well, maybe in your next life," she quipped. Neither she nor her mother believed in another life.

"It's the numbers . . . fall . . . from the sky." Verna's speech had become disconnected again, more typical over the past year or so. Miriam didn't think of her mother as demented. She could see the woman she'd known all her life was still in there, still making interesting, sometimes surprising, connections. It was just her ability to explain them that was frayed. Verna's hearing was almost completely gone. Miriam thought she had begun to read lips, then realized that probably wasn't possible.

"Real poetry," Verna said then. "Real . . . poetry. Can you see them: the round words . . . fat . . . pointy . . . standing up?"

Miriam couldn't see what Verna saw but believed there was something to see. At Casa Alegre all the residents were treated as if they suffered from dementia, Alzheimer's, or something similar. Memory was certainly an issue for most. Yet Miriam's experience with her mother over these past few years told her that dementia wasn't always what it seemed. It could be tricky, elude conventional diagnosis or prognosis. People who didn't recognize their own children often told stories of long-ago events in surprising detail. Those who repeated the same question again and again would stop doing that for a while, then begin once more. Those who sat as if catatonic day after day might suddenly turn their heads, smile, and utter a perfectly coherent greeting. Music therapy brought many from some faraway place into an engaged present. Who knew what went on in the human mind when its synapses stop firing as they should?

Living cells still contained cognition. Perhaps they took over. If Verna was exploring a connection between words and numbers, Miriam was curious as to what it might be.

Verna had long ago let go of that formulaic conversation so many older people rehearse, the "Hello, how are you? I'm fine, thanks for asking" that pretends information or sentiments are being exchanged. She no longer asked Miriam what she'd been doing when she came to visit, nor expected her daughter to tell her except on rare occasions. Mostly, it didn't seem to Miriam that her mother was interested in anything beyond the walls of her room. And then, suddenly, it seemed the world was in that room.

Before Miriam reached Verna's fiefdom today, Carina had stopped her in the hall: "Your mother has been asking me to take her out into the garden," she said. "I've gotten her into a wheelchair a few times. She brings a little notebook and stares at the ocotillo and at the lines of needles on the saguaro. Sometimes I think she's counting them." "The needles?" "Yes. And she makes marks in her notebook, but I can't tell what they mean."

Three days before Verna's 104th birthday, she failed to pick up her breakfast. Carina brought it to her room, only to find that the old woman had died sometime during the night. Her eyes were closed, her features serene. Carina sat for a while, reluctant to inform her superiors. She'd taken to Verna and wanted a chance to say goodbye before the room was transformed by the regulation bustle that followed death in this place.

She noticed the papers scattered across Verna's bed: pages, some with handwritten marks and others made on the computer, although she couldn't make out most of the words. One sheet of paper looked as if it had fallen from Verna's hand. Another was half hidden beneath her body.

Carina gathered the papers, taking care not to alter Verna's position. Casa Alegre called Miriam, who drove down immediately. Mile after mile, she replayed her mother's life, especially these last years. What hadn't been said or heard? What secrets had her mother taken with her? She arrived to a whirlwind of condolences and efficiency. The director reiterated what a long rich life her mother had lived, perhaps hoping for a compliment or two about how the institution had attended to her final years. They hadn't yet allowed the funeral home to take the body, he explained, thinking Miriam might want to spend some time with her mother.

Miriam thanked him. In truth she didn't know what she wanted. She didn't really believe Verna was still in that body on the bed, but she was curious. She knew there would be formalities to be followed. One step at a time. Casa Alegre had the required experience. At least there wouldn't be any more talk of a birthday party. The director said he would leave her alone with her mother. She should take her time. Miriam had pulled Verna's desk chair over to the bed and was holding her mother's cool hand when Carina appeared with a ream of papers. She looked like she'd been crying.

"These were all over your mother's bed when I found her this morning," she said, holding the papers out to Miriam. "I thought you'd want to have them."

Miriam got up to give her Carina a hug. More than just a caretaker, she knew she'd been a friend. She took the papers and put them in her bag. There'd be time for them later. After all the necessary arrangements had been made and Miriam was back in her car about to begin the drive home, she remembered what Carina had given her. Before turning the key in the ignition, she opened her bag and began reading.

Some pages were almost empty, except for a few illegible marks made with a ballpoint pen. The ink was uneven, as if Verna had been leaning back with the paper close to her face, holding the pen at an awkward angle. On other pages Miriam could make out a few words or groups of words, perhaps tantalizingly expressive of her mother's final thoughts. Verna had made a determined effort to leave a message of some kind, that was clear. Something that looked like *words* and something that looked like *numbers* seemed to be repeated several times, sometimes alone, sometimes paired. Miriam thought her mother had also tried to write *saguaro*, *ocotillo*, and *bird*. What was she trying to say? Was she aware that this was her last chance to communicate what was on her mind?

Miriam would never know. Could these scribbled pages contain the revelations she needed, the answers to so many unanswered questions? Although she studied them for hours, there wasn't enough there that made sense or warranted sharing. At least not with the living. The daughter was left, as daughters tend to be, wishing she'd asked more questions before it was too late. What had seemed hopeful turned out to be deceptive at best.

It was almost two weeks later that Miriam got the call from Casa Alegre's director: "I thought you would want to know that we found a tape when we cleaned your mother's room," he said, after the usual pleasantries. "Sorry I didn't call sooner, so much work you know. No, not music. Something your mother made. It was still in that old tape deck she had. I'm sure you'll want it. Will you come down, or should I mail it to you?"

"What do you mean? What tape? No, no, I'll come down. I can be there in a couple of hours." Miriam's heart was beating faster than usual. She could hardly wait to return to that place she'd hoped never to see again. When she arrived, the director was waiting for her at the front entrance. He had a thick manila envelope in his hands which he put in hers. "We have the tape deck," he said. "If you want to listen to it here, you're welcome."

"No, thank you," Miriam said, "I'll take it home. I appreciate you calling." And she clasped both the director's hands in hers as she said goodbye.

Miriam knew she would be listening to her mother's voice from beyond a chasm rarely crossed. She forced herself to take it slow, remove her coat and scarf, make herself a pot of herbal tea—she chose peach—and pour herself a cup, then place the tape carefully in her long unused tape recorder and carefully close its clear plastic door before sitting down to listen. She pressed the on button and Verna entered the room. She spoke slowly but coherently, in a way Miriam hadn't heard from her mother in at least a year. She wondered when Verna had made the tape, then put all such questions out of her mind and simply listened.

"I love you," she heard Verna say. "When you hear this, I'll be . . . you won't . . . I mean . . . no questions. I'll be as clear (long pause). I know we haven't always been able to reach . . . talk to one another. I'm sorry. I love you, Stella." Miriam realized her mother was confusing her with her younger sister, or her younger sister with her. Perhaps this tape was meant for her and all her siblings, perhaps for everyone she loved.

"The words . . . powerful . . . the poems . . . stories." Verna's voice seemed more emphatic now, more as Miriam remembered it before her mother's move to Casa Alegre. She wondered if she'd made the tape in one sitting or several, over hours or weeks.

Now she was speaking again: "It wasn't choosing . . . to write . . . be mother. I thought (interminable pause). I thought I could do it all. I mean . . . hope." The voice on the tape stopped. Miriam listened to the staticky sound of the machine continuing in on mode. She waited. Nothing.

So, this was it. The tension that had caused so much resentment through all of Miriam's eighty years had also been a dilemma for Verna. One that had no solution. There was no "I'm sorry," no begging for forgiveness, just that calm matter-of-fact voice telling her what was. And that her mother loved her. She held those words close. Or loved her sister. Between intermittent sips of tea, Miriam sobbed most of that night.

The next day she felt an energy she hadn't known in years. Right after breakfast she returned the stone mason's call. He'd left several messages in the weeks since Verna's death to ask what she wanted on her mother's stone. Now she was ready to tell him: "VERNA RIFKIN, 1913 - 2017. SHE DID IT ALL."

Erasure

"Something's going on . . . Something missing," were the words most frequently repeated throughout the halls and offices of Central Utah's Bureau of Land Management Field Office. "Not right," "a mystery," "some kind of hoax," "a joke," and unintelligible expressions mouthed behind glass paneling that muted their sound but was accompanied by facial expressions leaving no room for doubt as to the seriousness of the situation. Crisis time, for sure. And a crisis like none that any of them had experienced before.

Inhabiting that push and pull territory known as middle management, Cynthia had to contend with the absurd ideas of her superiors as well as the sincere questions of those beneath her. In both cases she was struck by how obviously coworkers tended to focus on their own careers with regard to the phenomenon rather than expressing amazement at how or when or why the event had occurred. Everyone had an opinion. They were wildly different from what she'd expected.

More like a conundrum or maybe even an omen. Much more than a secret, although an aura of secretiveness seemed to attend to every conversation. And every conversation, at work and in the broader community, began and ended with what was on everyone's mind. It was like Lourdes, France 1858 or Roswell, New Mexico 1947. Cynthia wondered how the discovery would unfold in the short and long term, if it would leave something permanently consciousness-altering in its wake.

Hard times tended to forefront personal issues rather than the larger picture. Granted, this larger picture was unusually large. Larger than anything she could remember. Cynthia attended meetings, even called a few herself. Phoned a friend at the Park Service. Contacted Intertribal cold. Even brought in folks from the Army Corps of Engineers. Muttered in frustration as bureaucracy doomed cooperation.

She joined her colleagues in asking questions, proposing possible next steps. She refrained from voicing an opinion that might mark her as unscientific or too "out there." She got along with people and was generally well-liked, which helped. On the job, she only really confided her deepest thoughts to Mike, her secretary with the title of assistant, a nod to his male pride. Cynthia hadn't been able to choose him for her team exactly but remembered his deep intelligence in graduate school and when the job opened up managed to steer it his way.

Cynthia's immigrant family and the Mormons who settled Utah had a similar history. Both had braved dangerous journeys to get there. Both were strangers when they first arrived. But for the Mexicans it was all more recent, still precarious. The Saints were the owner class now. The brown-skinned foragers from the other side of the southern border were second-class citizens. The unspoken secret that threatened them was that many weren't citizens at all. Conditions that separated and occasionally brought them together.

While her mother was alive, Cynthia sometimes asked the why of her name—why Cynthia? Mama always said she couldn't remember. Maybe it had been after a Hollywood star, but when curiosity sent the adult daughter to look at those who'd captured the public imagination in the 1940s, she couldn't find a Cynthia. From a Mexican immigrant mother—both her parents breached the magic line illegally and survived without papers until they died—she might have expected Maria or Concepción or even Xochitl. But then Mama tended to look forward when she was faced with a choice. And Papa assented to his wife's every desire. With a smile on his face. Dear sweet Papa. How she missed him, especially at this time of year when the monsoons swept wild through Utah's red rock canyons and dark clouds towered above. They'd hiked together often in this magical season, sometimes having to shelter beneath rock overhangs when the rain came down hard.

Although Mama chose her name it was Papa who went to the Public Records office in Provo to register his daughter. Doing right for his family was the job he'd set for himself from when he married at seventeen to his last tired breath at forty-four. He'd made it through fifth grade at the semi-abandoned country schoolhouse in Mexicali but never managed to learn more English than what he needed to work the fields or get hired onto sporadic day jobs as their life in these "Unided" States unfolded.

When the Mormon clerk asked how to spell Cynthia, he'd carefully enunciated the letters: S-I-N-T-IA. And so, Cynthia Gómez Morales started school as Sintia Gomez Morales, sometimes seated with the G's and sometimes with the M's, depending on a teacher's cultural aware-ness. And always missing the accent mark that was simply superfluous in this homogenized world. Cynthia's class-mates—the Hiram's and Josephs and Clara's—sometimes teased her, chanting Skinny or *Cinta* which meant ribbon. It didn't really hurt that much. Bullying back then wasn't anywhere near the level of today's abuse.

Still, as she grew Cynthia managed to anglicize the spelling of her name. Which is why the brass nameplate at the edge of her desk said Dr. Cynthia Gómez. Her degree prominently displayed, first name properly Americanized, surname her father's alone and the accent firmly in place. "Dr. Cynthia Gómez, Field Director Central Utah." In contrast, she drew on her parents' culture when naming her battered 1977 dust-colored Ford pickup. She called it Milagros because she liked giving names to the important things in her life, tended to endow them as female, and the old truck definitely needed more than one miracle to keep in shape.

Her parents dreamed of several children but had to content themselves with one. Cynthia obliged by giving them the satisfaction of a son as well as a daughter. From birth she was strong and square, a chunky toddler, tough youngster and compact somewhat box-shaped adult. Except for getting taller and a bit more worn, she was one of those people who wouldn't change much from cradle to her final years. Her inquisitive mind and generous nature brought rewards, to her and to her family. Mama and Papa saw their dreams materialize in her. And they doted.

Cynthia rarely stopped to ponder how far she'd come from her family's humble beginnings. Gratitude for her parents' unbroken labor was a constant, woven into her DNA. But her own part of the journey had never seemed that difficult or even unusual. Sure, she'd had to work hard to erase the immigrant stigma. And the painful fear that her parents might be deported was a constant presence in all their lives. They were careful about what they did and said, and who they said it to. They knew the smallest slip could be mean disaster.

Being a girl who was fascinated by science caused a few raised eyebrows along the way. But, by the late 1960s when it was time for Cynthia to choose a career, a lot of barriers were giving way. Even in conservative Utah. Her parents' unstinting love provided a bedrock of support.

Cynthia's lack of enthusiasm for boys, her resistance to their clumsy moves or even the advances of male colleagues later on, might have made for concern in a different family. Not in hers. She knew she was attracted to women long before she'd heard the word lesbian, from the moment she and another third-grade girl exchanged a shy kiss in their school locker room. She dreamed of making a good life with a good woman, the kind of life her parents modeled. Unlike other gay people she knew, she never faced intolerance at home, never had to struggle through fictitious relationships with male partners before falling in love with the women with whom she'd been happy now for more than three decades. Mama and Papa beamed and celebrated all their daughter's choices.

Cynthia credited her parents with her acceptance of who she was. She'd never come out to them, to use that phrase that described liberation but also the moment of angst she knew others had to navigate. Neither Mama nor Papa had ever asked her if she had a boyfriend or tried to mold her to meet the social expectations of a heterosexual culture. No frilly dresses or pointers on feminine wiles. They simply delighted in their daughter *tal cual*, as she was, were proud of her many accomplishments. And when Maggie came into her life, she was like another daughter to them. Cynthia was grateful that her partner, now wife, had those few years of knowing her parents before they died, Mama of a broken heart just months after Papa's sudden aneurism. Maggie's childhood hadn't been as loving as hers, and it had been good for her to have been able to enjoy accepting parents for however brief a time.

The older and younger couples lived within blocks of each other and often shared meals. They were friends.

Of course, she and Maggie talked about the current phenomenon. Every night, sometimes all night. Maggie was a beautician, owned and worked in a small salon on their town's main drag she called Hair Matters. She cut and styled hair for most of the women and a few of the gentler men. Suggested new colors, new identities. Gave them manicures. Massaged their tired feet. Nourished their dreams.

Cynthia knew that most of her contemporaries at the BLM wondered at the match. Not because they were two women but because they saw her as a professional and Maggie as less educated and engaged in a trade that wasn't on the executive list. But she knew the role Maggie played, listening to her client's troubles, sympathizing with their predicaments, guiding them toward honesty and self-awareness. To Cynthia, Maggie was that rare combination of teacher, aid worker, and therapist. Self-taught. A natural. Over the years the salon became a focal point for local struggles, political but non-partisan, welcoming and safe.

And then there was the interesting complexity their relationship introduced into people's lives. Its unexpected composition seemed to challenge their preconceptions but never in a way that taunted or threatened. Cynthia, of a Mexican American immigrant background, with her professional status and white-bread name. Maggie, of hardy Mormon stock, living in sin in the eyes of most of her kinfolk. Cynthia in her BLM uniform, Maggie in her uniform of cowboy boots, Levi's and a western shirt in primary colors and with mother of pearl buttons. Race, class, education, sexuality, and culture all thrown together in a way that stood proud and refused questions as to its legitimacy.

The phenomenon now on everyone's mind had its origins in hearsay. "Have you heard about . . .?" "Did you know that . . .?" Someone saw something and told someone else. Rumors coursed through the agency. It was Maggie who, over breakfast one morning, said she was surprised no one in the office had gone to see for themselves. Cynthia dropped her spoonful of fresh fruit back into its bowl. Why hadn't she thought of that? It was such a logical question. Almost as soon as Mike showed up for work that morning, she asked him if he'd make the trip with her. He grinned: "Sure." Her supervisor and others—from their office all the way up to the agency's headquarters in Washington— didn't explicitly articulate a sense of fear but it was obvious they felt such an unusual occurrence might rub off on them in some unwelcome way. As if by getting too close they might become implicated, even contaminated.

Milagros was up for the adventure and Maggie handed them a small car cooler with sandwiches and lemonade for the trip. Then she put her hand on Mike's forearm, kissed Cynthia, and waved goodbye as she headed to the salon in her yellow Dart. It was a balmy fall day. They could expect to be at the BLM office in Hanksville by noon, and it was only another half hour or so over a well-graded dirt road to the trailhead where they would begin their hike.

Cynthia had never been properly introduced to the guy slouched behind the visitor's counter at the Hanksville office, though she'd probably seen him at one or two large agency events. She identified herself and Mike, then told him they were heading into the canyon. She was surprised at his hands-off attitude. Despite the rumors, he hadn't been inclined to see for himself. "No, not really interested," was his odd response when she asked. As with others, she sensed there was something more behind his reticence. A wariness, even fear. He was curious though. "Stop by on your way back," he said, "and tell me what you find." She said she would.

She and Mike were mostly silent on their way to the trailhead, each immersed in their respective wonderings about what they might find. Mike, usually so talkative, hadn't uttered more than half a dozen words since leaving the Hanksville office. Neither did he have much to say as they ate their sandwiches, downed almost all the lemonade, filled their water packs and laced their hiking boots. Cynthia made sure Milagros was safely locked and they headed over the slickrock lip of Horseshoe Canyon.

Only a few years back, she would have raced along the 800-foot descent to the canyon floor. Now she made her way cautiously, careful not to twist an ankle or worse. She was grateful for the hiking sticks Maggie had bought her the Christmas before. She watched with discernible longing as Mike, ten years her junior, bounded from cairn to cairn.

At the bottom the route got harder although the terrain was flat. The early afternoon sun was intense, and the dry creek bottom covered in deep sand and loose scree that slowed their pace. Cynthia knew this canyon well. She had hiked it often over the years. It was one of her favorite places and, so far, nothing seemed amiss. The same sandstone walls to either side, a few familiar rock art panels like preludes to what lay ahead. After a half hour of dragging their feet through sand, they stopped to sit for a while beneath the shade of a rare tree. More bush than tree but affording what might pass for shade in this desert landscape.

They still weren't talking much. It seemed unnecessary to break the silence that surrounded them. Or maybe they were still immersed in thought, playing in their heads with ideas neither wanted to put into words. They sipped their water slowly. They breathed slowly. They moved slowly when they finally did move.

Farther along and to the right of the trail Cynthia spotted a large snake slithering through a waist-high crevice of rock. She was proud of her knowledge of regional flora and fauna, usually adept at identifying the snakes in this part of the state. Most were varieties of rattlers: Sidewinder, Midget-Faced, Hopi, Great Basin and others. She couldn't tell what she was looking at now, though, and entertained a fleeting thought that it might be a rare species or, although she wouldn't have put this into words, some sort of shapeshifter; not really a snake at all. Cynthia felt a strange shudder move through her body. She tried to steady her breathing, calm herself. Looking at Mike, she saw he was pale and sweating profusely. Lips pressed tight beneath his reddish beard. Hands curled into fists. She glanced back at what she could still see of the creature as it disappeared behind a boulder and they continued on.

It was a pleasant day, all in all, and Cynthia began to ponder the fact that they seemed entirely alone in the canyon. This outlier part of Canyonlands National Park wasn't a place that attracted crowds, but she'd never been here without running into at least a half dozen others making their way to the site that was their destination. The Great Gallery was the name the anthropology community had given to the 200-foot-long panel that would be visible soon, also on their right. The spectacular figures, first thought to be a couple thousand years old and more recently determined to have been made five times that long ago, were unique among the great variety of rock art scattered over this land. There were always a few adventurous hikers eager to see them.

But today she and Mike were alone. She was grateful for his company. There was something slightly ominous about this solitude. Cynthia chided herself. Well, maybe not ominous but unusual. Unusual didn't have to be a bad thing. Her scientist's mind was careful to stay with the evidence, not allow herself to be drawn into any of the quasi-theories she'd heard people toss about since the event had first been noticed. This sort of happening too easily lent itself to speculation of all sorts, none of it helpful.

And then they arrived. The giant figures became visible a couple of hundred yards before they stood in front of them. Some of the largest contained intricate designs enclosed in tapering torsos. All had small triangular heads and lacked arms and legs. They had been painted on the back wall of this shallow alcove with the reds and oranges and creams ground to a powder and applied with some sort of binder never identified. The black lines were produced by carbon. Astonishingly, no evidence of settlement existed at the site or nearby; this art or signage or whatever its creators meant it to be had been left by people passing through. Passing through but stopping long enough to leave so much more than a footprint, ceramic pot or arrowhead. Something that would speak to people through the centuries.

The alcove wasn't protected from the elements, which had undoubtedly changed dramatically over thousands of years. Wet periods and dry. Wind and sun. A big question had always been: what kept this panel so vivid over all this time, its colors so alive, its significance such a challenge to us today? Anthropologists and others hadn't been shy with their explanations, but these changed from era to era. The large figures might be deities or ancestors. A long line of small marks issued from a V-shaped mouth or vagina on the lower portion of the wall. People? Marks representing events or dates? Or something else entirely? A fight scene showed two smaller figures sparring.

For a brief moment Cynthia and Mike almost felt relief as they looked at the imposing panel. But in the next instant they saw what was missing: something so central to this scene they should have noticed its absence immediately. The largest being, the one some academic had dubbed the Holy Ghost Figure, wasn't there. It had disappeared. There was no evidence of vandalism, no abusive chipping away at the rock, the sort of damage the parks always feared and never had funding enough to protect against. The figure was simply gone, as if it had been erased. Or had never been there at all.

Cynthia and Mike gasped audibly. They looked at the panel, at one another, and back at the wall. This was clearly what had originated the rumors. Someone visiting the site had registered the figure's absence and told someone else. But the news was impossible to assimilate and those passing it on stopped doing so for fear of being called liars or worse. Cynthia sat on a low rock without taking her eyes from the scene before her. She searched for any sign of human alteration of the wall. Nothing. Still, the figure was gone.

Mike joined her. But he wasn't doing a lot of talking. There was no use stating the obvious. It was the how and why that bothered both their minds. They took pictures, closeups and panoramic shots. Documentation was important. Cynthia let her eyes move the depth and length of the panel. It was then that she noticed something else. One small red mark was missing from the line of dots issuing from the V-shaped form. She could tell by the additional space between two of the dots about halfway along the line. She focused her camera on that spot as well, snapping its shutter several times.

If only the park had been able to install night vision movement-triggered cameras at the site. There had been talk of doing so a few years back, but such plans rarely materialized; there was never enough money and the current administration had cut funding further. Yet even as she considered the missed opportunity, something told her such a camera wouldn't have documented anything unusual. No human with today's technology would have been able to remove that figure so completely without leaving a trace of how it had been done. Even her evidence-oriented mind told her this was something else, something they might never understand.

They sat there for more than an hour before Mike looked at his watch and they both agreed they should probably head back. It was never a good idea to remain after dark in an area where sudden storms were known to materialize without warning and poisonous snakes and insects were plentiful. They took one last long look at the place where the large figure had been and began the trek out of the canyon. They were as silent on the way out as they'd been on the way in, immersed in their thoughts of what they had seen or not seen.

It was late when they reached Hanksville. They decided not to stop at the agency center there. The guy hadn't seemed that curious, after all. If he had been, he would have gone to look for himself. And Cynthia would be writing a report he'd receive along with every other office. Closer to Provo they became more talkative. Far from the silence of the canyon, it was as if they were free to speak out loud about what others had mentioned so covertly over the past several weeks.

By the time Cynthia got home, Maggie was making dinner. She blurted out what she'd seen, her sentences unfinished, chaotic. The distance between having stood before the panel and being able to transmit the mystery it embodied was too great to breach. Maggie asked all the right questions, but Cynthia realized you had to have been there to have the vaguest sense of what couldn't be understood. That night she hardly slept. And when she did, her dreams were a mix of the palpable with some indescribable otherness. The scattered pages of an immense calendar fell from the sky, illegible writing filling some squares representing days. Or were they months? She tried reaching for the pages and saw that her hands were covered in blood. She woke with a low-grade fever. Still, she showered, dressed and went to work.

Over the following months and year, experts from different disciplines made their way to The Great Gallery. They looked at where the figure had been, tested the rock, used every method at their disposal in a series of studies that quickly exceeded all budgets destined to that purpose. Someone posited the theory that the lines and colors of the missing figure had simply faded after all these years, no mention of why the rest of the panel remained intact.

Self-proclaimed gurus were quick to offer explanations. Pilgrims visited the site, prayed before the empty portion of the wall and often left offerings: flowers, foodstuffs, notes of one sort or another. The Vatican sent a representative who treated the phenomenon like an apparition of the Blessed Virgin in reverse. An entrepreneurial evangelical preacher built a makeshift gate and tried to charge visitors to view the site; the National Park Service took him to court on the grounds that it was government land and the legal battle lasted until an exasperated judge dismissed the case.

Hikers began noticing other erasures, equally "impossible" on pictograph panels throughout the southwest. These too were documented, discussed, written up. Articles appeared in scientific journals. There was talk of some sort of mass psychosis, in which large numbers of people, for reasons as yet unknown, were registering the same visual illusion, perhaps induced by the lingering virus that was said to have left the consciousness of survivors dramatically impaired. Neither Cynthia nor Mike had been infected, though, and scoffed at the idea.

Life went on and had to be lived. Discussions of the missing pictograph began to feel redundant or too time-consuming, and gradually other events and ideas captured people's attention. A couple of years after Cynthia and Mike had gone to document the missing figure, the issue was discussed, if at all, with an edge of past-tense tedium, like some myth or legend, inexplicable but forever part of popular lore. The erasures, for there were many, were relegated to that realm in which undecipherable phenomena are considered metaphysical by some and scientific by others who say that when science catches up, it will be able to explain the apparent mystery.

Cynthia and Maggie adopted a nine-year-old girl whose parents had died in a tragic accident. They'd been Mormons but she was part Navajo. A long period of grief and confusion eventually gave way to a close-knit threesome, in which Brenda's mothers attempted to give their daughter the sense of wholeness and self-confidence Cynthia's parents had given her.

When Brenda was fifteen, the three of them made the hike to The Great Gallery. The large figure was still gone. And now another couple of marks were missing from the line of red dots. Cynthia took to talking with her daughter about the importance of noticing what's important or beautiful. "You need to look, really see. You never know how long you'll have the privilege," she would say, her voice fading along some distant horizon.

The Ring

In retrospect, I might have noticed a change the day before. Uneasy tingling in my joints, especially elbows and knees. Arthritis? Not really that painful. In diminishing flashes, I remember going to sleep thinking about aging, wondering where the next modest ache would mock the body that had served me so well.

It isn't until I wake the next morning, stretch myself the length of my bed and raise myself on one elbow, that I know something is jarringly wrong. Pieces that don't fit. Unnerving, then frightening. Not quite memories, the rhythmic tingling conforms a knowledge that seems always to have been in me, freed from the entanglement of time. What we take for granted, as they say.

The bed itself is narrower than when I settled into sleep. Narrower and also lower to the ground. And it is crude cement here, not our parquet bedroom floor. I turn to where my love's body always meets me, warm and smelling faintly of hypoallergenic skin cream. I touch air. I'm almost always awake before she is and take care not to rouse her as I slip from my side of the bed. But now I am alone in this strange place, and the sheets feel unfamiliar. In fact, they aren't sheets as I know them, but rough fabric smelling of desert wind and horses. My body, when I manage to pull my senses back into it, is one I cannot recognize—either by external touch or from within.

Thin. Small. Spindly arms and legs. Youthful. And then some sort of fragmented understanding descends upon me like rain: I am a child, but with rapidly fleeing sensations of another body, another self. As this realization breaks through, I fight to hold onto a corner here, a disappearing sliver of familiarity there. Edges of body knowledge curl into my secret places, burrowing out of mind, sight, sense.

Voices. At first, they come from an unknown lexicon, strange guttural tones I strain to decipher. Gradually I understand: a man asking for his breakfast, a woman answering in gentle coaxing tones but with a dynamic I can't unlock. Like putting a knife to an orange, beginning to separate a circular strip and suddenly the whole outer rind falls away. The language belongs, it is inside me, but the words hold silhouettes of other words, weaving under and over and through themselves, crossing out and writing above and below the line, glyphs hiding within glyphs, assuming definitive shape against this soft morning light. As I mouth each, its predecessor fades. Out of reach. Gone. A known world moves beyond my touch, disappearing with the sounds that speak for it.

Another world is taking its place.

Each departing word leaves a piercing sadness, raw in my throat, beginning to close in terror. Where am I? Who am I? What is this place, and why is it becoming more familiar as dawn unfolds about me? I am like the pollen of a large flower, its powder lifting on air, then floating back down to settle in random pattern.

Yet random is the single word I would not use to describe my plight. There is something frighteningly specific, concrete, systemic about what has picked me up and is imprisoning me now.

I am jolted back to the body sitting at the edge of a pile of shaggy blankets piled between the small bed and a doorway of hanging beads. No door, only a meager partition. It is from a still-obscure adjoining room that the increasingly familiar voices approach.

I stare at myself. Natural light, still thin, reveals matchstick arms hanging from hunched shoulders. I am dressed in a formless gray shift. I shiver. My hair is no longer scant and white, struggling to cover expanses of puffed pink flesh—a fading memory—but coarse and long and black. I pull its strands to cheeks and scrawny neck, then run my fingers through its heft. Horse-blanket straw. The feel of an old woman's deceptive salon-cut disappears.

A pale circle on my left hand's ring finger begs to be touched; but when I explore the absence of what is no longer there, loss rises anguished in my throat. Right thumb and forefinger search in vain, grow frightened and lonely. A bitter taste overtakes me. And the bitterness streams through pools, excess saliva my tongue tries frantically to control and swallow back down my throat. An unknown replaces what seconds before seemed dependable but strangely illusive: the temperature of a beloved body, a scent so familiar it might be my own.

The woman whose caressing tone I've begun to understand appears at the opening between this alcove and the chamber beyond, the one from where the voices come. She smells of olive oil and dirty kerosene. She holds a weight of ordinary days. She is speaking to me. Her words form pictures, gradually vertical in their clarity. She wants me to get up, fetch water. From where? How to perform a task I have never performed and cannot yet imagine?

Begin again.

Begin again.

These two words remain unspoken but scrawled in heavy black script, a palpable remonstration. As the woman's words enter me, I turn them over, grasp meaning here, something almost ordinary. What needn't be pictured to be done. She smiles. I smile back, not quite so afraid. My dry lips part, then close and separate again. In my cheek a frightened muscle twitches. I reach up with trembling fingers to press it into stillness. I want to pull sounds from my throat, tongue, teeth, lips that may bridge this invisible divide.

Taste rises again, the rancid taste of fear. My slim body heaves, as if to give up what it has been forced to swallow. Then it settles. Time sputters in my hands like a campfire going out. Its particles float to my eyes, anticipating questions before they form. With childlike certainty, I know each new understanding obliterates some fragment of a place before, perhaps erasing it forever. I try to hold on, but a dark wind threatens. The naked ring finger feels hobbled, taken by a force I cannot decipher. I am torn between a need to know who and where I am and a cloud of nostalgia already blanching into porous sands.

Sands. Yes, although this is a small apartment building in a neighborhood of others, although I sense many like it crowding in on all sides, this is a place of sand. Through an open window, other windows, other buildings, still-garbled street sounds, the repetitive chant of a male voice coming from a loudspeaker close by. I glimpse morning light turning old stone and modern steel to flaming orange. The names of colors are comforting. They anchor me. I hold a brief memory of watermelon mountains glowing briefly just before dusk, then they are gone. A thousand shades of brown. Cobalt sky as big as the one that rises here but sheltering a different sort of life. Gray greens that hold a faint scent of water swollen in their withered arms.

Gone.

All gone.

The woman is telling me to go to a courtyard and bring water from an earthenware jar almost as tall as I am. I follow my body. It tells me where to find the wooden stool, where the clay dipper hangs, how to lean into the jar's coolness and lift the water out, spilling it carefully into a basin at my feet. My body knows not a drop of precious liquid must be wasted. This is a dry place.

Dry doesn't frighten me. It feels familiar and comfortable, if also thin and precarious. But something hangs ominous beyond my immediate line of sight. The dull drone of city sounds bore into my inner ear: danger writ large. The torn strip of a vaguely remembered other place separates me from a terror I try to expel from consciousness.

Carefully replacing the large jar's cover, I carry the basin to where Mother flips fragrant rounds of bread on a hot surface. Although I am sure I have never seen her before, I now know she is Mother. And the man, whose words are clear as the surface of an ancient pool of water, Father. He inclines his head, motioning me to sit beside him on the floor. Breathing in the command of his gesture, I continue to stumble on shards of uncertainty, as if each movement toward obedience carries me along a path from which there can be no return.

There is no choice, and I sit beside the man who looks like me—ominously? comfortingly? I take the flat bread he offers, touch it to my lips, taste herbs and salt. Still, my eyes travel, searching my surroundings, turning corners inside out. The surface of this place is sewn shut, its seams invisible and indivisible, not a loose thread anywhere. Yet I know I have come from somewhere else. If only I could find the door, a loose end of the weave, hold on tight, follow it out.

Follow the colors or numbers: two paths and I don't know if either leads to the place I want, need, am forgetting even as I desperately try not to.

Home? What role does direction play in this game that isn't a game?

I do know this breakfast is different. A prologue to something special, or is it ominous?

Hello?

Goodbye?

Hello?

Time rubs up against my small body and a faint wave of nausea carries me once more into momentary dizziness. Memories of another time spar with memories of another place, another knowledge, another language and personhood. Briefly I balance atop one swaying tray of a giant scale, swinging dizzyingly from a height hidden in clouds beyond my sight. A web of questions presses against my body from all sides, an enormous vice hinged with iron clasps.

Among the questions are: Stay or return? And what happens next?

Where do I find my will?

How to grab and hold on?

Love, full and powerful as a hurricane's wind, gentle as the lightest touch.

Briefly the image of a woman sitting at the edge of a bed, sobbing against an inert body—mine—flashes before my eyes. I long for her. This is pain like I have never experienced it: brutalizing and total.

Ragged shadows, some rent apart in places, open their mouths in silent grotesquery: a sneer there, soft smile here. The faces, if they can be described as faces, show lips moving: insistent, magnetic. Eyes unplugged, then unmovable, erecting walls between these facial gestures and words like some rancid food I cannot keep down. The woman who weeps shakes her head, waves everyone away, gathers my body in her arms. Her face is like gray rock, crossed by crevices where rough shale chips and cracks.

The questions stop walking, turn their heads, look back and pierce me with their eyes.

Now they are no longer questions but statements: perfectly round and absolutely clear.

If I turn in toward the shabby apartment, my body will be reduced to a severed head, bloodied shoulders, stump of flesh. My stilled heart will be burdened by scars. My legacy: a statement written by someone else, repeated and recorded in my quivering breath. A destiny torn from some book of fate written long before my birth. My actions will never have belonged to me. My journey shudders like the furious water of a river crashing against rock.

Is this the same ancient rock?

No, it is smooth, polished by millennia of water, standing where it is meant to stand, precisely. Salvation seems to beckon from terror's center, from that point where loss and gain are indistinguishable. I summon every whisper of will, every strength of knowledge, and turn. Something snaps, like an invisible wishbone, large as a question mark. Memory puts its arms around me, drawing me back and away.

Now I am rousing, struggling to breathe, returning to life beside the woman who holds me in her arms. I begin to stir in her strong embrace, begin to feel once more its texture and heat. Blood rages through me, warming my parched skin. Again and again she touches me. My velveteen rabbit, I murmur, but only I hear the words. She presses an index finger to her lips, chokes on her own tears, presses me closer.

"Almost lost," I hear her whisper, and try to imagine what almost means.

Memories layer in random order: Marriages, both public and private. The moment she understood she needed her own workspace, that her name is Artist. When she began leaving her family's shadow and living in her own. When we got past the eight-year mark and I knew this time would be different, would not forget its name. How jealousy fled and didn't return. Where trust took up residence. How kindness became a family member, taking each of us by the hand. When we discovered, together, that only art can pave the road to that world threatening to slip between our fingers.

Place writ large.

As if on a screen, moving just beyond my eyes but on which I can see its shadow figures—free of strings or maneuvering hands—a young girl leaves a breakfast table, her parents, the last remnants of tea glistening in its shallow dish, an uneaten scrap of flatbread.

The figure of another man shimmers at the edge of the picture plane. As he steps forward, I see an unwieldy vest in his hands. He holds it close to the girl's chest—her incipient breasts straining in broken acceptance, her heart thundering—his monotone of jumbled words telling a story she hears but does not understand. This is about measuring, measurement, the size of numbers but not their older meaning. Wires stick out in burning disarray. Material speaks to the girl in a language she almost remembers but ignores.

The man says something about this being an honor for her, the first young girl . . .

The time has come.

In this interstice of moment and place, I realize I no longer understand the mother, the father, the man with the vest. Their eyes empty out, then leave their sockets of bone, fleeing a refusal to belong that tells me everything I need to know. As he fades, the man chokes on a guttural sigh.

A burst of dry thunder accompanies this brutal shift of time and place. Rivulets of pain run from my belly, along my arms, coming to a sudden stop beneath my fingernails. Pools of saliva flood back into my mouth, then, washing away the sharp taste of fear.

I turn my head, definitively.

Looking up into the eyes of the woman I love, I begin to take my first breaths beyond such perilous escape. On the floor, one soiled canvass edge just visible beneath the familiar bedframe, I catch sight of the suicide vest, its bulky contour fleeing until it no longer fills my field of vision.

Without conscious thought, in the almost automatic motion I have made so many times before, the tip of my left thumb curls to push the plain gold band into the fleshy pad at the top of my palm. That ring: alive with energy. One of a pair, identical, linked by the same date embossed on their undersides. I hear the sound of my own voice, words in the language I think I have always spoken, words that become a poem. Simultaneously I push them out into cracked air and try to keep them from utterance.

My dream fades, until only its broken contour scatters across the floor.

In a soft voice I begin to count: 0, 1, 1, 2, 3, 5, 8, 13, 21, 34. I am tired. So tired. The numbers approach my eyes, like shooting stars: sunflowers, hurricanes, galaxies. Somewhere in a distant sphere, Euclid laughs. I can see Fibonacci, prancing along the sidelines, eager to have his say.

Now color takes over. I have made my choice.

Silence pulls me into its arms. Less really does seem to be more.

With the tip of one bare toe, I push a corner of dirty canvass cloth from sight, its mass of wires unruly, perhaps contagious.

For the moment I have no inclination to explain. And how would I begin, if I myself still stumble across a map that is tissue-thin, threatening to shred and scatter.

Then I saw what the calling was: it was the road I traveled.

Rukeyser's words, in my birth language and accompanied by a cello's deep tones, enter the room on a sudden wind. From the South come another woman's words: *Gracias a la vida, que me ha dado tanto.* They are more than enough. I touch the ring again and dissolve into the embrace of the woman whose face is only now beginning to lose its cast of grief.

Both Sides, No Middle

"We live without sensing the country beneath us."
—Osip Mandelstam[1]

Thelma asked Diane to look for Sensodyne: her teeth hurt these days, maybe she isn't getting enough calcium. Or maybe she is grinding them in her sleep. Tension wracks their nights as well as their waking hours. Diane pushes the basket through one supermarket aisle after another, leaning on its handle in order to alleviate this feeling of fatigue that seems to drown her days in lethargy. She notices artistically arranged pyramids of cans and boxes; a way of keeping minimum wage employees busy and the store's shelves looking fuller than current scarcities allow. Every time Diane shops, she notices the absence or return of a few more basics: milk, butter, toilet paper. You never know what you'll find. She fights against hoarding or anxiety buying. "Relax," she tells herself, usually without success, "and take a breath."

At the same time, she ponders the vast variety of products, items that have gained mainstream middle-class popularity just during her lifetime. You can pay extra for just about any fruit or vegetable, in or out of season, exotic or ordinary. And you can buy it cleaned and packaged, cutting down on preparation time—and distancing yourself ever further from the earth where it was planted and grew. You can select a neatly wrapped cut of meat that guarantees you won't have to imagine killing the animal it came from.

---

1 "Stalin's Epigram," 1933.

You can buy a bottled power drink with so much caffeine it should be able to short-circuit brain and heart in one volcanic eruption. You can choose fat-free, 1%, 2%, whole, chocolate, soy, or almond milk, to name only the most popular. The list of over-the-top possibilities seems to increase in some obscene correlation to the number of people who have to decide whether to buy food or medicine because acquiring both is no longer an option for them.

Diane won't forget to peruse the pharmacy section for the Sensodyne and also those vitamins and supplements that might make up for the bounty of fresh fruits and vegetables she's always bought to keep her family healthy. She and Thelma know they are among the lucky ones, those who can still purchase a couple of apples or head of lettuce for more than their poorer neighbors have to pay for an entire meal special at McDonalds. The thin hamburger patty on a doughy white bun with its accompanying grease-drenched pocket of French fries and a coke might satiate a child's hunger but provides more filler than nutrition. Childhood diabetes has become almost as much of a pandemic as the cruel viruses that now bombard them in rapid succession. Diane and Thelma have given up arguing with people they know who still berate the poor for choosing fast food over a tub of spinach or a vitamin-packed bell pepper. Diane continues to be amazed at the facility and frequency with which the comfortable criticize the disadvantaged, even now.

In the fresh produce section, she has almost made it past the mushrooms. Her chest is tight and cold beads of perspiration bathe her brow. A flood of saliva pours from her tongue, fighting nausea and filling her mouth like a tsunami casting her onto an island where all moorings have disappeared. She swallows but the secretion invades her again and then again, leaving a crust of salt along her bottom lip. Involuntarily, she sucks in her breath, forces herself to look, squeezes every orifice in her body tightly shut, then averts her eyes as she catches a strong whiff of musty forest decay laced with her grandfather's Listerine breath. This corner of the market is always a challenge, probably always will be. Recovering the memory of childhood abuse in therapy has been a relief but hasn't gotten her beyond the lifelong phobia.

Her determined battle with the mushrooms barely behind her, the suddenness of unexpected contact shakes Diane from her shuddering reverie. A heavyset thick-necked male shopper has just jammed his cart into hers. Her first response when she looks up is the beginning of a smile, even that automatic "I'm sorry" ready and waiting from her earliest conditioning.

An accident, no?

Instantaneously, she knows it wasn't.

The familiar red baseball cap half hides the man's buzz cut. His tank top, stretched tight over beer belly and bulked shoulders, reads "Bar-b-q, Beer, Freedom" rather than "Make America Great Again," but it's the same message. She takes in his hostile expression—something between a smirk and a scowl—and realizes he's collided with her intentionally. Most people keep their distance in public places but there are exceptions. This guy has removed the mask he had to wear to gain access to the store. She can see the corner of it and a dangling ear strap jammed into one of his back pants pockets.

Habit takes over. "Sorry," she hears herself say, then averts her gaze in order to steady herself and decide upon the best course of action. Thelma has finally convinced her of the danger in confronting strangers to recommend the virtues of social distancing and masks to those who are so clearly making their individualist statements at the expense of everyone's safety. "No one's gonna tell me what I have to do" is the message, spoken or unspoken, that such people exude. The air they share seems loaded these days with those "I Dare You to Confront Me" intimidations. A day doesn't go by that Thelma doesn't beg Diane to curb her urge to engage such people and try to educate them. "You only risk yourself," she insists, "and us if we're with you." Diane knows her wife is right and has retreated from her waning conviction that every opportunity is a teachable moment.

The man who's hit her basket with his has pulled back a foot or two and then inches toward her again, stopping just short of collision. He is daring her to make the next move. His face is a menacing map of features perched at the very edge of contained rage. He says nothing, a smirk at the corner of his mouth, waiting to see what her reaction will be. When she maneuvers to the right, he takes a step forward on his left, blocking her way. She tries going in the other direction. He leans right then, filling the aisle. The guy is obviously enjoying the dance. He is quicker than she is and determined. It is a macabre game, one he has planned and undoubtedly engaged in before. The other shoppers disappear from Diane's radius of vision, leaving her alone in this stand-off. In the few minutes their encounter has lasted so far, the man seems to have visibly grown, taller and also broader, filling the space they share and also the darkest corners of Diane's memory.

In her peripheral vision, Diane catches sight of other shoppers turning and moving away, putting as much space between themselves and her predicament as they can. Not getting involved has become a common survival instinct in these times.

The man's stare is filled with all the gloating "I Told You So's" of that half of the population that would commit every crime to stay in power and mocks a virus gone rogue that threatens them all. Those citizens their president endows with permission to indulge their basest instincts. They lost the recent election by a narrow margin, but a margin nonetheless, and are simply refusing to vacate power. The whole country is living in a no-person's land of uncertainty and absent government.

The United States a failed state? Unimaginable even just a few years back.

The dictator and his fascist cohorts have taken cheating to a new level, even boasting of their gross manipulation. They defend their de facto control with black leather jackets and military style fatigues, monster trucks, submachine guns, compound bows, pistols, Billy clubs, swinging chains, rants meant to drown out any reason, a derisive belittling of anyone they deem "other," the simple heft of their ready bodies and the spittle from their angry mouths—all aimed at the most vulnerable. They don't hesitate to infect, murder, maim, shout insults and obscenities, and try to make the rest of us believe it's their world now.

Diane starts to speak but swallows her words before they can escape her lips. She backs up then, almost into the mushroom bin. A dagger-like current of electricity contorts her muscles in terror and repulsion. She jumps back, almost stumbles, but grabs the handle of her basket again and manages a tight turn. She heads toward the front of the store, steering the cart by sheer force of will, forcing herself not to look back. By the time she'd reaches the end of cereals and baking products and turns into oils, vinegars and syrups, she can feel in her cells that he is no longer close.

No. Threat, not confrontation, is the bully's goal. But by now the knowledge that he and perhaps others like him are in the store has lodged itself in Diane's lungs and between her hunched shoulder blades. Her breath turns shallow, painful. She tries to calm her respiration, reminding herself that the most serious error she and her friends commit is judging the logic of guys like him by their own.

Why me, Diane wonders? Woman? Lesbian? Just someone who looks as if she might be a reasonable human being? An easy target? Or all of the above? Perhaps this guy just felt the urge to attack and has targeted her at random. It doesn't really matter, she thinks, as she moves nervously from one spaced floor marker to the next, leading up to the check-out counter.

She is still drenched in sweat as she reaches the cashier, numbly places her purchases on the moving surface, bags them herself and heads for the exit. Her whole body remains brittle, as if permanent paralysis has invaded her tenderest places. She is conscious that she isn't yet in the clear, that she still has to cross the parking lot, put her groceries in the car and head home, vigilant in case the bully's car is following her. Or that she herself might allow her nerves to cause an accident. Her logic tells her none of this is likely. But that other logic, the one she has such trouble grasping? Who knows?

Diane has lowered her own mask to just below her chin for driving. Wearing it tends to fog her glasses and make it harder to breathe. By the time she reaches the familiarity of their street and house, and parks the car in the driveway, she feels steadier, less anxious. She has been able to put some distance between the incident in the supermarket and herself. Denial, perhaps. But what the hell. You can't live with the constant pressure of fear. She will tell Thelma about her encounter with the bully and the telling will release the tightness in her chest.

But maybe not in front of the kids. They are burdened enough these days by a world so changed she can hardly conceive of how it impacts their young lives. Sometimes she tries to imagine what this reality must feel like for a three- or four-year-old whose entire experience has been skewed by crisis. She knows she can't know what living like this means for someone with no memory of before. Fabiola spends more and more time these days with her imaginary friends. They talk endlessly in reassuring tones. They help her ward off uncertainty, comfort and console her. Sometimes Diane or Thelma catch their youngest, Rodrigo, staring into a beyond they know they cannot imagine.

Now Diane turns off the engine and steps out of the car. She presses the release that springs the hatchback and prepares to bring her purchases inside. Fewer items than uninterrupted shopping might have yielded, but enough to get the family through the week.

Suddenly a screech of tires, shattering of glass and cacophony of sound unlike any she can identify pierce the midsummer morning. A crash! Right in front of their house!

Diane turns, dropping the full bag of groceries she'd just hoisted from her car's trunk. For one frozen moment her eyes follow a stream of blueberries rolling down the drive. A jar of jam lays shattered at her feet and she quickly steps aside to avoid the shards of glass coated in fruity goo. She raises her eyes and looks to where sound takes her gaze, to two vehicles that have collided head-on, a mass of twisted steel in terrible embrace not a hundred feet from where she stands. One horn blares continuously. The front end of a vintage Volkswagen Beetle is crushed all the way up to its windshield. She registers a series of clunks and pops she doesn't recognize but whose intrusion brings stinging bile to her tongue. Then she focuses on the blurred figure of a woman slumped behind the driver's window, motionless.

Diane runs toward the tangled cars. Neighbors are hurrying in their direction as well. A disembodied voice: "Someone call 911!" Diane realizes she doesn't even know where her cell phone is. She keeps moving, propelled by the immediate need of two drivers she knows might be dead. All thought of the bully is gone.

The woman bent broken over the Beetle's steering wheel isn't moving. A thread of bright blood issues from the corner of her mouth. Too late, Diane mutters, not aware she is speaking out loud. She shifts her attention to the white SUV. She catches sight of a jerky movement in its front seat. She can't see the driver's face, but he seems to be struggling with something. The scene reveals itself to Diane in slow motion. She realizes the billowing mass obscuring the driver's face is an air bag that released at the instant of impact.

From where she is now standing, Diane can see a puddle of liquid spreading beneath the accordioned front of the VW. The unmistakable sound of dripping liquid somehow comes clear amidst the intensifying noise produced by the echo of the crash itself, the blaring horn, people shouting. Diane sees that gasoline is also spattering, then gushing, from beneath the chassis of the SUV. She points and tries to shout: "Look! Gas! Gotta get him out . . .!" This time no sound comes from between her lips. Panic erases the words before she can utter them.

But others have seen what she sees. Almost in a trance she realizes Thelma is on the scene, along with Ricardo from across the street. He has something metal in his hand and is prying at the SUV's door. It bursts open in seconds. Diane watches as Thelma helps extract the driver from the cushiony twist that has saved his life. She sees her wife and their neighbor carry the man to safety and lay him gently on the sidewalk. Someone she doesn't recognize runs over with a folded jacket and places it beneath the survivor's head. The blaring horn, gushing liquid, hissing steam, and chorus of voices create a dissonance that eliminates all else from her consciousness. What she hears and what she sees only partially match.

Diane has no sense of how much time has passed before a different set of sounds pierces the midmorning air. Approaching sirens. A fire truck followed by an ambulance. As if in a single choreographed motion, practiced professionals assess the situation. One touches the neck of the Beetle's driver. A twinge of despair tastes bitter on Diane's tongue as she watches the paramedic shake his head and walk away. She forces herself to shift her vision to the sidewalk where a team of rescue workers are lifting the driver of the SUV onto a stretcher. He seems to be mumbling something, the reassuring syllables of life.

Thelma joins Diane then and pulls her to their car where they stand leaning against it and very close to each other. "Too late for the woman," Thelma says, "but I think the guy is going to be all right."

Diane opens her mouth. She wants to tell her wife about her experience at the supermarket, what, less than a half hour ago? She swallows that story. She needs to tell her instead how much she loves her, but those words emerge in a whisper only she can hear. She folds silently into Thelma's arms, then looks back at the street where two police cars are now part of the swelling knot of vehicles, their drivers increasing a crowd that numbers several dozen.

What fills Diane is the knowledge that every single person milling about the accident has helped in whatever way they've been able. Breaking open the SUV door, carrying its driver to safety, calling for help, exuding an energy of concern and rapid action. Disaster has brought out the best in their neighbors, passersby, police, paramedics, people they know and those they don't.

Her mind travels to the year before, when Thelma was diagnosed with breast cancer and so many strangers as well as friends rallied, encouraged, helped in dozens of different ways without being asked. And she remembers a parade of lesser events, not as dramatic but just as needing of compassion. Now tragedy has once again invaded their lives. Sudden. Unexpected. No one is laughing or gloating. No one is enjoying the misery of others or getting off on someone else's pain.

Diane knows, without understanding she knows, that a great communal heart continues to beat among her people. The fascist hordes are there. They can't be denied and mustn't be ignored. But neither do they come anywhere near constituting the future. At moments like these they fade into a soup of irrelevance.

Some, like the woman driving the Beetle, will die. But life will continue to rebirth itself in their troubling world.

The Extinction

*"Literature does not treat the world as an object
of knowledge but as a subject of human concern.
And this itself is a cognitive accomplishment, a
way of bearing witness to the world."*

—John Gibson[2]

Winter morphs to spring in the southern hemisphere.
A spring like none Olga can remember. She sometimes
looks up at the ovenbird nest perfectly balanced atop the
streetlight pole across the street. The streetlight hasn't
come on in over a year, leaving the block in permanent
shadow. A burnt-out bulb with no replacement? The nest
is empty. Its small tan builders with their white breasts and
bright orange feathertails, who labored more than a month
to make just the right home, haven't been seen this season
either. The adobe complex, with its foyer and hidden inner
room, remains abandoned. Humans and animals: losing
our habitats.

Olga wants to make Miguel's birthday special this
year, gather his few remaining playmates and invent doings
that will delight them. Eight is a good age, she thinks: still
a child with all the innocence that implies, but perceptive
now in ways that sometimes take her breath away. So
much has changed, and so quickly. She weeps unasham-
edly when she thinks of her grandparents, parents, and so

---

2 *Fiction and the Weave of Life.* New York: Oxford UP, 2007.
p. 117.

many friends whose lives have ended during this sixth great pandemic surge: new mutations and inexplicable dangers looming every few months. There's a reason they're now calling it an extinction.

Sometimes Olga ponders the fact that her small family—her husband Daniel, Miguel, her daughter Iris who is five, and herself—are all still alive. Not even a fever or cough to set their nerves on edge. So far. Chance, she knows. Luck. They haven't taken more precautions than others. There is little if anything different about their lives. In fact, Miguel and Iris were able to return to kindergarten and daycare when other children were still struggling to socialize online. Libertad is a small country with a relatively sparse population. And people are disciplined. From the onset of the first virus, the one people refer to now as Coronavirus I, they've handled it well. But who is to say the worst isn't yet to come?

Countries might have been expected to stand or fall depending on how they were governed, the socialist societies adopting more rigorous safeguards and requiring their citizens to observe them, the liberal democracies following scientific guidelines aimed at reducing the number of deaths, the countries with the most fervently capitalist systems sacrificing lives in their efforts to preserve economies, their voracious leaders shrugging off statistics or lying to cover their tracks. Individuals might have been expected to weather the combined crises in line with their economic means, attitudes or levels of creativity. But this isn't what's happened, at least not everywhere. People continue to sicken and die regardless of age, vulnerabilities, economic status, philosophical positions or willingness to be vaccinated.

The overcrowded conditions that stoke dog-eat-dog behavior in one place have people helping one another somewhere else. Some are thriving on fresh fruits and vegetables; others are doomed by their isolation to eating out of cans. Many who need it haven't been able to get medical attention: this has proved fatal to some but, perhaps unsurprisingly, saved others. Merchants have generally found a way to keep selling but those who fix what is broken are in high demand. Neither educational levels nor privileged access make a noticeable statistical difference with regard to who has succumbed and where, although a minority race and poverty, as always, have produced the greatest devastation. Some depend on government aid while others seek new models of community organization. Everywhere survival seems to follow different paths and statistics are about the same. That is, as far as Olga can tell with so few trustworthy sources of information.

Her greatest sorrow is the loss of both their sets of parents; they'd been so close and so important to them all. Olga forces herself to remember her children's early lives, when her parents traveled from the capital almost every weekend to spend lovely carefree days with them in the small provincial city of Coruña. That sense of abandon and joy. Would it ever return? Can it return in a world so ravaged by illness and death, by climate crisis and economic tragedy and, even with a greatly reduced world population, more people walking aimlessly from place to place now than those who can cling to a spot they call home? A world where a few brief years have destroyed life as they'd known it, reorganized politics and economics, seems at times more like prehistory struggling beneath an awareness of pre-crisis denial. We knew, Olga, thought, but pretended not to.

Whenever Olga uses the term pre-crisis, Daniel is quick to remind her it wasn't a single sudden crisis that turned their lives upside down. No, this has been coming for a long time. They both talked about it, predicted it, feared it. They are scientists, biochemists, and Olga had also been in her fourth year of medicine when life stopped and then what was left of it struggled to its feet again. Following any reasonable discussion to its logical conclusion inevitably led to the realization that humans have been destroying their habitat for generations. Consciously, although most political and corporate leaders took refuge in denial. And then there was that unbridgeable distance between acknowledging an outcome and being willing to do something about it. Campaign after campaign had gathered strength and sputtered out. Daniel spends long hours in the fruit orchard and vegetable garden behind their house. He has always loved making things grow. Now it is a necessity.

Olga looks out the window at Miguel playing in the backyard. He is swinging slowly in the large rubber tire Daniel has secured to a rope hanging from the sturdiest lower branch of the big native pine. Her son moves listlessly, dragging his feet in the dead pine needles carpeting the ground where she's given up trying to coax new grass. He cups something in his hands. Could it be a small bird? Yes, a bird. He seems to be talking to the fledgling, though Olga can't make out what he's saying.

So many species gone now. Some falling from the sky like biblical fish. Others mutated, nameless, struggling to adapt to new habitats. Birds starting out on their yearly migrations and then returning months before they are expected, always in vastly reduced numbers. The lucky ones, Olga thinks. Or maybe not. Despite her irreparable loss, she too considers herself one of the lucky ones. She mostly feels that way when she realizes that her small family has been able to resist, but then a wave of grief will wash over her, like winter rain's cold sharp needles piercing her flesh. It might have been better to have been among the first to succumb. She wouldn't have had to juggle the painful memory of loss.

And explaining the extinction to Miguel and Iris. That takes every bit of ingenuity she can muster. What to tell them when they ask about Grandma and Grandpa? How to talk about the absence of so many people they loved? Their few religious acquaintances speak of a God that has always felt foreign to Olga, talk about "a better place" as if imagining such a realm somehow renders the inexplicable loss more acceptable. A few of the more fanatical even equate the scourge of death with something they call the Rapture, claiming that those who've died were lifted up into a heavenly realm where they no longer suffer: the chosen ones. Now, as 2025 winds its torturous way to a close, there are still a few people who are comforted by belief, who try to explain what has happened as some sort of test of faith. They are in a distinct minority. And there's an irony, Olga thinks, in the fact that the believers and non-believers have been equally affected.

Globally the extinction has validated the scientific view. In any case, few have time for such debates now. Too much to do, and so few to do it. And, although Olga and Daniel subscribe to the scientific findings, they don't offer much solace. In the final days of the last pandemic there'd been a rush to save what could be saved. Some infrastructure. Some lines of communication. Survivors were desperate to know where and how many they were. Some countries, whose governments hadn't been completely decimated, tried to severely restrict the flow of information, but those who could hacked and patched and scoffed at attempts to limit what connectivity they could muster.

Olga had been in constant contact with her father, until he no longer responded. Although she resisted the thought, she knew why. And then only the innocence and need in her children's eyes brought her out of deep despair.

When she'd first used the word extinction when describing to Miguel what was happening, he'd drawn a picture of four dinosaurs, two towering Tyrannosaurus Rex and two smaller creatures with white wings that faded into the paper. Olga knew he was drawing his immediate family, the people with whom he lived, those whose daily presence he counts on. Then he scratched black lines back and forth across the four prehistoric animals until you could barely make them out beneath his rush of furious energy. He'd become more and more agitated as he'd covered them with a crayon stub that barely survived his determination. Was he trying to preempt what he feared? He knew the word extinction from when they'd told him about the giant meteor and why dinosaurs no longer roam the earth. But how could an eight-year-old grasp the idea of an extinction that included people? One that takes people he loves, attacks humans as indiscriminately as animals and plants?

This is uncharted territory. Olga wants her son and daughter to understand. She knows their unanswered questions will torment them more than an explanation, no matter how terrible. But how can any of them understand an extinction that has left a smattering of humans to contemplate their future, if a concept such as future can even be imagined now?

Back to Miguel's birthday. Olga takes her eyes from her son swinging listlessly on the tire hanging from the tree. She tries to free her mind of her mounting anxieties. Focusing on an immediate task has become the best way of centering herself. Since her classes in medicine happen only sporadically now—when a professor is able and willing—and the biochemistry classes she herself teaches have also turned erratic, she has more time for the children. A delight, but often overwhelming. She knows she must prepare them for a very different world. Yet she herself knows so little about that world. What will it look like? Where are the suicides beginning to subside? Where are people showing the most creativity in what they are trying to save, recreate, reimagine?

Olga remembers a time, a couple years back, when she dared believe the survivors would design new models of social organization, models that spoke to human need rather than uncontrolled greed. She and Daniel had briefly joined a group of young people in Coruña determined to come up with ideas, launch local projects. But when several sickened and died, the group fell apart. From what she can tell, those surviving have mostly reverted to the old familiar ways of getting by. Will her precious children find their places in the world to come? Will their generation, or what's left of it, be able to create a more conscious and hopeful world?

Maybe begin by asking him if he wants a party? Who would he like to invite? "Grandpa and Grandma," he exclaims, and repeats the two beloved words: "Grandpa and Grandma." Olga turns away. She tries to force back the tears pooling and threatening to spill from her eyes. Then she turns back to her son, gathers him in her arms along with the tiny bird he is clutching, and holds them wordlessly.

By the end of 2024, the term pandemic had largely disappeared from world discourse and the word extinction had taken its place. Poets, those still alive, began using the new word in their poems. Songs rhymed the term in both trite and serious ways. Scientists began factoring the concept into their equations. Every discipline or area of inquiry felt new, untried. Just a few years back, when someone said extinction, it evoked prehistoric events, all before the advent of humans. Over the past several years things have moved so fast that language is less and less able to keep up; words become obsolete almost before they are familiar, can enter dictionaries or curriculums.

Olga forces herself to recall the exact sequence. One resurgence after another of the original virus. Then the first major mutation. And mutations some scientists hesitated to designate as such, moving back and forth between animals and humans, traveling through water and air, clinging to surfaces scrubbed clean with every known disinfectant, claiming tens of thousands and then millions of lives as they ravaged Africa and Asia, then central Europe, the Americas, Australia, even the international station at the South Pole and the isolated Inuit villages of the far north.

With the breakdown of instant communication, it took a while for Libertad to receive news of small communities that had somehow survived one wave or another. Or cities where populations had been decimated but not erased. A village near Egypt's pyramids of Giza got word of its survival out to the wider world when a camel train reached Tunis and an email transmitted the message to someone in Paris. What was left of Buenos Aires made contact with what was left of Montevideo, just across the river. On the Caribbean island of Cuba "*radio bembá*" or word of mouth kept a dwindling population current. Islanders after all was said and done, people who tilted their noses and gestured in a way that said we might be poor, but we're survivors. Men and women hardened by trips to sea in makeshift boats took the news to nearby islands. The single surviving member of one generation of a family in Melbourne, Australia somehow reached a niece of that family residing in Coruña, but she has not yet been able to get word back.

Olga thinks now of that moment, a few months back, when Miguel had been trying to help his father get dinner. Daniel was heating up leftovers, their son proudly setting the table. A glass slipped from his hand and shattered on the kitchen floor. In earlier times such a mishap would have elicited tears. Not now. Miguel had taken a few gasping breaths his father expected would be the prelude to several minutes of frustrated chaos. But instead of a tantrum, the child had suddenly stopped crying, looked at his dad and choked back his tears. Daniel, ever attentive to the ways in which this strange new time was affecting their kids, looked over at Olga and motioned with his eyes for her to take in the radically changed behavior. Later that night, in bed, he'd whispered to her: "I think he may believe he's to blame for what's happening. I hope he doesn't think it's his fault." Olga had wept then. "Iris, too," she sputtered, trying to calm her own tears "There was a time when I could have imagined preferring passivity to a burst of childhood temper."

Language collapses and expands. Shipments of foods and medicines leap borders or get bogged down in deserts and jungles. With so few people flying and driving cars or taking trains and buses, the reduction of pollution has brightened skies and vastly improved air quality. With so few modes of public transportation nothing is certain.

Monster storms have become less frequent. The survivors of an endangered planet have begun breathing more deeply. Slowly, the polar ice cap has stopped melting, seas have maintained fairly stable levels, and small island nations no longer feel endangered. But where the representatives of almost eight billion people had once staged international symposia and argued endlessly about a world that was getting hotter, less than six million now rejoice in the improved conditions. Six million out of eight billion people left on our planet! Still a sizeable global community. But so scattered, so disconnected, so battered by PTSD and so hopelessly grappling with that forever question: how do we begin again?

Olga finds herself alternating between trying to protect her small family bubble, nurturing her children in the hope of a future they can look forward to, encouraging Daniel when he becomes depressed or listless and counting on him to encourage her when her spirits flag. Having two young children to live for is a privilege and also daunting.

Her arms around her son, she looks down for the first time at the bird he holds in his hands. It is motionless, dead. Miguel starts murmuring to it again, seemingly oblivious to the fact that it is gone. They have talked about death a lot over the past year and a half. She knows he understands the concept, at least insofar as a child of his age is able. "Shall we bury it?" she asks him. "No," Miguel says, I want it to live. I need it to live."

Water: The Mirage

Felicia hears the truck in the distance and hurries out to be at the Commons when it makes its weekly stop in the stark circle between the half dozen houses scattered at the southern edge of what was once a thriving community. According to the distribution plan agreed upon at the beginning of the last quarter, she and her family will receive 12 tumblrs for the week. The new measurement invented for these times. Fragments of the discussion, the echo of those words announcing the ultimate decision, surface now in memory. Twelve tumblrs of water for eleven people. Not much, if you think about cooking, bathing, washing.

The whole scene comes into focus, then blurs again.

Water in each home, being able to drink it freely, is something they barely remembered now, although Felicia sometimes wakes to a faint smile on Kate's face, those weathered features time can't erase. Those mornings Felicia knows her wife has dreamt of water. That long-ago time when the precious liquid gushed from pipes and faucets, when you could fill a whole glass and then another, drink until thirst no longer turned your tongue pasty or plunged a twisting knife in your gut. A memory of plumped skin unwrinkled by a constant state of low-level dehydration.

Twelve tumblrs for eleven people, slightly more than one apiece. Felicia and Kate shares some of their own ration with the younger members of their family: Ben who moved in with Sophie and Dan after Martha died, Sandra and Cisco—who was called Sissy when they'd joined the household; sex-change surgeries were no longer performed in this New Time but they all respected his claim to the identity he knew was his and addressed him as a man—, and the four Contreras siblings who'd become part of their extended family when it seemed they could all do better joining forces and sharing provisions.

These scenes return with all their loud details perfectly chiseled, like a rain forest that creates its own ecosystem. Her metaphors and similes construct a particular depth perception, like the most traditional of stage sets.

Felicia never stops telling stories of Before to Geraldine, Arturo, Maria and Epi. She can't let go of the dream that all those who'd survived the Extinction must find ways to accelerate progress and bring back something of The Good Old Days. Not the greed and waste, she would tell herself, just the togetherness, philosophical adventures, laughter, art, scientific exploration, travel as pastime, some basic resources and a few of the gourmet delights they made possible.

Tumblr, she thinks, such a clichéd name for the bottle that is more than three quarts but increasingly less than a gallon. A name that means nothing but sticks to her lips like some catchy evocation of a non-specific quantity, an aggregate that has gradually diminished again over the past few months. Or years. Or lifetimes. Like those little square clear plastic tubs of blueberries that she sometimes remembers buying at the supermarket when supermarkets still existed. They started off as half pints, then contained fewer and fewer berries and more air but were sold for the same price. Or more. Few complained about the fact they were getting less product for more money. Complaints took too much energy. It was almost as if complaining threatened to make the scarcities more real or erased the hope that things would ever return to how they'd been.

All of civilization had been a hill you'd climbed, meeting challenges along the way, only to reach the top and careen down the other side, plunging and plummeting in ever more rapid descent.

Felicia occasionally wanders into memories like the one she is having now, enters their territory as if it were a living breathing space. Familiar and longed for at the same time. She might come across an idea she can caress there, find a friend, locate something solid she can hold in her hand for a while. Those forays are like visits to astonishment.

The truck arrives and Felicia takes a step back to let her neighbors crowd in front and receive their rations first. Stan waves to her as he unloads each tumblr, checking them off on the list affixed to his clipboard. Digital devices once used for recording such deliveries have long since vanished and been replaced with slower but more reliable methods. She knows he won't leave her without. As the human press against the truck's tailgate thins, she moves closer, smiles at Stan and raises her thin arms to receive the first of their weekly ration.

"How are things going over in Staytown," Felicia asks. "Bout like you'd think," Stan mumbles as he hands down the first of her tumblrs. His muttered words, practiced and nondescript, fall lifelessly onto the worn truck bed. But his smile is a ray of kindness filling the morning and embracing Felicia's yearning breath. She stands motionless for a few moments, the clear liquid sloshing within the scratched plastic mesmerizing her. Then she lifts the first tumblr onto one shoulder. It is weightless.

Weightless because it doesn't exist? Or because it does?

Felicia thinks about how the rich taste of water always

caresses her tongue from the moment she sees it sloshing off the truck, one tumblr after another. Then satiation gives way to an agonizing saltiness. The New Time has irrevocably changed perspective, shaping it in ways she couldn't have anticipated. Known for her quick wit and ready words before the Extinction, now she often stands silent before another's comment or question, contemplating her response, wanting to be sure before she speaks. Or just summoning the strength to speak. She is remembering then, letting her imagination take her back to that other life. Memory is more than a friend. It is a bridge. A bridge she crosses again and again to keep herself alive.

And imagination is her best friend. Always has been.

Slowly, Felicia walks to the house, deposits one tumblr, returns to the truck, comes back with another, and repeats her brief journeys until the dozen stand in a neat row before the kitchen sink where faucets haven't been turned on for years. Nothing comes through the rusty pipes. They remain a ghostly monument to another time, architecture of the absurd, a labyrinth of fading emotion.

Felicia calls her family together. She knows they will be eager to whet their lips, soothe their throats, water their gardens of dying cells. She calls them with the power of her mind, silently, breathless in parched air that pushes in on all sides, causing her body to tense and then relax like a large animal yawning.

And they come, one by one, each appearing to Felicia at their moment of greatest power and physical beauty. Kate has laughter in her eyes. Ben is a proud father. Epi swings back and forth on the tire they've hung from a sturdy cottonwood, her little feet stuck out before her, her invented song filling the air. She is forever young, the small girlchild with everything in her future, dreams stopped in their tracks, longings forever unrealized. Geraldine waves goodbye from the back window of an interstate bus as she goes off to study theater in a city that no longer exists. The whole eastern seaboard crumbled into the Atlantic a dozen years before, leaving few survivors and a holographic memory of great human-made structures to those old enough to have lived among them.

And Felicia herself? Who was she back then?

After everyone has consumed their ration, Felicia puts each bottle back in place, stands for a moment observing them, making sure they are equidistant one from another, admiring their uniformity, passing her fingers over their unsightly scratches as if willing them to disappear, ignoring the invisible water level in each.

She settles in the comfortable chair then, worn notebook in hand. Computers, even ballpoint pens, are things of the past. She opens the notebook to one of its last empty pages and writes lightly with a pencil stub that is almost too small now to grip between her fingers. She writes haltingly, admiring each syllable, each letter, each place where graphite murmurs against paper.

Felicia describes each of these people she loves, bringing them to life on ragged pages. She evokes deep canyons and wild animals and nights with every star brilliantly visible. Flourless chocolate cake. The yearly yellow blooms on a prickly pear cactus and the waxy white flower topping the century plant. Sometimes, just for the challenge, she tries writing with her left hand, but those attempts resemble the abandoned road winding back to the moment of her birth and she soon gives up.

Sometimes she forms numbers, just to see if she can still recall what they look like but can't remember the difference between a six and a nine, thinks seven might be missing an arm or leg. Once she attempted a poem but stopped when the knowledge that she would never read it to an audience, never share it orally or on paper, leaves the words floating like dust motes in the air. Just a few months ago she thought she'd sketch a house with living windows and an inviting half-open door, but when she thumbs back through the notebook, the scene has disappeared.

Lately, Felicia voices instructions to herself, but by the time she begins to follow them she can no longer remember what they are.

She urges herself to draw. Draw Stan and his truck, their neighbors clamoring for their tumblrs, she herself hoisting one large bottle after another onto her shoulder and bringing it into the house. She tries to recreate the conversation Stan and she had just minutes before. Or hours before. Or months or years before. She can no longer remember when everyone and everything disappeared. When she'd found herself alone in this limbo between life and memory, her own recall straining to reimagine itself.

She draws the chair, a smudge rendered unrecognizable by her fading eyesight. She tries to draw the notebook, the pencil, her barely moving hand. She draws time itself, swallowing place, and then place swallowing time. She no longer knows whether time or place comes first or how to navigate between them.

Felicia flashes for a moment on a picture she'd seen many years before of an elephant that had been eaten by a boa constrictor. You can't discern the elephant because it is inside the snake. And the snake doesn't look like a snake because it has stretched to envelop the elephant. Just as well, she thinks, because she doesn't think she can any longer realistically draw an elephant or a snake. She can't remember what they look like. But the memory of that drawing comforts her. It says nothing is as it seems.[3]

And that's fine.

Voices fill Felicia's head. Kate's beloved tone, telling her everything will be all right and, if it isn't, they will get through it together. Sophie and Dan who only whisper now. Martha, whose discourse races to catch up with the rest of them; Felicia sometimes thinks Martha was fortunate to have died before all these changes that have carried them to this place that has no name.

The truck with the tumblrs stopped coming 14 days ago.

The row of tumblrs is a mirage.

The notebook is full, and the pencil stub falls from Felicia's listless hand.

A fierce lightning bolt flashes sideways just above the horizon across a dark purple dust-filled sky. There is no one to exclaim over its crackling power. But a drop of dew clings to the withered arm of a cholla. Within that dewdrop—the equivalent of a digital pixel or multidimensional map of the universe—Felicia's memory, the people she's loved, stale water standing like sentinels in worn plastic carafes, a decrepit chair, a ragged notebook, and pencil stub all stretching their arms, struggling to wake.

Memory itself has yet to decide whether it will go another round.

---

3 From *The Little Prince* by Antoine de Saint-Exupéry, a novella first published in 1943 that has been translated into many languages and sold more than 140,000,000 worldwide.

Scheherazade's New World

In the small Spanish village of Cascarilla, in the fall of 1491, Magdalena played among the olive trees. She knew every twisted trunk and fruit-laden branch of her family's grove, her playground since she'd learned to crawl. She and her siblings began young to help with the yearly harvest, using poles longer than they were tall to shake those branches so the fruit would fall into nets spread out below, helping to separate the yield according to size, storing a part of it to ripen, packing the rest in wooden barrels to be sold at the local cooperative. The more lucrative business of pressing for oil was all adults. Magda's father had inherited the venture from his father who had come into it from his, back into a time no one remembers.

At eleven, Magdalena or Magda as she was called by family and friends, was short for her age, compact but muscular and quick. Her skin was tan and silky, her eyes dark. Those eyes had seen a lot and remembered it all. Her face was the chiseled countenance of a much older person. Her hair was startling in a family with uniformly dark locks; it was lighter than her parents' or siblings and streaked on one side with a reddish light that glowed like burnished copper when touched by sun or candlelight. People looked from one parent to the other, liked to say they didn't know where that red came from.

Magda's mind overflowed with images, questions, ideas; sometimes they tumbled out when least expected, astonishing those around her. She longed to accompany her younger brother Plutarco to the stone schoolhouse in the village. But she was a girl and had to content herself with what the trees and wind whispered in her eager ears, the wonders her younger brother Plu sometimes confided when he wasn't ignoring her pleadings, wasn't busy learning to be a man. He would sit beside her then in the shade of her favorite tree, tell her that despite Church teachings, some say the earth is round and those distant lights they see in the sky at night are worlds, perhaps like theirs, perhaps with children like themselves. They would talk about how bees pollinate flowers and make honey. He might recite a poem he'd learned, repeating the words until she too believed they belonged to her.

Cascarilla's hard-baked earth had absorbed the fierce rain of the night before. Magda's mother was at home, up before the sun to begin the daily chores of cleaning and feeding that measured out the rhythm of her life. She always had a hearty meal, perhaps oxtail and saffron-scented rice, waiting for her family at day's end. Magda's father was already in the fields, his bota skin with its ration of Rioja slung across his rough woolen tunic, a wide-brimmed felt hat against the sun, and an indulgent smile cast his daughter's way when he caught sight of her among the trees. Her called her *mi hijita*.

On this day, Magda had something on her mind. Eleven was a dangerous age. She'd overheard the murmurs of conversation, seen the appraising eyes turned in her direction. She knew she would soon be handed off to Hercules, a village boy who at seventeen had suddenly inherited his parents' land and needed a woman to help him begin the family that would become his own proud line.

Magda didn't want to have Hercules' babies. She dreaded their impending union, having to leave her family home for her husband's, that repulsive act she imagined from the allusions made by girls and jokes shouted out by cloddish boys. She dreaded growing thick with any man's child, following the inevitable road of all but the ugliest señoritas, those who might avoid such a prison by virtue of some blessed deformity. They were the ones destined to live out their lives caring for their own parents in that exchange of roles that happens when the young replace the old in responsibility.

Magda wanted to do her own longings proud, and this idea was what accompanied her constantly now in the low buzz that felt like an invisible halo circling her head. It sounded like their swarm of bees when she approached the hive near the long stone veranda that fronted the house.

Yesterday Plu had been kind. Before running to join his friends, he'd sat with her for a while under one of the oldest olive trees and carefully scratched an A, a B, a C, and a D, using a pointed rock against one that was flatter, almost as good as the sheepskin he practiced on at school. After each of the last three letters, he carved a smaller O or I. Magda tasted the sounds in her mouth, pushed them across her tongue, said them out loud to herself until their music remembered each shape and it felt at home in her.

Plu promised he would teach her to link the letters until they made words, the words until they formed sentences, the sentences until they became stories. Reading and writing was a dream she cherished even when she knew it was not supposed to be for her. She feared she wouldn't have time to learn every letter, and continued to store her unwritten stories away, building a library in her head that only she could see.

Not a week later, Magda took a fallen branch and reluctantly scraped at the earth until she'd made a deep hole, one where her secret would be safe. She dropped the stone into that hole, replaced the earth, patted it lovingly and turned back to her dream. She would leave Cascarilla that night. She didn't know if she would see her childhood home again, and that made her sad. But she understood that she was the only one who could save her life; no one else would. Was she burying her writing stone for someone else to find, for her to retrieve in some future she couldn't imagine, or simply to keep it safe?

I can't tell you how Magda learned about the Italian adventurer who was preparing to set sail for a new world, nor how she got from Cascarilla to Palos de la Frontera where his three handsome vessels were docked. That would require a novel, perhaps several. I will only say that her journey took the better part of a year, traveling mostly at night, making her way on foot from village to village, fleeing dangers and depending on the kindness of strangers. She had only her ingenuity, and luck.

The young girl cut her red-flecked hair short and pushed its strands beneath a farmer's hat. She easily passed for a boy if you didn't brush up against her budding breasts or notice her broadening hips beneath the fraying tunic. In the shadow of a doorway or shelter of a bridge, betrayals as well as discoveries inspired stories, and those stories would give her the strength to go on. Clouds were whimsical animals, rocks wise old sages, trees graceful beings who urged her on, and fields oceans daring her to cross.

Magda begged. She stole. She employed her considerable wiles, and the body Hercules thought would be his, in order to make her way. Palos de la Frontera was a busy seaport. It took her several days to find her way around the place. Finally, she charmed a young seaman who snuck her aboard the Pinta. She'd met him on the dock and determinedly traded her easiest currency for the promise of another world.

Did Magda have an idea of what that other world might be like? Only in her fantasy. She could see the words. New had tasted good from the moment she'd heard her father say it so many months before. To be sure, he'd been speaking to her brothers, not to her. They listened but went about their lives, not tempted to leave Cascarilla. Magda caught the syllables—*nue-vo mun-do*—in mid-air and reassembled them between her teeth. They stayed with her, scratching an itch she didn't know she had and eventually hatching a desire she was compelled to follow.

On the 60-foot Pinta, the young sailor who's snuck her aboard kept her out of sight for as long as possible. He brought her just enough of his ration to keep her alive. She was always hungry. The vessel was small but had its hiding places. Sometimes he shared her with his mates. Magda endured them all, the drunken and surly as well as the gentler and one young gypsy whose tenderness almost woke her desire. During those three long months at sea, she kept her mind on the promise of that new world. It helped that the vessel's lurching never made her sick. She was of hardy stock, not easily frightened or physically upset, and the journey to Palo had toughened her body as well as her resolve.

It was during that sea voyage that Magda realized she had something besides her body that she could use to get what she needed. Magda's imagination served her well. Her stories were like magnets. The tales she'd invented in the olive groves of her childhood and the months of escape grew to embrace complicated situations, flamboyant protagonists, surprising twists of plot, and details that delighted those among the Pinta's crew who knew she was onboard. She might deter wine-fouled breath or a groping hand by whispering *Once upon a time*, and the man who'd crawled into her hiding place would settle back to listen. She had stories for them all: about the sights and scents of home for those who felt lost at sea, about beautiful women for those who who missed that particular pleasure, even about the succulent dishes of southern Spain for those who were tired of salted anchovies, dried cod, and hardtack bread.

A month into the voyage, Martín Alonso Pinzón, the Pinta's captain, got wind of the unusual stowaway and ordered she be brought before him. Magda was thinner than when she'd boarded the ship, and filthy. Her scalp was covered in scabs and her hair, grown now, stood out in matted clumps. She knew she must smell bad, and tried to keep her distance from Pinzón, slight of stature himself but a commanding presence.

The man in charge quickly gave the young girl to understand she had nothing to fear from him. He wasn't about to throw her overboard or punish her in any way. Instead, he berated his crew and told them to provide her with a place to wash, proper food and a clean set of clothes. Men's clothes but better than the shift she'd worn since coming aboard, foul smelling and ripped here and there by lusty hands.

In return Magda gave the captain stories he wouldn't forget. Each night he would request her presence in his cabin, light his pipe, sit back, and listen. He never tried to take her into his bed. Years later, back in Palos de la Frontera and in the final moments of his life, the captain's last memory was not of his exploratory triumphs, his wife and progeny or his mistress of many years, but of the brave girl in rags he'd discovered on his first voyage to another world and the images she'd painted for him. They'd exceeded anything he'd seen in a lifetime of adventure.

Magda, on the other hand, didn't dwell on the stories she'd told Pinzón or the many she'd gifted the other members of the Pinta's crew. She never told the same tale twice. When Columbus's three ships put into port in what they soon learned was not India but a small island in the Caribbean, she quickly made her escape from the motley crew of men who'd been her friends or foes during the crossing. Here, finally, was the new world she'd risked so much to reach. Although men were still women's tickets to survival, she trusted no one but herself.

This was a very different climate and landscape from the one she'd grown up on in Cascarilla. Almost anywhere you went, you could smell salt in the air. Stately palms took the place of gnarled olives; they bent with the constant northeasterly wind that caused them to bow in a single direction. Some produced coconuts, a large fruit with a hard and hairy shell, liquid that satiated thirst and sweet white flesh Magda hadn't tasted before. The breezes on the island were softer and more caressing than those at home, yet violent storms could break without warning, lashing the land with wind and rain, toppling homes built on stilts to protect them from destruction.

And Magda too was different. Soon this, not the place that lived in her memory, was home. From eleven to thirteen she had become a woman with a woman's presence and sensibility. From younger sister in a family that ruled by tradition, she was now someone who could pass for twenty, and did. She made herself useful, cooking, cleaning, washing, raising and selling small animals, delivering babies, caring for children, and making herself useful as a trustworthy messenger and interpreter. She made friends with the natives and her prodigious memory served her well, for she learned their language before the first winter turned to spring. As a female from somewhere else, she found people tolerated her strange ways, allowing her a freedom that local women didn't have or know how to demand.

Magda died of smallpox in 1503. She'd survived the influenza that had decimated native and European populations on the island of Santo Domingo a decade earlier, but the strange affliction that caused high fever, fatigue, and open sores on people's skin was finally too much. Within a week she was gone. Still in her early twenties, she'd been living with Tiburón—or Shark—a Taino man thirteen years her senior, who loved her stories and gave her two children, Ramón and Isabela. Gentle and attentive, he'd reminded her of her brother Plu. They'd had a good life for as long as it lasted. When Magdalena succumbed to the plague, Tiburón buried her close to their small wooden house, hoping he would still be able to hear her stories in the night.

It was Isabela who inherited the streaks of red in her mother's hair, her talent for stories and fierce passion for independence. She dreamed of visiting Magda's Spanish homeland, but was never able to make the trip. Travel was still for merchants or explorers, invariably men.

Isabela was naturally musical. She taught herself the vihuela, a guitar-like instrument her father had taken in trade from one of the galleons arriving from the old world. Their merchants were always eager for the indigo, vanilla beans, nutmeg, and other spices plentiful on the island. Isabela sang to her dead mother and to the living, sometimes setting her own stories to the music that issued from the vihuela's strings when her long fingers danced across them.

Isabela played for herself and the villagers who were drawn to her music. As a woman, she had no access to a stage. As a half breed, born of a Spanish mother and Taino father, she had no access to what her age defined as society or culture. The art she created lived in the ears of those who came under her spell. It foretold and echoed in generations to come when life for women would be different. She too became a desirable young woman, married, and gave birth to a daughter with reddish hair and a penchant for storytelling. But, although she dreamed of a time when her desire would find release, that time never came for her.

Generations succeeded one another, each with its female descendants whose glints of copper in their hair and way with words set them apart. Women were most often the vessels of that power, although a few men—taunted for being feminine or weak—also possessed the gene. For some the storytelling brought unwanted attention, accusations of difference that resulted in isolation, taunt, or worse. Others learned to use the knack to their advantage. Men were aggravated but some were seduced. Women were jealous although one or two would listen and nurture their own talents for using stories as a way to try to make up for how their womanness kept them down.

After a while, Magda's long-ago history was lost to her great granddaughters and their great granddaughters, shrouded in the unexplored shadows of before. Memories of her disappeared with minds and hearts long gone in her labyrinthine family line.

The sixteenth century ended, and the seventeenth took its place. Conquerors, claiming land and subjects for Crown and Cross, landed aggressively in virgin territories, destroying lives and ways of being. Indentured servants arrived, looking to pay off their travel debt with work, and finding their best years consumed by the effort. Africans were kidnapped by the millions and, if they survived the brutal passage, forced into lives of slavery. Native tribes were all but annihilated in the name of progress. By the time the eighteenth century approached, the poor and even women and children were traveling from the old world to the new, looking for a change that only came for some. Stories held all their lives together, recorded their pasts, empowered their futures.

These travelers, whatever their condition, passed secrets in both directions. You can trace your own lineage on this map. If you give free reign to your imagination, you will unearth your own stories. Some of you will pass them down to your children at bedtime or on special occasions. For some, they are part of your narrative, as precious and ordinary as a smile. A few of you will even write or sing or dance or paint or sculpt or perform them, imbuing them with a physicality that can be repeated or held in wait.

Once upon a time instantly takes you from where you are now and transports you to a moment in the past, often the distant past. It is up to the storyteller to enable you to see when and where. Sometimes she intentionally keeps you guessing; the story is meant to be a game with two players and it's too late now: you can't escape. Sometimes the storyteller gives you everything—what the place looks and smells like, what season it is, the air's temperature, the protagonist's motivation, how others respond, what they wear and how they speak. She rides roughshod over your imagination, but there will be time enough for you to exercise that muscle. It is what you commit to memory and store for future reference that matters.

In Cascarilla so long ago, Magda's parents cried for their lost child. Plu mourned his sister's disappearance, secretly hoping she might be in a place where she could go to school. Hercules quickly forgot the girl he'd been promised and took another young village maid to bed. One of their daughters surprised the community with a glint of red in her hair.

Generations succeed one another in the old world just as they do in the new. Sometime toward the end of the nineteenth century, the most skilled women weavers of stories began to be known as Scheherazade's. If time is lineal as some think it is, Magda would not have understood the reference. If it's not, she might have smiled to herself. At mid-twentieth century, Puebloan ceramicists in the Rio Grande Valley of the US American Southwest started fashioning clay storyteller dolls with varying numbers of rapt children nestled in their laps, perched on their shoulders, or hanging off their arms. A literary genre now shapes, and sometimes diminishes what was once imagination turned fascination on the lips of a woman who didn't know how to read.

The stories live on, telling a truth that runs in our veins like blood, sometimes spilled in pointless battle, sometimes preparing the way for stories to come.

Another World

I'm afraid to tell you where it was. I mean the exact coordinates. It's not that I don't want to share my secret. On the contrary, I could use some validation of my discovery, some acknowledgment that the place and its time exist. It's just that a powerful but unspoken code of silence seemed to surround it from the beginning. Like if I say something, give the slightest hint, I'll never be able to return.

Return to that place or return home? At first, I asked myself that question dozens of times, wondering which would be the greater punishment: never again being able to visit the world I'd unearthed or not being able to find my way back to John and the girls? I didn't think I could forfeit either.

It all started several months ago on one of those clear fall mornings so typical of the desert Southwest. The monsoons had been heavy, and the scent of sage and piñon were thick in air that was still beginning to warm even so early in the day. John was asleep when I slipped unnoticed from bed. I felt like a walk before breakfast, just an hour or so to get myself energized. As quietly as I could, I pulled on a pair of Levi's, my old Rosie the Riveter shirt, and the wide-brimmed hat John surprised me with when I told him how much I enjoyed hiking our foothills trail. I grabbed my walking stick on my way out the door.

Heading up the ravine, I noticed the tiny tracks of darkling beetles sharing my path. I could hear the faint call of a canyon wren and then the response of its mate. Or, who knew, maybe its mother or sibling. A brilliant stand of deep red claret cup cactus blooms surprised me from what seemed like a crevice in the rock too narrow to hold enough earth to support its vibrancy. I made my way slowly, as I always did, drinking in every scent and sound.

When I reached the strangely shaped boulder that I knew meant I'd come a half mile or so, I stopped and leaned down to tie the lacing that had come undone on my left boot. I think it was the left because I remember something unusual catching my eye on that side. The lacing resisted my pull and that's when I lowered myself onto the base of the boulder so I could give my full attention to the small task.

I saw a shadow. There was something wrong with its shape. The early morning sun creates highlights and darker features perfectly reflecting each changing moment. If something isn't right, you know it. I'm not in the habit of questioning light and its absence. Each unfolding of day or night presents itself in its expected configuration and, unless altered by sudden dust or rain or some other weather event, is unlikely to defy reality.

The weirdly shaped shadow stood out like an open sore on the earth's face. I couldn't not see it.

My boot lace retied and secure, I walked over to the shadow. It didn't change as I moved, which seemed strange and quickened my breath, compelling me forward. As I got closer, I felt a pull, as if a living force stronger than my will was leading me somewhere and I was obliged to follow. Don't get me wrong. I'm not talking about some higher power. If anything, the pull was coming from below, and I briefly flashed on the popular sci-fi greeting "May the force be with you." Nor was it a propulsion of nature. The shadow didn't move or change as it would have were it produced by the sun's angle or other natural phenomena.

I vividly remember those first moments of approach. For weeks I relived them in slow motion and could describe them as accurately as when I initially experienced their insistence. What I found more difficult to reproduce with accuracy was the bridge from here to there, from this time to that other. What I'm trying to say is I have no idea how I got from a pleasant early autumn morning bathed in desert light to a time and place I couldn't talk about for fear of being called mad—or becoming the butt of cheap jokes. One moment I was on my home landscape, one I had known for years, intimate and beloved. The next I was somewhere else.

It was a somewhere else that all but stopped my breath. My desert disappeared and a wetter greener environ took its place. Large trees and plants I didn't recognize stretched as far as I could see. It wasn't raining but water dripped from branches, a little too slowly. Gravity itself seemed to operate differently. The sky was dark with towering clouds, thunderheads that would have been menacing where I come from. They rivaled those I'd seen in paintings by the sixteenth century Spanish master El Greco, ominous backgrounds in his canvasses of Toledo, yet no one seemed to be concerned or running for cover.

What really caught my attention were the people. People? I'm still not sure that's the right word. They moved as if in unison, with a cadence somewhere between wildly erratic and a puppet's obedience. Yet I saw no evidence that they were being manipulated or controlled in any way. Their faces, mask-like in impact, projected emotions I tried hard to decipher. They neither smiled nor frowned, yet their expressions were relaxed. And when I speak of them in plural it's because they seemed of a group. It wasn't that there was no sense of individuality. I noticed differences in size and shape. Some seemed older, more worn, perhaps a bit frayed around the edges, while others shone with a newness that was almost blinding.

They all had what I thought of as accentuated eyes and full sensuous lips. In fact, all their features were generous: broad nostrils, voluminous ears, and especially large prominently knuckled hands, some of which seemed to be gesturing to me in greeting. I immediately thought prehistoric, neanderthal or some such anthropological designation. But no. There were no overhanging brows, no stooped posture reminiscent of my own species' descent from the trees. These beings were voluptuous, graceful, elegant in their presence and movements. Their skin was exotic: a rich copperish brown, sensuous olive, ebony, chocolate, or creamy tan. A few had long hair arranged in elaborate do's; other's heads were shaved.

Clichéd as it seems in retrospect, I asked the nearest person: "Where am I?" She or he—everyone I saw appeared androgynous—turned and looked directly at me, moving their lips with a certain deliberateness as if expecting that I would read them rather than only listen to the sounds of the words. "That's not really the right question," they responded in a voice of choral harmony accompanied by sculptural gestures that rippled through the silence. Its tones evoked my favorite Brandenburg concerto. "The right question is when."

While I was pondering this, I felt an upheaval in every part of my body, much like a smaller version of what happened when volcanic movement uplifted parts of the earth's crust millions of years ago. Kaleidoscopic images swirled before my eyes and a deep rumble exploded at the base of my throat. For some indeterminate span of time, everything went dark. More than dark, colorless.

Before I had a chance to question or react, I was sitting on the built-in strawbale bench in the vestibule of our home, untying my hiking boots and massaging my tired feet. I looked at the boots. They appeared older and more trail-worn than they had when I put them on earlier that morning. I ran my fingers over their suede surface but only managed to dislodge a bit of red earth. That red earth I knew so well.

How long had I been in that other world? I didn't know. It felt like years but when I checked my watch, I saw that a scant hour had passed. It was as if I had walked to the boulder and back, no interim adventure involved. Yet my journey haunted my memory in a sort of timeless reverie.

John was still in bed but beginning to wake. "Can you start the coffee?" he called out, when I entered our bedroom, boots in hand. Time here seemed ordinary again. There was nothing in my husband's manner or my surroundings to indicate I'd done anything more than go out for a brief morning stroll. No evidence of where I'd been or what I'd seen.

I started the coffee, made breakfast, and tried to engage with the day's routine as if I wasn't carrying a memory so heavy it gnawed at me constantly and from every direction. Magda and Liz both commented that I "wasn't myself." John told me several times that I seemed distracted. That was putting it mildly. How could I not be? No matter how hard I tried to dislodge the experience, I couldn't. It stuck to me like some mystery map begging to be explored.

The rest of that day is a blur. The next morning, I woke even earlier. I hadn't slept well and had no trouble getting out of bed. I wanted to retrace my steps, but something told me neither to hurry or delay. I sensed that I'd need to be in the same place at more or less the same time to be able have another chance at transit to that other world. All I could think of as I made my way through the small ravine and onto the stretch of flat trail was not missing the precise spot, being able to see what I hadn't been aware of seeing the day before. I passed the claret cup without stopping to immerse myself in its beauty, paid no attention to whether the laces on my boots were securely tied. All I could think of was a destination that summoned me without revealing its location.

When I arrived at the flat boulder, I suddenly felt as if I were on automatic. No longer concerned about finding my way, the transition happened smoothly, without tension or resistance. One moment I was in my habitual desert landscape. The next I was in that other world, if indeed it was another world, immersed in green, a moist but invigorating chill in lethargic air. Its inhabitants seemed happy to see me. I thought I observed expressions that resembled smiles, eyes that danced with a gracious light. Nothing extreme. More comforting than anything else. One being gestured for me to join them beneath a tree the branches of which hung almost to the ground, a great profusion of blue-green leaves that formed a protective tent.

I did and immediately felt at home. Not home as place but as sensation. An ambience of wellbeing. We didn't talk much. I had too many questions and wasn't sure how to formulate them or if I would understand the answers. I realized that what I'd been told was true, and my greatest curiosity now wasn't so much about place as about time. Was this some long gone world or a revelation of future? Or maybe just a waking dream, some figment of my imagination? But although the first person with whom I'd exchanged that very brief conversation had told me in no uncertain terms that the issue was when, not where, I hesitated. On each approach to the subject, something stopped me from explicitly asking. It was as if I knew I would be breaching some undisclosed code of behavior.

Nevertheless, that second visit confirmed my initial experience, etched it more solidly in my consciousness. And it took up emphatic residence in my cells. After exiting much as I'd arrived—that is without any great effort on my part—I made my way along the familiar trail and into the ravine still warmed by the same early sunlight as on my ascent. Only now my eyes seemed more alive, more capable of seeing. I noticed a peregrine's nest high in the rock. Its refuge broke sharply with the horizon line, and I wondered how I could have missed it before. As I gazed, the falcon swooped down with something I couldn't make out dangling from its beak. I caught sight of several tiny, upturned mouths opening to devour what the adult bird delivered. My eyes seemed to function telescopically. The life cycle, I thought, essentially the same for us all.

On my way back to the house I almost ran head on into a cholla leaning out over the trail. Between two of its weathered rain-swollen arms stretched a large spider web, its silky threads glistening in direct sunlight. I stopped and searched for the creature that had woven such perfection. The web was empty. One edge was torn, as if its maker had been dislodged and fallen to the ground. I looked around the base of the cholla but couldn't find the spider, dead or alive.

Everything seemed strangely illuminated on that second return from the mystery place, the grace of its odd but welcoming creatures still alive in my memory. Desert rocks and plants were individually bathed in light and the overall effect assaulted my eyes in a way I hadn't been aware of before. And this visual hypersensitivity didn't stop when I got home. On my computer monitor the words of a poem I'd been struggling with for weeks pierced me like tiny darts; they didn't hurt but I'd say they had turned insistent, as if demanding I nurture their candor, bring them to fruition. Every painting on our walls seemed to vibrate, its areas of color outlined in black lines like the ones used by Rouault.

My family appeared different too. The hair on John's head and even the freshly washed forest of graying curls on his chest called to me, imploring touch. My impulsive caress seemed to surprise him, but he clearly appreciated the gesture and leaned down to nuzzle my neck with his face. When I separated the eggs to make my signature morning omelet, the yellow yokes seemed as distant from the clear whites as if they'd never inhabited the same shell. The braised onions, small squares of potato and cooked spinach waiting on a nearby plate kept curiously to themselves, reminding me of the way Liz, when she was a toddler, couldn't abide one food touching another.

Morning after morning, I continued my eager walks, anticipating the moment when I would let myself slip between boulders and find myself in that other place. The androgenous beings always welcomed me. And I began to distinguish small differences in look or movement. Some were slightly bent as if by age. Others, smaller and more limber, exuded an aura of playfulness. Some remained aloof while others were eager to sit and be a while. Not necessarily talk, just be. Occasional bits of conversation flowed between us, but I noticed that our most important communication happened without words or even gestures. We seemed to have a telepathic connection.

My visits weren't constrained by beginnings or endings. They lasted exactly for as long as they needed to, and then I would simply be released, sometimes gently sometimes urgently returned to the habitat I'd always known. The one thing I never experienced in the mystery place was violence of any kind. Not emotional or physical, not in word or deed.

After what must have been a month or so of those daily sojourns, the difference between my two worlds began to take a toll. It gnawed like an itch I couldn't scratch. John and our daughters had begun to look at me differently. It might have been my imagination, but I felt an unfamiliar caution coming from each of them. At times it seemed as if they were just worried, at others they acted patronizing as if I had grown old and even my loved ones were talking about rather than to me. I took care to act as I always had, to be attentive to their needs, to show my love in those many small acts that express our caring.

I could tell they weren't convinced.

The strange place gave me something vital, something indefinable but necessary. But this was my home, my family. I felt like I was being forced to make a choice. One morning I decided not to go on my walk. I waited until John and Liz and Magda had come downstairs and were sitting around the kitchen island waiting for the breakfast I'd offered every day of our years together.

"I know you're wondering," I began, not really feeling I did know anything for sure.

Forks stopped midway to mouths. Glasses of orange juice were set carefully on the counter. Liz's intake of breath was audible. The three of them looked at me expectantly.

"It started about a month ago," I began. "It's not that I've wanted to keep it from you, just that I haven't known how to talk about it. Because I know you're going to think it's unbelievable. I mean you probably won't believe . . ."

"Just spit it out already." Magda, still an adolescent, was conspicuously short on patience.

John looked at me silently. All I could see in his eyes was love. Any vestige of condescension was gone, and his unspoken gratitude urged me on.

I began at the beginning, with how I enjoyed getting out in the early morning, how the desert was at its best then, its sights and scents and textures there for the taking. I told them in as much detail as I could remember about the first time that I found myself moving through the rock, the world I'd discovered, the feelings of wellbeing that obviated more than the most elementary questions, the acceptance I felt on the part of the inhabitants of a place and time I was still unable to define.

My attempts at describing the people, or beings, were what least satisfied John and the girls. The absence of binary gender identities seemed especially confusing to them. And when I mentioned their prominent facial features, I thought I detected a shadow of discomfort in Liz's eyes. "You mean they were all Black or Latino?" she asked. Her apparent acceptance of my story momentarily blinded me to the racism in the tone of her question.

I was careful to acknowledge the logic in what they asked. I tried not to dwell on their astonishment. It probably just reflected the fact that they were accustomed to my writer's creativity and concluded that this story I was telling was simply something I'd invented and come to believe, some alternative scenario as harmless as it was odd. After all, they knew me to possess a vivid imagination. Nothing wrong with that. It could be interesting, even entertaining at times.

But as I shared where I'd been every day for the past month, the reaction of my listeners paled beside a realization of my own. I began to feel a shift deep inside. My answers to my husband and daughters' questions became less detailed. I found I could no longer remember exactly what that other place looked like, the strange vegetation, the ease with which its people had communicated with me. The issue of when—whether the place existed in the past, in some unknowable future, or outside linear time altogether—was no longer even a question I could formulate with ease. I could still talk about those visits, but in the way you might repeat someone else's story or describe a scene in a photograph you've seen your entire life. Not like something you yourself have experienced.

John took me in his arms and said something to the effect that whether it was real or a dream was irrelevant; he knew that I believed I had lived the experience I'd described and that was enough for him. Magda leaned over and gave me an embarrassed hug but retained her attitude of let's humor Mom. Liz looked like she was reserving judgment. It was time to get back to the business of eating breakfast, then go about our respective days.

With something like a dull ache rising in my chest, I realized their responses were no longer my primary concern. Something within me was different and I hated acknowledging what it was. Instinctively, I knew I would never again be able to access that magical place or time where I'd been sure I was on the threshold of understanding life's biggest questions. Getting right with my family had cost me a world.

Gradually, over time, I realized that something within me was indeed different but that could be a good thing. It was no longer the experience itself but how it had changed me. I found I could call upon it when I needed the expansive possibilities of its map, and it enabled me to see my family and the world with new eyes.

New eyes never take away. They always give.

About the Author

Margaret Randall (New York, 1936) is a poet, essayist, oral historian, translator, photographer and social activist. She lived in Latin America for 23 years (in Mexico, Cuba, and Nicaragua). From 1962 to 1969 she and Mexican poet Sergio Mondragón co-edited *El Corno Emplumado / The Plumed Horn*, a bilingual literary quarterly that published some of the best new literature and art of the sixties. She is the author of more than 150 books.

When she came home in 1984, the government ordered her deported because it found some of her writing to be "against the good order and happiness of the United States". With the support of many writers and others, she won her case in 1989. Throughout the late 1980s and early 1990s, she taught at several universities, most often Trinity College in Hartford, Connecticut.

Randall's most recent poetry titles include *As If the Empty Chair / Como si la silla vacía*, *The Rhizome as a Field of Broken Bones*, *About Little Charlie Lindbergh*, *She Becomes Time*, *The Morning After: Poems & Prose in a Post-Truth World* and *Out of Violence into Poetry* (all from Wings Press). *Che On My Mind* (a feminist poet's reminiscence of Che Guevara, published by Duke University Press), and *More Than Things* (essays, from The University of Nebraska Press) are other recent titles. *Haydée Santamaría: She Led by Transgression* was released by Duke in 2015. *Exporting Revolution: Cuba's Global Solidarity* was published by Duke in 2017. *Time's Language: Selected Poems: 1959-2018* came out from Wings in the fall of 2018; it covers 60 years of her poetry. Wings also published her collection of poems written out of the COVID experience, *Starfish on a Beach: The Pandemic Poems* in October of 2020. Her memoir, *I Never Left Home: Poet, Feminist, Revolutionary*, was released by Duke in March 2020. New Village Press published her *My Life in 100 Objects* in September 2020. 2021 saw several new books, including: *Out of Violence into Poetry* (poetry) and *Thinking about Thinking* (essays). *Artists in My Life, Stormclouds like Unkept Promises* (poetry, with photographs by Barbara Byers) and a new revised edition of *Risking a Somersault in the Air* (a 1984 collection of conversations with Nicaraguan writers) appeared in spring 2022. Short stories are a new genre for her. She began writing them during the pandemic of 2020, produced a couple dozen in rapid succession, and then stopped as suddenly as she'd begun.

Two of Randall's photographs are in the Capitol Art Collection in Santa Fe.

She has also devoted herself to translation, producing *When Rains Become Floods* by Lurgio Galván Sánchez, *You Can Cross the Massacre on Foot* by Freddy Prestol Castillo, *Voices from the Center of the World: Contemporary Poets of Ecuador* and *Only the Road / Solo el camino*, an anthology of eight decades of Cuban poetry. Red Mountain Press in Santa Fe and The Operating System in Brooklyn have brought out her translations of individual Cuban poets. And she rediscovered the poetry of Rita Valdivia, a young combatant in Che Guevara's rebel army, and made it available to an English readership. Randall received the 2017 *Medalla al Mérito Literario*, awarded by *Literatura en el Bravo* in Ciudad Juárez, Mexico.

More recent honors received by Randall include the "Poet of Two Hemispheres" prize, given by Poesía en

Paralelo Cero, Quito, Ecuador, in April of 2019 and the Haydée Santamaría Medal, given by Casa de las Américas, Cuba, in May 2019. In May 2019, the University of New Mexico gave her an Honorary Doctorate in Letters. In March 2020 AWP named her the year's recipient of its George Garrett Award. And that same month she was honored with the 2019-2020 Paulo Freire Democratic Project Award by Chapman University's Donna Ford Attallah College of Education.

Randall's web page is www.margaretrandall.org. She lives in Albuquerque with her partner (now wife) of more than 35 years, the visual artist Barbara Byers, and travels extensively to read, lecture and teach.

Wings Press was founded in 1975 by Joanie Whitebird and Joseph F. Lomax, both deceased, as "an informal association of artists and cultural mythologists dedicated to the preservation of the literature of the nation of Texas." Publisher, editor and designer since 1995, Bryce Milligan is honored to carry on and expand that mission to include the finest in American writing— meaning all of the Americas, without commercial considerations clouding the decision to publish or not to publish.

Wings Press intends to produce multi-cultural books, chapbooks, ebooks, recordings and broadsides that enlighten the human spirit and enliven the mind. Everyone ever associated with Wings has been or is a writer, and we know well that writing is a transformational art form capable of changing the world, primarily by allowing us to glimpse something of each other's souls. We believe that good writing is innovative, insightful, and interesting. But most of all it is honest. As Bob Dylan put it, "To live outside the law, you must be honest."

Likewise, Wings Press is committed to treating the planet itself as a partner. Thus the press uses as much recycled material as possible, from the paper on which the books are printed to the boxes in which they are shipped.

As Robert Dana wrote in *Against the Grain*, "Small press publishing is personal publishing. In essence, it's a matter of personal vision, personal taste and courage, and personal friendships." Welcome to our world.

WINGS PRESS

Colophon

This first edition of *Lupe's Dream and Other Stories*, by Margaret Randall, has been printed on 60 pound "natural" paper containing a percentage of recycled fiber. Titles have been set in Charlemagne and Caslon Semibold type, the text in Adobe Caslon type. This book was designed by Bryce Milligan.

On-line catalogue and ordering:
www.wingspress.com
Wings Press titles are distributed to the trade by the
Independent Publishers Group
www.ipgbook.com
and in Europe by Gazelle
www.gazellebookservices.co.uk

Also available as an ebook.

*For more information about Margaret Randall,
visit her website at www.margaretrandall.org.*